ISBN 978-0-9956212-1-3

Printed and bound in Great Britain by Clays Ltd, St Ives plc.

Books by Rob Sinclair

Dark Fragments

The Enemy series:

Dance with the Enemy
Rise of the Enemy
Hunt for the Enemy

For my mum and dad. Thank you for all of your support
and advice (even the times you were wrong).

PROLOGUE

'Were you ever happy?' she asked.

'Of course,' I said.

'And what made you happy?'

'Lots of things. It depends what point in my life you're asking about. I was a happy kid, certainly – my upbringing wasn't particularly hard or painful.'

'And what about in your adult life?'

'Alice made me happy.'

'Always?'

'No, not always. We were together for twelve years; we had ups and downs like everyone else. But in the early days, before marriage and mortgages and children and ... complications, our relationship was perfect.'

'And since Alice?'

'Since Alice? Since Alice I've never been the same.'

'You mean you've never been that happy again?'

'No. Not like I was back then.'

'What would that person, the old you, think of you now? What would he say if he were to meet you?'

'He wouldn't recognise me. We're such different people. But then I could never have foreseen that my life would turn out like this. I could never have imagined that one day in our home, in our bed, I would find Alice murdered.'

CHAPTER 1

'What's two plus two plus two plus two?' Harry said.

'Two!' Chloe blurted out.

'No, idiot.'

'Harry, be nice,' I said. Chloe gave her brother a withering look.

'Come on, Dad, what is it?' Harry said as he skipped a few steps in front of me. Chloe was by my side, her tiny hand snug inside mine.

'Eight,' I said.

It took Harry a few moments to determine whether I was indeed correct.

'Yes!' he finally said. 'Okay. So what's a million and a million billion thousand?'

'A lot,' I said.

'No!'

'Yes, it is,' I said.

'Is,' echoed Chloe.

'A lot isn't a number, Dad. Play properly.'

'Okay, what was the question again?'

'I can't remember.'

'Two!' Chloe blurted out again.

'Chloe!' Harry said in disgust.

'My turn then,' I said. 'If I have three pounds and an ice-cream costs one pound, how many ice-creams will each of us have?'

'Ice-cream!' Chloe said.

Harry snorted. 'That's too easy.'

'What is it then?'

'One.'

'No. You'll have none. 'Cos I'm eating them all! Unless you beat me to the ice-cream van.'

With that, Harry and Chloe both screamed in delight. Harry burst off at pace through the park gates and toward the van a couple of hundred yards ahead. Chloe let go of my hand and started running – more like shimmying really – after her big brother. After a few paces, though, she stopped and pouted.

'He beat me,' she said sulkily.

'Keep going – you only have to beat me!'

With renewed impetus she set off again. I couldn't help but beam as I watched my kids dashing away, not a care in the world except for making sure they got an ice-cream. The innocence of youth truly is wonderfully blinkered. It's infectious too. Spending time with my children, especially impromptu time, was like a drug, making me forget – at least temporarily – the many troubles in my life. And I really needed the respite.

Usually our childminder, Mary, who I thought was a sweet and caring woman but who the kids thought was old and boring, would pick the children up after school on a Monday. Not today, though. It might have been October, but the weather was balmy and sunny (though to be honest, even if it had been minus ten out the kids wouldn't have said no to ice-cream in the park). And I'd had a crappy week … scratch that, I'd had a shitty month, and Harry and Chloe were as ever the perfect pick-me-up.

Not that they were a breeze to look after – what kids are? At eight going on eighteen, Harry was far too smart for his own good, and had little patience for his three-year-old sister. Put them together for more than a few minutes and there was bound to be an incident of some sort. Harry, being the eldest and the biggest, tormented his sister like crazy, but she was slowly starting to show her own cunning too. Within a few years she'd be able to give him a run for his money, for sure.

With me in a blinkered state of relaxation, the three of us sat down on a bench to tuck into our treats. Needless to say, Chloe somehow managed to smear sticky ice-cream all over her pretty pink dress – not that she batted an eyelid. Harry chose a hideous blue ice-lolly that, he showed us proudly, turned his tongue, teeth and lips a vibrant blue. Simple pleasures.

And then they were off again, hurtling around the grass emitting spates of giggles and the occasional disgruntled shout, Chloe chasing but never quite catching her brother.

As the time edged toward six I decided we should head back to the house. My wife, Gemma, would be home and wondering where we all were. We set off side by side, all three of us seemingly content. And yet, as we walked toward the park exit, I felt like I was walking from one life into another. Back to reality.

That gloomy feeling was further cemented when I saw the black Range Rover pulled up outside the park gates. As we approached, its engine thundered to life. By that point I could feel my heart heaving in my chest.

They wouldn't have come here, would they? When I'm with my kids?

A mixture of fear and disgust filled me. I stared at the blackened windows, unable to see anything of who sat inside – although I knew full well to whom the car belonged.

We were almost adjacent when the Range Rover began crawling away. Then, after a few seconds, the driver put his foot down and the engine roared as it propelled the heavy vehicle away at pace. I watched as the car sped down the road … toward the turn for our street.

I held my breath. The car slowed. Its brake lights blinked once. Twice.

No, please, don't, I willed. *Not my home.*

But at the last moment the car revved again and shot off into the distance. Soon it was out of sight. I felt my body loosen as a wave of tension was suddenly released.

'Dad?' Harry said.

I turned to face him, trying to regain my composure, but he must have seen the look on my face. He indicated to Chloe, and I looked down. Her face was creased and upset. I was grasping her hand, I realised, squeezing it as tightly as I could. I hadn't even noticed, hadn't heard her murmurs. I'd been too consumed by my own world. My own problems.

I let go and saw the mangled form of Chloe's hand quickly regain its normal shape.

'Honey, I'm so sorry,' I said to her. 'Did I hurt your hand?'

Chloe, bottom lip protruding, just nodded.

'Dad, is everything okay?' Harry said.

'Yes,' I said. 'Everything's fine. Let's get home and see Mum.'

I hated lying. I especially hated lying to my children. But what else was I supposed to say? I had to shield them from harm. That's what a father does. And if that meant shielding them from the truth, then so be it.

Sooner or later, though, I knew something would have to give. And as we headed for home, my instincts whispered that it was going to be sooner.

CHAPTER 2

I didn't get the nightmare often, not anymore, just once every few months. In the past, in the early days, it had come every night. People say that time is a great healer. I'm not sure I felt healed through the passage of time, but it at least created a certain detachment and distance that grew as the days, weeks, months and years went by. Yet when the nightmare came, it was still as powerful and real as the very first time, still able to shake every bit of confidence and resolve from my battered mind.

The nightmare was a single frame, a moment frozen in time – a memory I'd tried over the years to bury deep in my mind but that still tormented me. Nothing could ever have prepared me for seeing Alice – my wife, the love of my life – like that. Her lithe, naked body draped over the sheets of our king-sized bed. The rings of red on her neck from the killer's hands scorched onto her delicate skin. Her wide open eyes, all life drained from them, staring up at me, pleading for my help.

In the nightmare I couldn't speak, couldn't move, couldn't breathe. I was entirely frozen, powerless, just as she was. Just as I had been in the moment seven years ago when I'd first looked down at Alice's lifeless body.

My eyes shot wide open and my head jumped up off the pillow as I escaped the horror of the flashback. After a few seconds, I realised where I was and a sense of relief washed over me. I looked over at the bedside clock: seven twenty-five a.m. The alarm would be going off in five minutes.

A groan from the other side of the bed.

'Ben? What time is it?' Gemma murmured.

'Almost time to get up,' I said, looking over at her.

Her light-brown hair was crumpled and messy and strewn over her face. She gave a half-smile. Not a warm, happy smile. More a grimace at having been disturbed.

'I'd best get ready,' she mumbled, then got up from the bed and headed to the en-suite bathroom.

She slipped off her nightie as she walked and I watched her, the way her hips rocked gently, sexily, remembering how that teasing saunter had first drawn me to her. I was still hugely attracted to Gemma – how could I not be? Staring at her toned, naked body, I felt arousal bubbling every time. But our relationship was far from rosy. In my late thirties, I certainly wasn't over the hill, not by a long stretch, yet lust and passion were becoming forgotten. It wasn't that I still expected Gemma to be tearing my clothes off every night, but her interest in me was cooling by the day.

Cooling? No, it was damn near frozen already. Not that Gemma was entirely to blame for that.

'Daddy?' came the tiniest of voices from the bedroom doorway. Chloe. 'Is it up time?'

Chloe was the most kind and caring little person, in many ways a true mirror image of her mother. Whatever my struggles to keep the fires of passion burning with Gemma, one thing I knew for sure was that she was a great mother.

'Yes, sweetie,' I said. 'Go and wake your brother.'

I waited for Gemma to finish in the bathroom. She came out looking fresher and brighter – awake. She gave me the faintest of smiles as we silently walked past each other. I took my time in the shower, then dressed in a pair of jeans and a blue hooded sweatshirt. By the time I got downstairs, Gemma and the kids were sitting around the kitchen table munching cereal.

'Are you going to work today at all?' Gemma asked, her tone unsympathetic.

'Probably not.'

Gemma tried her best to hide her eye roll. Or at least I gave her the benefit of the doubt on that; maybe she'd intended for me to see it.

'You're not taking Harry out of school again, are you?' she queried.

'Again? It's only a couple of times a year.'

'You think?'

'You know it is.'

'Well, sure, the trips down to that wretched place may be a couple of times a year, but what about the rest of it? This moping around of yours is getting worse, and dragging the kids into it with you isn't helping anyone.'

'This isn't the time or the place,' I said, scowling and looking over at the kids, who were busy pretending not to be there.

Gemma blushed, ashamed. She was right, though. Gemma and I had had various ups and downs over the years and I knew she'd been a lifeline to me after Alice's death. But recently the weight of the world was bearing down on me once more. I loved them, all three of them, I really did. Whatever problems I had, the last thing I wanted was to bring Gemma and the kids down with me. I needed them.

'It'll get better again,' I said, reaching out and putting my hand on Gemma's. 'I promise.'

I wanted my words to be true, not just a desperate hope. Gemma smiled at me, but the look she gave told me she saw the doubt in my eyes. She whipped her hand away.

'He's not going with you,' Gemma said. 'Come on, Ben, he's eight years old. He needs to be at school with his friends. The cemetery is no place for kids, you know that.'

I looked over at Harry, who was staring sheepishly at Gemma. He turned toward me.

'Sorry, Dad,' he said. 'I should go to school.'

I felt my heart sink, not necessarily at his words or their meaning, but at knowing that Gemma had swayed my own son against me.

Really, though, was Harry wanting to go to school rather than accompany me to a cemetery the worst thing in the world? Probably not. I wanted the best for the kids. I wanted them to grow up in a stable and happy home. I'd worked hard over the years to make sure that was the case. We weren't the perfect family but then what family is? I was doing the best I could under the circumstances.

Still, I felt a duty to do right by Alice too. I owed it to her. And it wasn't that much to ask of Harry, or Gemma.

I could feel my anger building. I wanted to retort and remind Gemma that Harry was my son, not hers … but I wouldn't. I couldn't. Doing so wouldn't change either of their decisions. And there was no need to stick a dagger in Gemma's heart like that. Alice may have been Harry's biological mother, but it was Gemma who'd looked after him for the last six, nearly seven years, who'd washed him, fed him. She was there when he learned to walk, when he spoke his first word. She helped to teach him to read and write. She was Harry's mother.

I stared at Gemma for a good while but said nothing. Her expression remained hard and defiant.

I looked over at Harry. His head was bowed.

'You can come if you want,' I said to him. 'I'll make sure school understands.'

'He's not going with you!' Gemma said.

Harry just gently shook his head.

I got up from the table and gave both of the kids a kiss on their forehead. Then I moved up to Gemma and kissed her softly on the cheek.

'I love you,' I said.

Gemma said nothing in return. Without another word spoken, I turned and headed for the door.

CHAPTER 3

Fitting for the occasion, the weather was best described as utter shit. It was October. It was dark, gloomy, windy. It wasn't pelting down with rain but the air was filled with dampness. And misery.

I'd ridden around aimlessly for hours – it just didn't feel right, Harry not being with me. It was nearly midday by the time I built up the courage to head to the cemetery on the outskirts of Sutton Coldfield, the town where we lived, just a few miles north of Birmingham.

I parked my motorbike in one of the few spaces near the central chapel, took off my helmet, and then forced my way against the biting wind over to where Alice's remains were buried. By the time I reached the plot water was dripping from my hair, and even though my leathers were keeping the heavy drizzle off my body, I was shivering vigorously. I took off my backpack and pulled out the bunch of fresh flowers I'd picked up from a local florist on the way. Next I took out a picture of Harry, taken on our recent holiday to Spain.

Harry had been a little over twelve months old when Alice was killed. He couldn't really remember her, I was sure of that. I could tell he held a fondness for her, though, a false memory if you like, built up from us looking at pictures of them together and the stories I told him about Alice. He probably imagined himself in those pictures, the familiarity tricking his brain to the point where he really believed he could remember being there. Memory is a funny thing. It feels reliable and absolute, though it's anything but.

I was upset that Harry wasn't with me, but I knew he had his own life to lead, and I knew deep down that Gemma was only looking out for Harry's best interests. She was his mother now. In all the years that had passed I hadn't been able to let go of Alice, of what had happened to her or of the impact of her death on me. Maybe it wasn't a bad thing if Harry could.

As I stared at the picture in my hand, my brain took me back to the day Harry was born. I'm not sure I've ever had a day with so many ups and downs. Alice had been nearly eight months pregnant. We had been visiting her parents up north for the weekend and had arrived home in the Midlands tired and groggy from a horrendous journey down the M6. Alice, fiercely headstrong as she was, had insisted that she help with unpacking, knowing I was drained from the gruelling drive. In the end it was nothing more than an accident. She'd slipped on the stairs with the suitcase – a seemingly innocuous fall, if she hadn't been so heavily pregnant.

I've never heard such screams of despair as came from her in that instant. It was as though all the possible horrors of life had suddenly flashed before her eyes. I'll never know what she truly felt in those moments – how any mother felt knowing that the baby she had been carrying with such love, with so much hope, might be taken away.

Within seconds we had both flown into a mad panic. One way or another the baby was coming, there was no doubt. I called an ambulance immediately, but barely seconds after putting the phone down we were in my car, heading the short distance to Good Hope A&E, which was less than two miles from our home. It felt like we had no other choice. We couldn't bear the thought of waiting even another two minutes for the ambulance to arrive.

By the time they got Alice onto a gurney, she was already fully dilated. I remember imagining that the baby's head was pushing out – not that I dared look at the business end of things. Moments later, there was a whole new problem brewing. The umbilical cord was wrapped around the baby's neck. If Alice kept on pushing – almost impossible for her not to do, given the huge contractions that were consuming her – there was a real chance the baby would suffocate.

The subsequent half hour went by in a blur. Alice somehow found the strength and focus to sign a consent form before she was rushed into an operating theatre for an emergency caesarean. Completely lost and ghostlike, I stood by Alice's head, squeezing her hands and looking into her teary and bloodshot eyes. Trying my best to avert my gaze from the gaping, bloody hole in her stomach that was being accidentally reflected in the monitor in front of me.

Her body bucked up and down as the doctors tugged fiercely at her midriff, pulling apart the layers of fat, muscle and tissue to reach the baby. My impression of a delicate procedure was miles from the reality and the look of horror in Alice's eyes grew with every jolt.

And then, when it was over, when we should have been greeted by the cries of our first-born, there was only a deathly silence. The baby couldn't breathe properly. In an instant he was rushed off to another room with barely a word spoken to us. I held tight to Alice's hands as the doctors and nurses who were still present worked on stitching her up.

Minutes later a nurse came back into the operating room, a small bundle wrapped in a light-blue towel cradled in her arms. She beamed at us and I knew what it meant. Tears began to stream as uncontrollable joy washed over me. She handed me the baby. My baby. *Our* baby. Harry. And when I looked into Alice's eyes, no words were needed.

From that moment, Harry had always been such a happy baby. It was almost as if the trauma of his birth had mellowed him, like he was trying to apologise for having put us through so much angst. And Alice, exhaustion aside, was such a natural and loving mother. I know everyone says that but it was true. She was so proud of her son, as I was of her.

Yet Harry's mother – his biological mother – had been taken away from him, from me too, so cruelly and unexpectedly. Seven years had passed since her murder. Gemma thought it was morose that I still came to the cemetery twice a year, on Alice's birthday and on Harry's birthday. Or maybe she was just jealous? It seemed only right to me that a mother should get to see her son growing up. And I would continue to visit her grave even if Harry wanted to break free.

Each time I came, I left a picture of Harry next to the flowers so Alice could see the fine young boy he was becoming.

I felt a tear roll down my cheek. A fierce gust of wind blew it off my face and it flew away in the cold, damp air.

Harry had always come with me before. Had always been there by my side.

But this time, all Alice would see of him was a picture.

CHAPTER 4

I laid the flowers down by the gravestone, then propped the picture in place in a plastic frame cover. I took away the old picture from five months ago when I'd last been there, on Harry's birthday. The picture was now dirty and faded, parts of it almost entirely scratched away from the battering of wind and rain it had taken.

I looked at the gravestone and silently read the gold letters that said little of Alice's life. Just a few facts that in a hundred years would mean nothing to anyone. Then I turned to leave, unable to muster any words.

I was nearly back at my bike when I saw them.

The black Range Rover – the same one I'd spotted at the park the previous day – was clumsily pulled up on a grass verge some twenty yards past my Yamaha. This time, though, it wasn't just there so the occupants could spy on or spook me. Two men were already out of the vehicle, walking toward me. Both wore long black coats that reached down to their knees, jeans underneath and shiny black shoes – similar attire, but there was a considerable difference in height between the two men.

I'm a shade over six foot one. Not a massive guy by any stretch, but above average. The taller of the two men, though, was a giant: six foot six, maybe as much as six eight, and almost as wide as he was tall. His thick neck burst out around the collar of his coat and his arms – probably the size of my thighs – strained the fabric of his sleeves.

I knew from past encounters that his size was largely muscle. He was one of those freaks of nature, just naturally gigantic and strong. No amount or combination of drugs or weights or effort could ever make me or ninety-nine per cent of people that size. Hundreds of years ago he probably would have been a fabled warrior, perhaps a leader of a clan, a king of men even. In today's society he was just a brute. An oddity.

The other man? Well, he couldn't have been more ordinary to look at. He was shorter than me by four or five inches at least. He had an unassuming face, thick-rimmed glasses and mousy hair cut neat and short. He wouldn't have drawn a second glance from any passerby were it not for the man-mountain that strode with him.

And yet it was the smaller figure of the two whom I was loath to see: I truly detested him and I hugely feared him. That was why, when the men reached me, my heart was already pounding in my chest and I could feel the nerves building, my hands and legs shaking in response.

'Mr Stephens. Funny place for a walk,' Callum O'Brady snorted in his thick Irish accent.

'What are you doing here?' I answered back, sounding a lot more confident than I felt. Whatever power O'Brady had over me, I knew that showing weakness to him was the last thing I could afford to do.

'Your good wife said you'd be here.'

'You've been to my home?'

'Well, we didn't come across her while out getting milk and bread, my man.'

'You've got no right going to my house. Talking to her. She's got nothing to do with any of this.'

'Calm yourself,' O'Brady said. 'I didn't bone her. Though I could tell she probably needs a good screw. I think you need to take better care of her.'

'Oh, she wanted it all right,' the big man said in his grating southern accent. 'A proper naughty girl that one.'

'Fuck you,' I said, my heart skipping a beat at my ill-thought-out response.

The big man stepped forward, fists clenched, but O'Brady put an arm out to stop him.

'Not nice, Stephens,' O'Brady said. 'I'm being civil here. But if you're going to be a prick about it then Elvis will happily pummel you into the ground.'

Elvis. It wasn't his real name, of course; I had no clue what that was. I also had no idea why O'Brady had chosen that moniker for his most trusted muscleman – I wasn't a party to that in-joke.

'Fine,' I said. 'I'm sorry. But that's my wife you're talking about. Of course I'm going to defend her.'

'Understood. We're both family men. Like you.'

Elvis grunted. I imagined him with his litter of little apes – some kids had no chance.

'Just please don't go to my house again,' I said. 'I don't want Gemma or the kids brought into this.'

'What, are you ashamed of your business partners?' O'Brady scoffed.

'You know it's not like that.'

'Yeah, at the moment you're probably right. Because it's starting to feel like we're not business partners at all. It's starting to feel like you're treating me like some sort of dope. Taking me for a ride. Is that what you're doing, Stephens?'

'No. Not at all. I –'

'I need the money,' O'Brady stated.

My shoulders slumped at the inevitable turn in the conversation.

'You'll get it,' I said.

'But I haven't got it. That's the problem. So where is it?'

'I'll get it. Just trust me.'

'Trust you? Well, isn't that the whole basis of our relationship? Isn't that how it's worked from day one? If I hadn't trusted you, we wouldn't have started out in the first place. But you're wearing my patience thin now. I need the money. You've got two days.'

'Two days?! I can't just –'

'Two days, Stephens,' O'Brady said, turning to leave. 'Or your precious wife will become more involved in this than you'd care to imagine. Elvis.'

I opened my mouth to protest and never saw the fist from the big man coming. It smacked into my midriff and I let out a painful exhale. Before I knew it I was on my knees, the world spinning and blurry. I took deep breaths, trying not to puke.

By the time clarity started to return the Range Rover had already backed off the verge and was heading out toward the road.

Two days. That was all I had to find one hundred thousand pounds. If I didn't, I could kiss goodbye any semblance of a normal life that still remained.

For years I'd tried to keep my life on an even keel. I'd never truly overcome the trauma of Alice's death, though with the help of Gemma and the kids I'd certainly come close to salvaging a life for myself. At one point it had really looked like I would come out the other side on top.

That was all in the past now, though. I'd been dragged right back down to the bottom once more. Callum O'Brady had been there every step of the way, and was only too happy to watch me fall.

I was in a bind. It wasn't just my life on the line, it was the lives of every member of my family. With O'Brady on my back, I firmly believed that.

I had to get that money.

CHAPTER 5

I headed away from the cemetery with my mind on fire. I was in too deep to get out on my own. I needed help. Yet that was easier said than done. Could I really push my pride aside and ask for the help I so desperately needed? If the solution was that simple then I would have done it years ago. Pride comes before a fall. Well, I was certainly falling.

There was always another option. One I'd considered many times over the last seven years but had always been too much of a coward to see through.

Could I really do it this time, though? It would certainly be a way out for me. In time, it would release Gemma and Harry and Chloe too. O'Brady surely wouldn't care. He'd find some other mug to bleed dry, and no-one else would bat an eyelid.

Could I really do it?

Did I want to?

Instead of heading back home, I turned right out of the cemetery toward the A38 dual carriageway. I twisted the throttle and the 1000cc engine of the Yamaha growled and whined with pleasure as the bike shot forward at speed.

I'd bought the Yamaha two years previously, against Gemma's wishes. She thought it was dangerous and pointless. We already had two cars to get around. She told me – only partly in jest – I was having a mid-life crisis a decade too early. I'd always wanted a bike, though, but had long put off buying one in favour of spending on more sensible things. Finally, two years ago, I'd put better judgment to one side and gone with my heart for once.

Riding the bike was a release from the real world. I loved the feeling of getting away from everything. Alice's dad, whom I still saw every few months when the kids went to visit him and his wife, often warned me of the dangers of motorbikes. In fact, it had become one of his favourite pastimes, it seemed. He'd been a rider for many years and had been through his fair share of scrapes. The stark warning he'd first given me was simple: everyone comes off. And he wasn't wrong. I'd fallen off the bike twice. Not at great speed, otherwise I surely wouldn't have lived to tell the tale. Both times had nonetheless shaken me.

The second time had been worse than the first. I'd leaned into a corner at a little under thirty miles an hour and the back tyre had inexplicably lost traction. I don't know why. The conditions were good and I wasn't travelling too fast. Whatever it was, I'd ended up off the bike, scraping along the ground until I came to a crashing stop against a parked car. The friction had burned through the right leg and arm of my leathers and taken away a good chunk of skin from each of my limbs.

A couple of weeks in bandages had seen me through, but the scars on both my leg and my arm remained as a warning. If I hadn't had the leathers on, the fall would likely have taken away flesh and muscle too.

In the aftermath of the accident Alice's dad had been only too keen to share stories of skin grafts and amputations and life-long physical deformity. I'd seen and heard first hand just how dangerous motorbikes could be. But as I headed toward the A38, those stories and memories and my own caution couldn't have been further from my mind.

I reached the roundabout and headed right toward a long stretch of dual carriageway that had little traffic, particularly during the middle of the day. Within seconds the powerful bike eased past one hundred miles per hour. The road was regularly used by bikers who congregated at the Bassetts Pole roundabout from where I'd just come. I'd never been part of that social scene, but I could see why they enjoyed the roads around there so much. I'd put the Yamaha through its paces on numerous occasions but had always stopped short of its full potential.

This time I wasn't going to hold back.

Dark Fragments

I pulled on the throttle further and the bike gained another twenty miles per hour with ease. I edged it into the fast lane to overtake a lorry and the bike wobbled in the heavy slipstream. I whizzed past a car, the bike still gaining speed, and barely heard the honking horn above the din of my engine.

I didn't slow down. In fact, by that point I was home free with not a car or bike or lorry in sight ahead. I turned the throttle further, adrenaline making my heart pump faster. My hands squeezed the grips and my legs tensed, as though doing so would somehow help to keep me on the speeding machine.

I closed my eyes.

I thought about O'Brady. Alice. I thought about Gemma and the children. I thought about my life and how it seemed to be moving from one disaster to the next.

I needed a way out. For me. For those I loved.

I turned the throttle as far as it would go. I squeezed my eyelids tightly shut, trying to close everything out. Trying to shut out the thoughts, the memories, that would change my mind.

Body braced, I waited for the inevitable.

After a few seconds, no matter how hard I tried to keep a blank mind, the doubts began to creep in. I tried to push them away, but it was no use. It was like trying to sweep away the tide: no matter how much I pushed, the waves just kept coming and coming, crashing ashore, destroying all barriers in their path.

How much longer would it take? I wasn't sure I could hold out. By my calculation the next junction was still about a mile away. Perhaps twenty or so seconds. Or would I come off the bike before then? With the growing doubts in my mind, I contemplated whether to just pull on the handlebars and head straight for the central reservation. Would I feel pain or would I be obliterated the second the bike tipped me off?

I couldn't do it. Something was stopping me. With my eyes still closed, with the engine fully revved and loving every second of having been set free, I willed something to happen. Willed my life to end right there.

And then it happened.

A stone in the road perhaps. Or a gust of wind, though it was impossible to tell because the air was already howling past me at such speed. Whatever it was, it knocked the bike off balance. The Yamaha wobbled from left to right under me.

If I'd just let myself go, if I'd let the bike do its work …

But I couldn't. An image flashed before me and my eyes shot open. Immediately I braked and fought for control. The engine whined then growled then spat. The rapid deceleration made me shoot up and forward in the seat, and it was only because I was so tense and my hands were so tightly gripping the handlebars that I didn't fly off. As the speed shot down, the wobbling worsened for a second or two until I finally regained control. In just a few moments the bike was almost at a complete stop.

As my heart pounded in my chest and my whole body shook, I heard the blaring horn from the car I had passed, and its driver and passenger screaming expletives, as it overtook me. Then came the lorry, its thundering bulk slapping a waft of cool air into me.

I watched them head off toward the junction, just a couple of hundred yards in front. Just a few seconds away if only I'd had the nerve to keep on going. I hung my head down, dejected.

I'd bottled it. I'd failed. Again. I was a coward. What other explanation was there? I'd always been a coward and I always would be.

And my cowardliness had left me facing a path ahead that was bound to be more painful than the death I couldn't face.

CHAPTER 6

'Do you have any regrets?' she asked.

The woman sitting across from me on the other side of the desk was in her early thirties, I guessed. She wore a navy-blue suit, an unpretentious blouse underneath. Her straight hair was tied back neatly and on the end of her nose was a pair of silver-rimmed glasses. She looked formal and stoic, yet her manner was pleasant and engaging.

Still, I didn't answer her question for a good while. There was so much to consider before I could answer fully. Really, it was a closed question. A yes or no answer would have sufficed. Yet I knew that wasn't what she wanted. This wasn't the first time I'd seen her and it wouldn't be the last. I was getting used to our sessions now. Used to her questions and her manner, and to me talking. She wanted me to open up, to tell her about my life and the things I'd done and give an explanation, some sort of reasoning. She said she was there for my benefit. To assess me. To help me. I wasn't sure I trusted any of that. But I hadn't held back. I'd given her what she wanted.

'All of the things I did were me,' I said at last.

'What do you mean by that?'

'If you put me into those situations again and again then ninety-nine times out of a hundred you'd get the same results. I can't make excuses for my mistakes. Would I rather they hadn't happened? Yes. I wish I could take back some of the things I've said and done in my life. Who doesn't? But it was all me.'

'I'm not sure that answers the question,' she said, her tone more authoritative than it had been before. 'Do you regret what you've done?'

'You're looking for a simple yes or no?'

'It's a simple question.'

'But it's not a simple answer.'

'How so?'

'I regret how my actions have had such an impact on those closest to me, yes. Do I wish I could change things? Of course. If I could go back and be a different person in every situation that has gone wrong in my life then I would. But I can't do that. I wish I could, but I just can't.'

'So the answer is yes?'

'The answer is: yes and no.'

'Can you explain why?'

'Yes I regret how my life has turned out. But no, I don't regret all of the things I've done. They were ... necessary.'

'Necessary?'

'Yes. I did what I had to do.'

CHAPTER 7

'Are you fucking crazy?' Gemma screamed.

Her berating me was understandable, under the circumstances – but the venom in her voice surprised me still. I was standing in the doorway to the lounge. She was across the room, standing by the fireplace. Even at that distance I felt myself cower at the ferocity of her voice, my tail well and truly between my legs. I knew there was simply no point in fighting this one. I was in too deep and I needed her help.

I had still been a shaking wreck when I'd finally had the guts to make my way back home. I wasn't sure whether that was because of the perilous situation I'd put myself in out on the A38, or anxiety over what was now to come. Perhaps it was lingering regret for having failed to take my own life.

If Gemma had sensed my inner turmoil, she didn't mention it. In fact, she'd simply gone into full attack mode the moment I'd laid my proposition out to her.

Not that I could really blame her for that.

'I don't know what else to do,' I said meekly.

'Just what trouble have you got yourself in this time?'

'This time?'

'Damn it, Ben, it was a figure of speech. You need to tell me everything. The truth. Who is he?'

Where to start? I mean, so much of the story was fucked up. I didn't know how to explain my relationship with O'Brady to Gemma, let alone how I'd pretty much thrown away our life savings with that thug.

But I had no other option than to tell her *something*.

'He's a businessman,' I said.

'Oh yeah, of course he is. And I'm the fucking Queen.'

24

'To me you are,' I said, managing an unconvincing smile.

'Not the time for lame jokes, Ben. How the hell do you owe a thug like that so much money?'

'It was a business deal. It didn't go well.'

'Gambling? Did you lose all of our money gambling?'

'No! Of course not.'

That would have been a simple explanation: losing the money gambling and borrowing from O'Brady to fuel a die-hard habit. Certainly easier to explain than the murky and trouble-riddled relationship I'd built up with O'Brady over the years.

'You know that's not me, Gemma. I was doing this for us.'

'So? What was it?'

'It was a property deal. A development. You know I've always been interested in doing that. I should have told you, I know, but ... I don't know why I didn't. I was scared you wouldn't want me to go through with it. And I wanted to surprise you when it was done.'

'Yeah well, you've certainly done that.'

'O'Brady and I both put money in. It didn't go well. We both lost. But ... I guess he lost more.'

'So how do *you* owe *him* money? If you've both lost money on some crappy development, that should be the end of it.'

'It's hard to explain.'

'Try me, Ben. If you want my help, you're going to have to try me.'

'He says it's my fault it went wrong. He says I owe him for his losses.'

'Was it your fault?'

'No. I don't know. Maybe. Either way, he's not the sort of man to argue the toss with.'

Gemma gave me a blank stare. I held her gaze, not knowing what else to do or say. Well, I could tell her more, but I was certain that wouldn't help my position. I knew that the more details I gave, the more of the mess I revealed, the less likely it was that she'd help.

Eventually she shook her head and looked away.

'How the hell did you even meet a man like that?' she said.

I was quite impressed that she'd read O'Brady for the scumbag he was. From what I'd gathered, he'd been on the doorstep for less than five minutes. Gemma hadn't even invited him into the house, her naturally suspicious instincts on high alert. Luckily for her – and for me – O'Brady had been accommodating of her lack of accommodation. I was sure if he visited again, she wouldn't get away with such a slight. O'Brady was a dangerous, violent and vindictive man. Even in the brief time he'd been on our doorstep, Gemma had figured out just what a slimy character he was.

'Ben?'

'I don't know. It just happened,' I said.

'Oh yeah. I've heard that one before.'

'What's that supposed to mean?'

'Nothing.'

'No, it's something. What does that mean? When I have I ever let you or the kids down before?'

Whatever she could say of me, my love and devotion for my children was one hundred per cent unwavering.

'Forget it,' Gemma said. 'This isn't the time. We need to figure this mess out first.'

'*This* mess? Like there's more?'

'Just stop!' she shouted. 'Look at us! Look at the way we are! Always fighting, always on each other's backs. Just drop it. I can't keep living like this.' She moved away from the fireplace and slumped down onto the armchair by the bay window, her head in her hands.

'I know,' I said, frozen in the doorway. 'I'm sorry. It *will* get better.'

'When?' she said, lifting up her head, her eyes teary.

'Soon. But we need to get that money. Seriously, Gemma, we need that money tomorrow. These guys aren't messing about. I've seen what they're capable of.'

'I can't believe you didn't tell me before,' she said. 'Why have you kept this to yourself? We could have prevented all of this.'

'I know. I'm sorry.'

'Are you?'

'Yes. I really am.'

She sighed, wiping at her tears with the sleeve of her jumper. I made to go over to her. I wanted to hold her and comfort her. But as I stepped forward, she held up a hand to stop me.

'Don't,' she said.

I stayed where I was. My heart thudded in my chest with anticipation as I awaited her next words.

'I'll do it,' she said. She closed her eyes and turned away from me. 'What choice do I have? I can't have those men coming to the house again. What if the kids had been in? We need this to be over.'

'Honey, thank you so much,' I said, striding up to her. Before she had the chance to protest I leaned over, grabbed her with both arms and pulled her into me. I'm not sure it was exactly a loving hug – I was consumed with relief more than anything – and I couldn't help but feel a fraud because of that, even though my next words to her were genuine. 'I love you. I really do.'

'Yeah,' was all she said to that. 'Where's my phone?'

I grabbed her mobile from the mantelpiece and handed it to her, then stood straight, watching over her, willing her to make the call.

I stared as she scrolled through the contacts list. I could feel my hands shaking, my legs too, as adrenaline rushed through me. Only then, in that moment, when Gemma was about to come to my rescue, did I realise just how far the situation had spiralled and how close to the bottom I'd come. But this was it, the turning point. If we could just get through this one, things would finally be on the up.

The phone was to her ear. I waited with baited breath so that I'd be able to hear the muted blips of the dial tone followed by the familiar voice. The tension was unbearable.

But I should have known better. I should have known that life wouldn't ever work out that smoothly for me.

Before the call had connected, there was loud knock on the front door. Frustration gripped me when I saw Gemma pull the phone away from her ear and press the red button to stop the call. Barely a split-second later, though, I was overwhelmed with anxiety. Because there was a much more immediate concern.

Who the hell was at the door?

Gemma was clearly thinking the same thing. She was staring at me, her eyes wide in fear, her mouth open.

'Is that …?'

She didn't need to finish the sentence. I knew she was thinking the same thing I was: O'Brady.

'He said I had two days,' I said, willing the scumbag to have kept to his word. But could I really trust him?

I knew the answer to that. No, I couldn't. Not at all.

'Oh yeah, 'cos he seemed like a really genuine bloke to me,' Gemma said.

'He wouldn't come again,' I said, wishing my words to be true. If he really was back at the house … well, I didn't even want to think about what that could mean. 'I told him he couldn't come here again.'

'You're not filling me with much confidence here, Ben.'

Three more knocks on the door. Heavy knocks. Purposeful. I could feel my heart jerk with each thud.

I walked over to the window and lifted the edge of the curtain to peek out. From the bay window of the lounge I wasn't able to see the front door, but I could see the car parked on the street beyond our driveway.

On seeing it I knew without doubt who was out there.

'Ben, let's just call the police,' I heard Gemma say from behind me.

I let go of the curtain and it flopped back into place. I stared at the closed drapes for a few seconds, then hung my head down, my brain spinning with thoughts of what to do next.

'Ben?'

I turned, avoiding eye contact with Gemma, but I saw that she was standing too, directly in front of me. I edged past her toward the lounge door.

'I'm calling the police,' Gemma said. 'We have to. It's the only way.'

I was just about at the door. I stopped and turned. Gemma had the phone in her hand and was doing her best with shaky fingers to key in the short number.

'No, Gemma. Don't,' I said.

Her hand froze and she looked up at me. Her face was a weary mess. She looked broken, defeated. She'd known Callum O'Brady for all of five minutes and this was what his presence had done to her.

That's how I've felt for years, I thought.

'Ben, they can help us. We have to call the police.'

'There's no need to call the police,' I said to her, my voice calmer than it had been moments earlier. 'They're already here.'

CHAPTER 8

I opened the front door and stared at the woman on the other side. A woman I recognised. A woman I knew so well that just seeing her sent my mind into overdrive.

She wore a smart cream blouse tucked into tight-fitting navy suit trousers. Her silky brown hair was straight and held back in a ponytail. Her unblemished face had just the faintest traces of make-up on it. An altogether formal look, but she carried it off well. She was pretty, I'd always thought that, and with her penetrating chestnut eyes she had an aura of confidence about her.

I stared at her for a couple of seconds without saying a word. Then, like a computer synchronising, a sudden rush of memories raced through my brain: all the times we'd spent together, everything we'd gone through – the good, the bad and the ugly. This was a person to whom I was inexplicably connected. And yet there was an uneasy distance between us now. There had been for years.

'Hello, Ben,' the woman said. My sister. My twin.

'Dani, come in.'

I felt Gemma's presence behind me.

'Dani!' she beamed, brushing past me and giving my sister a tight hug.

Dani's cheeks blushed red and she gave me a sheepish smile. It was certainly the warmest welcome she'd ever had at our house. If only she'd known the turmoil that had been going through mine and Gemma's minds just moments before, she might have understood the overly warm embrace from my wife.

Or maybe she did know? Maybe that was why she was there?

I wasn't sure whether I wanted that to be the case or not.

'Long time no see,' Dani said to me when Gemma let her go.

Her voice – authoritative and with a slight huskiness to it – matched her formal appearance. She may have been pretty but she was far from a dainty lady. I leaned over and gave my sister a brief hug, awkward and clumsy on both our parts. Gemma ushered Dani into the lounge.

'It's good to see you, Dani,' I said, coming into the room behind them. 'I mean, Detective Sergeant Stephens.'

'You too, Ben,' she said, taking a seat on the armchair on which Gemma had moments earlier been sobbing. 'Although it's Detective Inspector now, you know. I got promoted a while back.'

'Oh,' I said. 'I hadn't realised.'

'Yeah well, it's been a long time.'

'Yeah, I guess it has.'

'So what brings you here?' Gemma said, sounding more happy and relaxed than she had done in an age. She'd always got along well enough with Dani, although the two of them had never been real friends. I hadn't seen Dani for nearly four years and Gemma was acting like her sudden appearance was the most normal thing in the world.

'Oh, you know,' said Dani. 'Thought it was about time I had a catch-up with Ben. Water under the bridge and all that.'

'Yeah. About bloody time,' Gemma said.

I was becoming annoyed by Gemma's happy and calm manner. She knew my relationship with Dani was anything but straightforward. A lot of unspoken angst lay between us siblings – regret too – built up over a long time. I loved Dani, of course I did; we were twins. But there were plenty of reasons we were never going to be best friends. Her turning up out of the blue was, in many ways, a nice surprise, and I was glad of the brief intervention in what had been a crappy day. But letting her back into our lives was a big and not-so-simple ask. If that was even what she wanted.

Gemma looked over at me and twigged when I gave her a prompting look. She got to her feet. 'Would you like a drink, Dani?' she asked. 'Tea, coffee? Wine?'

'Oh, I'd love a glass of wine, but I'm still technically on duty.'

'Of course,' Gemma said. 'Don't want you getting into trouble. Soft drink then?'

'Coffee would be great. Black.'

'Me too, please,' I said to Gemma as she headed to the door and out the room.

I watched Dani as she looked around the room, as if gauging what had changed since her last visit. I wasn't sure whether her lack of eye contact with me was deliberate or not.

'This isn't a social visit then?' I asked.

'Yes and no,' she said.

I waited for further elaboration but it didn't come. 'So?' I said.

'Let me just get settled in first,' she said, looking over at me. 'It's been a long time, Ben. It's really good to see you.'

'You're right. It has. And it is.'

'How are the kids?'

'They're great.'

'That's it?'

'Well, what do you want me to say? If you were that interested, you could come and see them every now and then.'

'Yeah, because you've always made me so welcome.'

I tutted, annoyed by her flippancy. But that was my sister. We may have been twins, but in many ways we couldn't have been more different. She was the eldest by a full twenty minutes. I'd long wondered whether that was the reason she always acted so superior. She'd wanted to be the big sister all the time. Guiding me, telling me what to do. I'd run out of patience with that approach many years ago.

No matter what I'd done to please her and others, Dani had always been the star of the family, and that pissed me off. We were both clever, both got near-identical results at school, university too, but she was the one who got all the plaudits. Who did what she was told, everything our parents wanted. In truth she was more outgoing than me, more engaging. She was kinder and more caring. Fuck it, she was a nicer person, and that was what really riled me. Why couldn't I be the nice one, the one everyone liked?

Just thinking about it was making jealously worm its way to the forefront of my mind. I mean, even the way she was sitting nonchalantly on my damn armchair: she should have been awkward and self-conscious, coming into my home out of the blue after so long, and yet she exuded confidence; she was completely in charge of the situation.

Gemma came back into the room with the drinks and placed them on the coffee table in the middle of the floor.

'You two catching up?' she said.

'Something like that,' I said.

'You really need to come more often, Dani,' Gemma said. 'The kids would love to see their auntie. They ask about you. Chloe too, even though she's never met you.'

Dani smiled, though I could tell Gemma's final words had knocked her confidence a little. She was my sister, yet she'd never once come around to meet her niece. Chloe got birthday and Christmas cards from Dani, but so what? She was hardly going to be up for an Auntie of the Year award on that performance. Dani said nothing in return.

When we'd last spoken, some four years ago, Dani had owned a swanky pad in central Birmingham – a flash apartment in one of many new-build blocks around Brindley Place and the canals. I could only guess she still lived there. Alone. She'd certainly been free and single the last I'd known – always more focused on the career, to which she was inseparable, than in finding a partner and settling down. In truth, though, I had no idea. For all I knew, she could have got hitched, moved out, had kids. I'd have been entirely none the wiser.

Yet she'd been keeping tabs on me and my family over the years. She'd never even met Chloe, who'd been born after I'd last seen Dani, yet my sister had known when and where to send her a birthday card. More than once I'd wondered whether Gemma had kept in sporadic contact with Dani. I wouldn't have been surprised, nor would I have been angry at Gemma for doing so. But Dani's knowledge may just have been down to the detective in her, prying into our affairs from afar to keep informed.

'So is there a Mr Policeman yet?' Gemma asked, apparently still not ready to drop the perfect hostess act.

Dani laughed nervously. 'Oh, you know me. Always looking for the right one.'

'You'll find him,' Gemma said, giving an uneasy smile.

The fact was I wasn't sure Dani would ever find someone to settle down with. She'd had boyfriends of course, and her looks had always got her plenty of interest from men. But none of her relationships lasted. I'd never believed she'd truly been into any guy, and my impression was that none of her boyfriends had got over the fact that she had to be so in control of every aspect of life.

In the past I'd had cringe-worthy conversations with our mum about whether Dani might even be gay. I'm not sure my old-fashioned mum could have coped with that. But that wasn't the case at all. Dani was into men. She was just into her job and herself more.

It was the one aspect of Dani's near-perfect life that our mum had never been able to get over. All she'd ever wanted was to see her daughter married off to a prince so she could produce some perfect offspring. It had never happened. When Mum had been diagnosed with motor neurone disease nearly five years ago, I'd wondered whether Dani might have rushed to tie the knot with some random guy, just to give Mum that one last piece of satisfaction. But she hadn't.

Mum had passed away less than twelve months after her diagnosis. In just a few short months the disease had eaten away at her body and mind, tearing her apart organ by organ, limb from limb, so that she faded away to nothing before our eyes. Not long after she passed, Dani and I had parted ways indefinitely. Caught up in our own selfish grief, we'd pushed each other away when we should have been there for each other. But such is life. I guess we'd never thought at the time that our separation would go on for so long. As the weeks, months and finally years went by, it had simply become the norm.

Which brought me back to a very important point.

'What are you doing here, Dani?' I said, aware that my tone had been harsher than I intended.

Dani stopped mid-sip and both she and Gemma looked over at me. I thought about backing down, apologising for my abruptness, but I didn't.

'We need to talk,' Dani said.

'About what?' I said.

'Gemma, do you think you could give us a minute?'

Gemma frowned and gave me a questioning look. I nodded to her.

'Yeah, of course,' she said. 'I've got a phone call to make anyway.'

Her words, taking me back to the conversation we'd been having before Dani had turned up, were a welcome relief, soothing some of the bubbling tension that was filling me. I needed Gemma to make that call. It was the only way I could see to get Callum O'Brady off my back.

Gemma got up and left the room. I heard her feet padding up the stairs.

I looked over at Dani, waiting for her to get to the point. She took another sip from her coffee, then set the cup back down on the table.

'So?' I said. 'We need to talk about what?'

Dani sat back in her seat. All pleasantries were now dispatched. Her face had taken on a cold, hard look. I knew she had a lot to say, but for some reason she was struggling to start. I didn't push. I waited.

'Ben,' she said eventually. 'I don't know quite how to tell you this. There's been another murder.'

CHAPTER 9

I'm not quite sure what I felt on hearing my sister's words. Panic? Relief? Anger? Whatever the complex combination of emotion that washed over me, I'm certain it would have knocked me off my feet if I hadn't already been seated.

My sister stared at me. I could feel her steely gaze burrowing into my mind. She was a police officer after all, used to questioning people, getting them to open up. But more than that, she was my twin. Many twins claim to have an almost telepathic relationship with their sibling. That's simply bullshit. I'd never been able to read my sister's mind. Once, when we were younger and much closer, I could have hazarded a guess at her thoughts. I wondered what she was thinking in that moment. In fact, I really wanted to know. But I had no idea.

I sensed she was wondering the same thing of me. The truth was, I wasn't sure *what* to think. My brain was in turmoil. Alice had been murdered, in our own home, in our bedroom. That was seven long, harrowing years ago. No-one had ever been convicted of the crime. No-one had been charged. No-one had even been arrested.

It's hard for me to describe how that made me feel. Knowing that the killer of my first wife, Alice, the love of my life, had never been brought to justice, was still walking the streets. It was something I tried to think about as little as possible. Yet here was my sister, in my house for the first time in years, bringing all of those unanswered questions, all of the heartache and the turmoil that I tried each day to lock away inside me, back to the surface.

Dani broke the uneasy silence: 'We think it's the same killer.'

'We?'

'The police. The investigation team.'

My sister had understood the simple question. She'd had nothing to do with the investigation into Alice's death. Not officially anyway. How could she when she was my twin? On top of that, she had been Alice's best friend. It was through my sister that I'd met my first wife.

Alice's death had hit us both hard. Dani and I had been a lot closer to each other back then than we were now. For months, as the investigation faltered and stalled and eventually stopped, Dani – from the sidelines – had done her best to keep me informed of what was happening. Of all of the ultimately fruitless leads that had been followed. Even of the identity of some of the potential suspects who'd been thrown into the mix but then disregarded without so much as a single arrest.

We both knew she'd crossed the line professionally back then. That was a big step for her – glued to her job as she was. She was a stickler for the rule of law, but had pushed her own ethics and professionalism aside in that time of need. Whether that was more for my benefit or hers I wasn't sure. Either way, it was certainly a disciplinary offence to have divulged so much to me; possibly she'd even broken the law. I'd never asked that of her. It had been a natural sibling response. She'd wanted to help me, and with her hands tied behind her back by the police's internal code, telling me those details in secret was the only way she could.

I sensed from her answer that whatever the circumstances of this new murder, she was now on the sidelines just as she had been seven years ago.

And here she was, in my house.

'I'm guessing you're not here in an official capacity then?' I asked.

'I was, initially, assigned to the new case. But when it became clear it might be linked … obviously I can't be on it now.'

'But you've come to tell me about it?'

'I wanted you to know. I know we're not exactly on good terms but you're still my brother. And I still want to do whatever little I can to help catch Alice's killer.'

'How can they think it's linked?' I said. 'Fingerprints? DNA? There were none found in our house, other than mine and Harry's and Alice's parents', right?'

'The same here. No trace of third-party DNA. No fingerprints.'

'No suspects?'

'No. But the circumstances are … similar.'

'Similar? In what way?'

'No evidence of a break-in, no evidence at all as to how the killer entered the property, in fact. Both scenes were wiped clean professionally. I'm not just talking a quick clean with a feather duster – like I said, no trace of the killer. Plus, the way both victims were killed, strangled and then … arranged.'

I cringed at my sister's words.

'You mean … ?'

'Naked. On the bed. A single white dove feather placed on her chest.'

I took a moment to digest Dani's words. The white feather. Dani had told me that the police had feared Alice's murder could have been the work of a serial killer, the white feather being a calling card. I thought they had probably been watching too much TV. The hypothesis had never been made public and the police had found no other similar murders. Nor had there been any since, at least to my knowledge.

Until now.

'There's more,' Dani said. 'We have a witness.'

'A witness to the killing?' I asked.

'A witness who thinks they saw the killer, yes.'

My sister paused. I waited for her to carry on. 'And?' I said when she didn't.

'And that's about it. I can't say much more.'

'What do you mean you can't say much more?'

'I shouldn't really have told you what I just did even.'

'Then why did you?'

38

'I'm trying to help.'

'Help who?'

'The police. The victims. You.'

'Yourself?'

'No. Not that.'

We both paused for a beat and I let the information Dani had relayed sink in. But the vague facts she had given me really didn't add up to much. What I did know was that Dani wasn't in my home purely for my benefit. After all these years I just couldn't believe that was the case. She'd had plenty of opportunities to make amends with me, as I had with her; I could have done it at any moment. For whatever reason, I'd chosen not to. As had Dani, until now.

'So you still don't know who killed Alice?' I said.

'No, we don't. Not yet.'

'What did the witness see?' I asked. 'The killer's face? Have you got a suspect?'

'No,' Dani said. 'Nowhere near that far yet, I'm afraid.'

I shook my head. 'But you think it's linked?'

'Like I said, there're a lot of similarities. The crime scene. The movements of the suspect. How he was seen spying on the house – just the same as with Alice. Though it's always hard to know how realistic such sightings are. I mean, they only ever come to the witness's mind after the event. But I have to say, overall, when I read the police reports, it was like I'd been sent back in time seven years.'

'And that's the official line that's been taken, or is this just your own personal hunch?'

'It's official enough that the link is being investigated further.'

'It's a horrible thing to think,' I said, unable to hide the bitterness in my voice, 'but I hope it is the same guy. Maybe this time they can catch him.'

'I hope so too. But there's something else I need to talk to you about.'

I raised an eyebrow. 'What?'

'This isn't on record. None of this is. This is me talking to my brother. I'm not officially on the investigation now anyway, right?'

'Spit it out, Dani.'

'I've been reading back through the case files from Alice's investigation, trying to piece everything together in my mind again. Looking for anything that can help, any similarity to the recent killing, any discrepancy even.'

Dani trailed off and stared into space. I imagined that I could hear the cogs turning in her mind as she thought through what she wanted to tell me. I looked down and saw that my knuckles had turned white, my hands were clasped together so hard in anticipation.

'I read back through all the statements that were taken, yours included. I don't know how I didn't spot it at the time – I mean, I can't even remember if I read all those statements. Maybe I did and I thought nothing of it, or I just glossed over it – everything was such a blur back then. But this time … this time it was so obvious.'

'Saw what? What are you talking about?'

My sister stared at me – a hollow and unforgiving look.

'You lied, Ben. You lied to the police. And I want to know why.'

CHAPTER 10

I didn't say a word in response. Above our heads the ceiling creaked as Gemma walked across the floor of our master bedroom. I willed her to come downstairs to break the icy silence. After a few seconds the noise above died down, but I heard nothing from the stairs off to my right so she must have been in the bedroom still. It seemed I wasn't going to be saved so easily.

Dani had me right where she wanted me. I thought about trying to bluff, but I could tell from the look in her eyes – her bad-cop look – that she was going to press for an answer.

'So?' she said. 'You need to explain, Ben.'

'I'm not sure what you want me to say.'

'I want you to tell me the truth.'

'What do you think I lied about?'

'Don't play me for a fool. You know exactly what I mean. You and Gemma.'

'I didn't lie.'

'No? Well, it was as good as lying. Not one mention of her in any of your statements. You were seeing Gemma back then. You were having an affair. Did you not think that was relevant to the investigation?'

Of course Dani knew better than most people the troubles that Alice and I had gone through. She had been Alice's best friend after all. My infidelity had pushed Dani's loyalty to the limit.

My heart was racing. I really didn't know what to say, largely because I knew that the more I said, the worse I would likely make things for myself. I huffed and glared at my sister. I realised with certainty that her being in my house wasn't a call from the blue, a long-lost sister wanting to rekindle her relationship with her twin.

This was Detective Inspector Danielle Stephens one hundred per cent.

'No,' I said as calmly as I could, 'I didn't think me seeing Gemma was relevant to the investigation. It wasn't then and it isn't now.'

'Are you stupid? Of course it's fucking relevant. It gives you motive. You know you were a person of interest.'

I laughed with incredulity. 'Motive? Motive for what? I don't even know who this new murder victim is. Are you saying she's linked to me?'

'I'm not taking about the new murder and you know that.'

'Alice? You think I had a motive to kill Alice? My wife? Are you crazy? I loved her more than anything.'

'Loved her enough to be screwing Gemma behind her back.'

'It wasn't like that,' I hissed.

'Yeah, of course not.'

'It wasn't. And this is exactly why I never said anything when I was interviewed at the time. Like you said, I was a person of interest. Not because of anything I'd done but simply because I was Alice's husband. Have you any idea what that put me through? Why derail the wider investigation to focus on me, which it inevitably would have done if I'd talked about Gemma? I wanted the person responsible for Alice's murder to be caught, not for sordid rumours to be played out to all and sundry.'

'But it would have been the right thing to do. You can surely see that. And it looks a lot worse coming out now.'

'Is that a threat?'

Dani didn't say anything. I could tell she was mulling over her position.

'No,' she said eventually. 'I haven't told anyone. And I'm not planning to. This isn't my investigation.'

'Then why are you here? Why have you brought it up at all? Am I a suspect?'

'A suspect in what?'

'In Alice's murder? In this new murder?'

'Should you be?'

'Of course not! What a stupid bloody question.'

'It was you who raised it.'

My cheeks turn red. I realised I wasn't winning myself any favours with my reaction to Dani's questioning.

'No, of course you're not a suspect,' my sister said. 'This second murder – the victim is completely unrelated to you as far as I can see. It's the killer who's the common denominator. But you can't assume that someone else won't start digging back through the files from Alice's murder. And if they spot your *omission* too, it could still come back to bite you. If that happens, there's little I can do to help you.'

'I know that. I wouldn't expect you to anyway.'

'But you have to tell me,' Dani said. 'Is there anything else I need to know? About Alice? About that night? Anything that could possibly connect Alice to this new victim?'

'I don't know this new victim. You said so yourself.'

'That doesn't answer my questions.'

I looked away. I couldn't keep eye contact with my sister any longer. I'd been trying to ride over her words but they were bringing painful memories to the surface, taking me back to the bedroom, back to that horrific night. The sight of Alice splayed on our bed, her dead eyes staring at me. I squeezed my eyes shut, trying to think of something else. Gemma. I thought about *her* naked body. That didn't help. Neither did thinking about Gemma upstairs right now and the phone call she should be making. Trying to sort out another in a long list of problems in my life.

Maybe someone should just put me out of my misery once and for all, I thought. I certainly didn't have the guts to do it myself.

'Ben?' Dani said. 'Is there? Is there anything else you need to tell me?'

I stared blankly at my sister, thinking over the question. The days and weeks after Alice's death were a blur. Truth be told, I would have a hard time recollecting exactly what statements I'd given back then. But I did know one thing: Dani was right. I'd made a very deliberate effort to leave out Gemma's name and our relationship from all of the many statements I'd given. The reasons for that were far more complicated than what Dani had alluded to. I really didn't want to start going into that now.

I heard footsteps on the stairs and looked over at the open doorway to see Gemma descending. My heart jumped at the welcome sight and I willed her to come into the lounge. She looked up as she passed the doorway and it appeared at first that she was about to continue past, down the hallway to the kitchen. But when she made eye contact with me, whatever she saw in my eyes did the trick of drawing her into the room.

'How'd you get on?' I asked Gemma, knowing she wouldn't answer the question but wanting to get away from the painful subject of Alice's murder.

'Let's talk about that after.'

'Oh. Sure. Okay.'

I looked over and saw an added spark of suspicion in Dani's eyes but she didn't say a word.

'You two still catching up?' Gemma said, sitting down next to me.

'Actually, I think we were just about done,' I said, looking over at Dani.

'Oh, that was quick,' Gemma said, her eyes darting over to Dani for confirmation. My sister nodded. 'You can stick around if you want,' Gemma added. 'The kids will be back soon. It would be great for them to see you. You could stay for tea?'

'No, she's still working,' I said. 'Isn't that right?'

Dani gave me a less-than-impressed scowl in return, but I could tell she wasn't going to push the subject any further now that Gemma was back in the room.

'Yeah, that's right,' Dani said. 'Thanks for the invite, Gemma, but I really do have to get back to it.' She got to her feet.

'I hope you'll be back soon,' Gemma said with a warm but uncertain smile. 'It's about time you two put your differences to one side.'

'Oh, don't worry about that,' Dani said, her gaze fixed on me. 'You're going to be seeing plenty more of me.'

And with that, she headed for the door.

CHAPTER 11

'Were you suspicious about your sister's sudden reappearance?' she asked.

'Of course I was,' I said. 'Especially when she started to bring up details about Alice's murder investigation.'

'And why exactly did that make you suspicious?'

'Because I got the distinct impression that Dani knew more than she was letting on. About that new murder. About Alice's.'

'How did it make you feel, for Dani to turn up like that, out of the blue?'

How did it make me feel? It was a typical question from her. Everything was always about how I felt and what I thought. How on earth do you answer a question like that, though? Thinking about an event with hindsight is never the same thing as experiencing it at the time. Plus I'd always been a private and in many ways insular person. I was no good at talking about emotions – either my own or those of other people.

It wasn't that I didn't empathise with others, or that I wasn't interested in the impact that I had on other people. Analysing feelings was just such an alien and unnatural process to me. It was the way my brain was wired. Lack of artistic side or something like that. At least that's the way I always saw it.

I remembered in English literature lessons at school the part I detested most was having to analyse poetry and prose, debating the reasoning for the language used and what the author really meant by his or her words. What image do you think the author was trying to convey with those words, Ben? Errrr, that the sky was blue and it was a windy day. No, Ben. The author was conveying the struggle of slaves trying to free themselves from oppression in post-war America. Bullshit. Not everything has to have a hidden meaning or a deep and thought-provoking premise. Some things just are. Some things just happen, and no amount of analysis after the event can ever truly explain the reasons.

But on the flip side, I had to admit that the more I spoke to this woman, the more benefit I was getting. I'd never opened up about myself in such depth before – not with Alice or Gemma or anyone. The more I talked, the more I let out. Catharsis. I was purging myself.

'How did it make you feel?' the woman asked again. 'When Dani turned up.'

'It shook me,' I said, falling back in line and trying my best to think of a full and honest answer. 'Both in terms of what Dani told me about the second murder, and her questions about what I'd said to the police all those years ago.'

'Why had you lied to the police?'

'I didn't lie. Not exactly.'

'It was an omission of the truth.'

'Which isn't a lie. It doesn't matter how you try to spin it, I didn't lie to the police or to anyone else about Gemma. I simply didn't tell them. How could I when they were in the midst of trying to find Alice's killer?'

'You were scared the investigation would focus on you?'

'Of course I was. I mean, it already had focused on me to some extent. You see that all the time, don't you? The grieving spouse is always at least considered. So yeah, sure, I didn't want my name dragged through the mud. It was more than just self-preservation, though. It would have devastated Alice's parents. They're Harry's grandparents, a big part of his life. I'm sure my relationship with them wouldn't have been so smooth if they'd known I'd been seeing Gemma behind Alice's back.'

'So they never knew?'

'Never. Gemma and I, we didn't see each other much after Alice was killed. I'm sure you can understand I wasn't in a great frame of mind at that time. And when we did start seeing each other properly again, we didn't announce our relationship to our families until many months after.'

'Was that your decision?'

'It was a joint decision. It took both of us to make it work. I'm sure the revelation at the time wouldn't have gone down well from Gemma's point of view either – with her parents.'

'Was another reason for not admitting to the affair that you were ashamed of what you'd done?'

'Yes, it was,' I said.

'Why do you think you felt that way?'

'I committed a cardinal sin. I had an affair.'

'Was that out of character for you?'

'Absolutely. I've always been loyal. I'd never had any kind of affair before. When I made the vow to Alice on our wedding day to be faithful for the rest of our lives, I truly meant it. I truly wanted it.'

'So what happened?'

'It wasn't just one thing that happened. I guess life doesn't always work out as smoothly as you hope. I wanted to be faithful. But I never imagined just how hard marriage would be. How hard it is to keep it working. To keep the passion. Plus we'd had Harry. Having a baby isn't exactly a relaxing experience. Gemma came along and … it sounds ridiculous, but sleeping with her seemed like the answer to some of my problems.'

'And what do you think now?'

'I think the affair was a mistake,' I said. 'Plain and simple. I shouldn't have done it. I should have found the strength to walk away. I didn't. But my infidelity didn't take away any of the love I had for Alice.'

'Isn't that just an excuse you're using with the benefit of hindsight?'

'Maybe.'

'If Alice hadn't been killed, what would you have done? Would you have broken it off with Gemma?'

'I don't know. I really don't know.'

'So these are just excuses then?'

'Excuses? Yes, of course they are. There are so many pathetic, lame excuses I could give for why I slept with Gemma – the same worn excuses that everyone has heard a thousand times in soap operas and movies and books. The thing is, though, the thing that nobody else knew, was that I'd heard all those excuses before too. From Alice.'

'From Alice?'

'Now, I'm not using that as an excuse, I'm just painting the picture of reality here. The cold, hard truth is that Alice cheated too.'

CHAPTER 12

Alice was the love of my life, I've always believed that. Yet my relationship with her had been less than perfect for some time before her death. But that's life, isn't it? You have to expect that. It's how you deal with the ups and downs that counts.

Yes, Alice cheated on me. Before I cheated on her. Maybe that had clouded my better judgment. Maybe my being with Gemma had, in the very first instance, had an element of revenge to it. But I believed I had at least partly vindicated myself, given that in the longer term Gemma and I had forged a legitimate relationship despite the shady start to us being together, even if the relationship we forged was at times rocky.

It was Alice's infidelity, though, not mine that was the start of our downfall. We'd been trying to conceive, but it just wasn't happening. For months it had been getting us both down. Day by day the distance between us widened.

We'd both been for tests. In many ways I'd hoped there might have been a problem with one of us, some medical cause for our difficulties in getting her pregnant. It would at least have told us what was wrong, perhaps given us some options. We'd talked to each other about IVF, surrogacy, adopting, weighing up our thoughts on each. I was happy to explore any and every option. Alice was more hesitant, but ultimately she desperately wanted children.

In the end all the tests came back negative. According to the doctors we were both perfectly fertile and there was no explanation for why we hadn't conceived other than bad timing and rotten luck. Which only added to our frustration and contributed to the slow build-up of unspoken resentment.

My job hadn't helped matters. I'd been working on a large project that had seen me shipped off down to London for the best part of twelve months, during the week at least. Alice was mapping out her menstrual cycle week by week, marking out the days when we *had* to try, no matter what. Not only had I missed many of those days, but the planned and forced nature of our sex life was beginning to take its toll.

Alice was becoming a sex-crazed beast, a dog on heat, but her almost frantic desire was all about the end goal with little passion left in our brief and deliberate bedroom encounters. And with her increased, albeit forced, appetite for sex, my libido was in gradual decline.

I knew how important conceiving was to her, though. I knew it was important for *us*, for our relationship and our future. And that was why I told myself I had to stick with her. We had to keep going together. There was no other way.

So when I arrived home from London one Thursday night, a day earlier than expected, I'd been fully expecting not just a warm welcome but a hot one – for Alice to pounce, tear off my clothes and drag me upstairs to our bed; it was, after all, slap bang in the middle of her cycle.

It was a little after eight p.m. and dark out on the chilly autumnal evening. Alice had no idea of my impending arrival but I'd texted her an hour earlier from the train. She'd told me she was already home from work at that point. So when I was greeted by an entirely dark and chillingly cold house, my suspicion was immediately aroused. The fact the house was so cold suggested the heating hadn't been on since the morning, which meant Alice hadn't been back after work as she'd claimed.

After sorting the heating out, I went into the lounge, my coat still on to keep me warm, plonked myself on the sofa and mulled over what to do next. Of course, it was possible Alice's text had been a little white lie. There were countless explanations as to why she hadn't told the truth. I thought about ringing, or texting her, but I couldn't decide what to say. Would I come straight out and ask for an explanation? Or would that just start an unnecessary argument?

In the end, I didn't need to worry. Less than five minutes after I'd got home, I heard the front door opening.

I remained seated. It would surely take only a few seconds for her to realise the lights were on and I was home. I heard the front door being gently pushed shut and a moment later Alice appeared in the lounge doorway. I got to my feet and gave her a beaming smile. I had been away since Sunday afternoon and I was genuinely pleased to see her. But as I strode up to her I saw her face fill not with happiness at my unexpected appearance but with worry.

'You're home,' she said as I wrapped my arms around her and gave her a loving hug. 'You didn't tell me.'

'I wanted to surprise you,' I said, then planted a long kiss on her soft, sweet lips. She tasted of wine. 'Surprise!'

She gave a half-laugh and kissed me back, but then quickly backed off. 'Have you eaten?' she asked, moving away to take off and hang up her coat.

'Just a few snacks on the train,' I said. 'Could do with something really. Have you? I thought you were home already?'

'Oh. Yeah,' she said. 'It was just … I didn't want to worry you.'

'About what?'

'I've just had a really crappy week at work, that's all. I knew you were under pressure as well. I didn't want you to worry about me.'

'So you lied to me?'

'Yeah, I mean … I guess I didn't see it as a lie. It's nothing, Ben. I'm glad you're back.' She gave me a smile but it wasn't convincing. 'Come on, let's go and see what we can rustle up.'

Alice turned away and went to walk down the hall toward the kitchen. I grabbed her arm and swung her around, pulled her close to me and wrapped my arms around her.

'Or maybe,' I said, kissing her lightly, teasingly, on her neck, 'we could rustle up something upstairs instead.'

Alice giggled coyly and I carried on kissing her.

'Or maybe just down here,' I said. 'In the lounge. Or on the kitchen table. Hell, let's do it out in the garden.'

Alice laughed and pushed me away. 'What's got into you?' she said, smiling. But seconds later the anxiety that had shadowed her when she'd first walked in was back.

'I've just missed my wife,' I said, moving back in for the kill.

But Alice put her hand out to stop me.

'What's wrong?' I said.

'Nothing. I just … I'm just tired.'

'Come on,' I said, giving her my best attempt at a sultry look. 'I've not seen you all week. And it's one of your highlighted days, isn't it?'

'Yeah, I know. You're right, it is. But maybe later? We should eat.'

'What's wrong, Alice?' I snapped, my tone harsher than I'd intended.

'Nothing's wrong,' she responded, frowning. 'I don't have to drop my knickers just because you're horny.'

I tutted and stepped back from her.

'What's wrong?' I repeated.

'Do we have to do this now?' she said, trying to sound more placid.

'Yes, we do. We're doing this now. Tell me what's wrong.'

Alice put her head in her hands and let out a long sigh. When she looked back up just a few seconds later, she was welling up with tears. I tried to catch her eye but she averted her gaze and stared straight past me.

'I think you'd better sit down,' she said.

CHAPTER 13

Three hours later, I was fast losing all sense of purpose and reality as I drowned my sorrows in a seedy strip club in Birmingham. Of course I knew the alcohol was clouding my better judgment and only making my busy mind angrier and less rational, but in the moment it was the only solution I could see.

'It was a mistake,' Alice had said, back at the house. 'A stupid, horrible mistake.'

I'd already prepared myself for the moment. Everything about the situation had screamed what was to come. Yet the blow when Alice told me she'd slept with someone else the night before had still hit me like a thousand-ton train. I was left entirely numb. No anger, no sadness, no regret, just nothing. At first. But inevitably all those other feelings had quickly surfaced as my mind played over her infidelity.

'Who is he?' I snarled.

'It doesn't matter. Please. It's not an affair. It was a mistake. It'll never happen again.'

'Of course it matters. Who is he?'

Alice hung her head. 'Craig. From the office.'

I sat stunned. I knew him. I'd met him a few times when I'd accompanied her on nights out with her colleagues. He was a little weasel, an arse-licker who thought he was all that, both in his job and when it came to attracting woman. In fact I could recall countless times when Alice and I had joked about what a twat he was. Yet she, a married woman – supposedly happily married – had somehow fallen for his cocky charm.

'We were just drunk,' she said.

'I've been drunk plenty of times, Alice. It's never led to me sleeping with someone behind your back.'

Alice cringed. Tears had been streaming down her face since the moment I'd sat and waited for the inevitable. I felt for her – seeing her so weak and vulnerable. But I wondered whether some or all of her appearance was just an act. Did she really regret it? Or did she only regret that she'd had no choice but to confess?

'It'll never happen again,' Alice repeated. 'I mean it. That's where I was tonight. I think Craig thought it'd be open season for him now. He asked me out for a drink. That's where I was when you texted.'

'Did you sleep with him again?'

'No! How can you even ask that? I only said yes to him tonight because I wanted to talk to him. I wanted to tell him what a mistake it had been. That there was nothing between us, and there never would be. And that I love you.'

'It's a strange way of showing it.'

'I know I don't deserve your forgiveness, Ben, but it really was a mistake. I never wanted it. We all went out for some drinks. I told you where we were. We haven't had a team night out for months. We were having a good time and I needed to let my hair down. The last few months have been really hard. I've been on my own week after week.'

'Oh, so it's all my fault now?'

'No,' Alice said, putting her hand on my knee. I brushed it off. 'Not at all. I'm not saying that. But you have to admit it's been tough. And then there's the whole baby thing. I've just been so down. And I've had no-one to turn to.'

'Well, I can see how jumping into bed with someone else could solve all that for you. What, you were hoping Craig could do the business and get you pregnant where I've failed so miserably?'

'That's not it at all,' Alice snapped, her tone tinged with anger and a hint of resentment. 'That's just ridiculous and you know it.'

I huffed and stared at her. She held my gaze for only a second before turning away.

'We were just drunk,' she said. 'He kissed me and I don't know what I was thinking, but I kissed him back. Then, at the end of the night, he said he'd help me get a cab. We ended up back at his apartment and –'

'Did you use protection?'

I immediately felt uncomfortable at my own words. I really didn't want to hear any more of the sordid details of how they'd wound up with no clothes on and his dick inside her, but my mind was still mulling what I'd said just a few moments before. What she'd said too – about the difficulties we'd been having in conceiving. And it was something … no, it was the *only* thing left that I had to know.

Alice stood up from the sofa, facing away from me. She didn't say a word. I could hear her sobbing. I waited for her to respond to my question. After a few moments, I realised her silence had given me the answer. Disgusted, I got up from the sofa, grabbed my coat, and was out of the door without either of us speaking another word.

Several beers and whiskies later, the conversation was still playing over and over in my mind. The sordid encounter she'd had flickered in my thoughts as I replayed my own interpretation of my wife sleeping with that creep.

Had she enjoyed it? Had he made her come? Had she moaned and screamed out his name as she rode on top of him, the two of them climaxing in ecstasy? Had they lain panting, smiling, glowing, in each other's arms afterward?

Or had it just been a fumbling, humping mess for two and half minutes, followed by an awkward conversation and a quick exit?

I would never know. Because I would never ask. But that didn't stop my mind imagining the many unpleasant possibilities on non-stop repeat.

I downed the whisky shot in front of me and asked the barmaid – a chesty young lady with an impossibly tight top, cleavage spilling over – for another. She frowned, probably realising I was already wasted, but nodded and got the drink. I ordered a cold beer too and took two long, satisfying sips before necking the spirit.

I swivelled on my stool to face the stage, where two topless women were busily acquainting themselves with a shiny upright pole.

I'd never been a fan of strip clubs. I'd never really felt the need to pay to see a woman's breasts when I had a beautiful wife at home. Still, over the years I'd been to plenty. Always as part of a larger group, though; never on my own before. I stared over at the dancers, their toned bodies writhing and gyrating on the stage and up and down the poles. I felt nothing. I saw nothing. My mind was too busy thinking over my wife's betrayal. And, increasingly, filling with ill temper directed toward one person. Not Alice, but Craig Fletcher.

My eyes scanned my less-than-salubrious surroundings. Even as far as strip clubs went, the place was a dive. It was in a rundown back street in Digbeth. Once a heart of industry, the enclave near the centre of the city had gone through decades of downfall, and it had only begun recovering in the last few years. Full Spread was a club from a bygone era. With trendy wine bars and lounges, nightclubs and new apartments springing up here, there and everywhere, its days were surely numbered. And yet even on a cold Thursday night it was pulling in plenty of punters.

I looked at the men sitting around the stage, some in groups, many on their own. I wondered what had brought them all to this dark and dingy and sleazy place. Had any of them just found out their wife had cheated on them? Or were they the cheaters? Perhaps visiting this place was the dirty little secret they kept from their spouses.

One of the groups of lads was getting overly rowdy and two burly bouncers came over to their table. The boys quickly settled down on their seats. I was disappointed that their bravado hadn't escalated – it would have been fun to watch the fight.

Action had certainly kicked off the only other time I'd been to the club. I'd been with a group of four other guys from our office. It was late, we were horrendously drunk, and one of the more senior guys in the team had insisted we come. I'd assumed he wasn't getting laid at home – he'd been banging on about going to a strip club the whole night. It was unspoken knowledge that some of the dancers at the club would give a little extra if you were prepared to pay for it and I'd assumed that was why he'd chosen the place. The fact he'd even said he'd pay for all our drinks meant no-one had seriously objected.

As invariably happens, though, when you put a group of five drunk men in front of scantily clad woman, it didn't take long for our obnoxious sides to show. Before long some of the guys were hurling abuse at the dancers, and then one decided to give a waitress a slap on her backside as she walked past.

Next thing we knew, four bouncers were descending on our table. Bizarrely – and this is a testament to just how deranged alcohol can make you – three of our group, just regular guys, scrawny office workers, saw it as a challenge and squared up for an improbable fight. Luckily one of our group knew better. At first I thought he was just being a peacemaker. That wasn't the whole story, though.

'Guys, for fuck's sake,' he said as he struggled to hold back two of the men stupidly egging on the bouncers. 'We need to apologise and go. Seriously. Do you know who owns this place?'

The answer was, I didn't. None of us did. Not then. We were eventually frog-marched out of the club and hurled into the street. The peacemaker then filled us in on the details of who owned the club. Which was the exact reason I was back there tonight. I wasn't interested in crying into my drink as I ogled the girls, pitying myself and the position I'd found myself in. I was there to see someone.

As I continued to scan, my eyes set on the table in the raised area of the club. Roped-off, it had a panoramic view overlooking the whole grubby expanse. I gazed over at the group of people clustered around the two tables there and found the man I was looking for. The man I'd come to see.

Callum O'Brady.

CHAPTER 14

'What made you want to meet a man like Callum O'Brady, Ben?'

'Anger,' I said. 'A need for revenge. It's stupid, puerile, I know. But that's the answer.'

'I can understand feeling that way, but to actually act on it? That's something quite different. It seems so out of character for you up to that point in your life.'

'What, you think I'm too weak to have done something like that?'

'If anything I think it showed a certain amount of weakness that you thought Callum O'Brady was the solution.'

'You're probably right,' I conceded. 'But I was desperate. I had to do something.'

'Do you see yourself as a violent person?'

'Not at all. I never have been. Like any kid I got into scrapes when I was younger, but I can count on my fingers the number of times I've thrown a punch at someone in my life.'

'What about your sister? Your father?'

'Dani? She was always physically superior to me. I mean, I'm bigger and stronger, but she's so much more athletic and agile. She was great at every sport she tried. I wouldn't call her a tomboy exactly, because as a kid she did all the things girls do too. But she's always been able to handle herself, that's for sure.'

'Did you ever fight with her?'

'Of course I did.'

'Physically?'

'Yes, but only when we were very young. I quickly learned it was a no-win position for me. Yeah, I'd get angry with her, and we'd come close to an all-out physical fight, but as we grew older I'd always back down before it escalated. I was doomed to come off worse. If she knocked me out, I would be

the guy who got beaten up by his sister. And if I knocked her out, I would be the guy who beats up girls. She could always get away with so much crap because she knew I was in that bind.'

'Did you harbour a grudge against Dani because of that?' she asked.

'In a way, yes. Not that she would ever have noticed that. She was too busy trying to be the superstar of anything and everything.'

'And what about your father?'

'Did I fight with him? Did he hit me? What's your question exactly?'

'Both of those questions, yes. Was he a violent man?'

'No,' I said. 'I didn't fight with him. And he didn't hit me. But was he a violent man? He was more used to violence than I am, I'd say, but no, he wasn't violent.'

'How do you mean?'

'He was a good man. A real man. He grew up in a different age to me and Dani. Our upbringing was comfortable; our parents weren't rich, but we didn't want for anything. My dad, though, couldn't have had it more different. He was brought up in a tough working-class neighbourhood. His parents, my grandparents, were really poor. He told me so many stories of his childhood there – the violence on the estate where they lived, the constant struggle to make ends meet. He was the first kid from that area to break the mould and get out and make something of himself.'

'You're proud of him?'

'Of course. Actually, I think I was in awe of him too.'

'Why was that?'

'Because in many ways I wanted to be like him. But I just didn't have the same edge he did. The same edge Dani has.'

'Can you describe what you mean by that?'

'Dad told me once about his family moving to a new area when he was thirteen, fourteen. The other kids shunned him, made him an outsider. So what did he do? He challenged the biggest, hardest kid on the street to a fight. My dad wasn't that big but he was clever. He went for speed: hit the guy hard and fast before he knew what was coming. And that was it – he was accepted.'

'You're proud of your father because he could handle himself in a fight?'

'Well … yeah. I know that sounds silly, but I bet nearly every guy has macho tendencies like that. Everyone wants to appear heroic and brave.'

'That's how you saw your father?'

'In some ways, yes. I would never have done something like that as a kid. But it was a different world back then. Fighting was more or less a hobby for boys. They didn't have mobile phones or games consoles where you get to beat up the bad guys on screen and shoot thousands of aliens.'

'So they just beat up each other instead? It sounds horrible,' she said, her face screwed up. *'Don't you think? To be brought up so close to and so used to physical violence? You know, a lot of people would say such violence has a habit of creeping into home life too. Isn't it better that we live in a more liberal and less violent society today?'*

'I'm not sure I agree. There was something pure about how life was back then. It's a natural instinct in humans to act like that. They were just boys. The way we bottle up emotions in this day and age, the way we shy away from conflict, it makes things worse, because the end result is so much more extreme.'

I saw a flash in her eyes at my words and I knew what she was thinking. She didn't say anything and I carried on.

'We have horrific violence today,' I said. *'These kids were fighting, but they were fair fights, noble. It was all about testing each other. They didn't take knives and bottles, they weren't out to inflict serious harm on each other. There was nothing cowardly or malicious about it.'*

'So when you reached out to Callum O'Brady,' she said, *'was that you trying to take the bull by the horns, so to speak, to be more like Dani and your father?'*

'Maybe at the time I thought so.'

'And now?'

'In hindsight, I think it was the opposite.'

'How so?'

'Like you said, it showed weakness on my part. Dani and my dad would have just sorted out the issue themselves. They would have figured out a way on their own, without needing someone like O'Brady.'

'But you couldn't?'

Rob Sinclair

'At the time, O'Brady seemed the obvious and immediate solution. I guess you never quite know how a good person is going to react when they get put under immense stress. In the heat of the moment going to O'Brady was the only option I could see.'

CHAPTER 15

I threw back the rest of my beer then got up from the stool. As I began to walk, I realised just how drunk I was. The room swayed with each step I took and I wobbled clumsily across the floor, but somehow managed to keep my blurred vision focused on my destination.

As I approached the rope barrier, I stopped. I'm not sure what I'd expected to happen. I could see O'Brady sitting up on the platform in front of me. He had two glammed-up girls next to him – one hanging off each of his shoulders like fashion accessories. To my right sat another man, also with a girl by his side. They were busy examining each other's tonsils. To my left sat a giant, scowling man I would later come to know as Elvis.

O'Brady's steely glare was fixed on me as I hovered by the rope, but neither he nor his company made any attempt to accommodate me. Taking matters into my own hands, I put one leg over the rope, my mind made up that I'd just go right up to them. No sooner had I done so, however, than I was grabbed suddenly from behind.

I did my best to shrug off the man who'd taken hold of me, but his huge hand and thick fingers held firm.

'I'm here to see Mr O'Brady,' I slurred over to the group, trying to break free from the vice-like grip.

I looked up at O'Brady. He was still staring at me.

'I have a business proposition.'

O'Brady looked on but said nothing, his expression devoid of emotion. The man holding me jerked me backward, taking me off my feet, and began to pull me away, my scrambling legs dragging on the floor. My ill-thought-out plan was already on the rocks.

But just then O'Brady nodded. In an instant the man holding me pushed me up and let go. I was caught by surprise and wasn't ready to take my weight and almost fell backward into him. He kept me upright and then nudged me toward O'Brady and his group.

As I moved away I turned around and looked at the bouncer who'd grabbed me. He stood, arms folded, with a smug look on his face. I shook my head, showing my distaste for him, acting way cockier than I had any right to be in that situation. He raised his eyebrows. I wondered then whether that indiscretion would come back to bite me.

I stepped forward over the rope barrier and up the three steps toward O'Brady's party. All six people were now staring at me coldly. The three women had distanced themselves somewhat from their chaperones and were glaring at me, clearly unimpressed by the intrusion.

I got to within six feet of O'Brady's table before he held a hand up to stop me.

'Mr O'Brady. My name —'

'Do I know you?' O'Brady queried in his raw Irish accent. He squinted his eyes as he spoke as though trying to gauge the answer to his own question.

'No, I —'

'Then we have no business,' he said.

'But I … a proposition —'

O'Brady leaned forward. 'We. Have. No. Business,' he said.

'Won't you at least hear me out?' I said, my gaze flicking over to Elvis who was now on the edge of his seat, clearly eager for a nod from his boss to allow him to take action.

Despite the vast amount of alcohol coursing through my bloodstream, I felt a moment of clarity and suddenly realised that maybe O'Brady was right. I could already see that I was getting in way over my head.

'Okay,' O'Brady said, to my surprise. 'So what do you do?'

Dark Fragments

I frowned at the question. 'I'm a … I'm a management consultant,' I said, cringing at my own words. 'But that's not –'

'Ah, you can feck off then,' O'Brady said, waving me away. 'Waste of money the lot of ya.'

Elvis got to his feet. My face must have been a picture as I looked up at the gigantic figure looming over me. I backed away, my eyes not leaving Elvis. He matched my every move, stepping forward with each step I took back. I stumbled down the stairs, and only when I got to the bottom did I turn around and make a beeline for the exit.

Heart racing, head pounding, I stepped out into the street and felt a sense of relief as the cold, fresh air hit my face. A second later, though, a wave of nausea coursed through me. I wasn't sure whether it was from the drink or the perilous situation I'd just put myself in. I grabbed hold of my knees and put my head down between my legs, waiting, hoping, that the feeling would pass and I could keep my stomach contents inside me.

When I felt able I straightened up, took a deep breath and looked around the street – deserted – then behind me at the door of the club. With no sign of Elvis or the other goons, I felt a further wave of relief.

I went to turn around to trudge toward the twenty-four-hour taxi rank five minute's walk away. It was time to go home. As I did so, though, I saw the man. Well, not the man – his balled fist hurtling toward my face. With no time to react – and too inebriated to have been able to even if I'd known it was coming – I put up no defence as the fist crashed into the side of my head. I was down on the ground before I knew it. I took a kick to the gut that knocked the wind out of me. My eyes bulged wide and I heaved, trying to catch my breath. Everything in front of me flickered into a wall of bright white light.

Seconds later I was out.

When I came to, a bulky bouncer was standing over me. He was dressed from head to toe in black, his leather-gloved hand outstretched toward me.

'Come on, son,' he said, his voice deep and husky and not unkind. 'Time for you to go home.'

He put his hand into my armpit and tugged. I groaned and got to my feet groggily, letting the bouncer take most of my weight.

'What happened?' I said.

'What happened? You've had a bit too much to drink, mate. Home time for you.'

'No. Someone hit me,' I said, holding my hand up to my head.

I pulled it back and looked at the dark, moist patch on my hand. Blood. Coming from a gash above my left eye.

'Nah, mate. You're just drunk. You fell over. Hit your head.'

I patted myself down. Realised my wallet was gone. My phone, keys, everything else was still in my pockets, though.

'What are you on about? I've been mugged. Someone's taken my wallet. Did you not see?'

Another bouncer sauntered over. His face was hard and unwelcoming compared to his colleague's.

'Time for you to go, son.'

'I've been attacked!' I protested.

'Time for you to go,' the bouncer repeated, his tone harder.

I held his glare for just a second. I wanted to stand and argue. I didn't know what was going on or why they weren't listening. Perhaps they really hadn't seen what had happened and just assumed I fell. Or maybe they were lying – but why?

Whatever the answer, I knew they were right. I wasn't welcome.

I turned and stumbled off down the road, looking back every few steps to make sure no-one was following me. The bouncers stayed by the club entrance, their eyes fixed on me the whole way down the street. When I got to the end of the road, I turned and ran.

CHAPTER 16

When my alarm went off at six thirty a.m. the next morning, my head was a painful, pounding mess. Much of that was the alcohol I'd drunk, I realised, but I was sure the punch to the head and the kick to the stomach hadn't helped matters.

Despite my drunken state and the wounds on my face, I'd managed to find a taxi driver willing to take me from the city centre back to Sutton Coldfield where Alice and I lived. Although in recent times it was considered a suburb of Birmingham, the town had a rich history in its own right. It was the size of most small cities with a largely middle-class population and some pockets, particularly in the northern parts, of real wealth. Not the type of area where you'd expect to see men with bashed-up faces wandering the streets in drunken stupors. Yet that had certainly been me the previous night.

My memory was hazy, but I could recall a brief argument with the taxi driver who'd stopped the cab and ordered me out some half a mile away from my house. He'd obviously realised what was coming. Just a few steps further I'd been hunched down, hands on knees, spewing my guts up all over someone's front hedge.

The embarrassment I felt on remembering my antics was palpable. But I really hadn't intended to act that way. I certainly didn't make a habit of anti-social behaviour; it was simply a testament to the dreadful state I'd been in. I supposed the one saving grace was that my drunken foolery hadn't been anywhere near my house. I could only imagine what the reaction on our street would have been if a neighbour had seen me spewing in their garden. Not that that made it any better for the poor sod who was waking up to a sick-filled hedge.

I groaned as I lifted myself upright and pain shot through my abdomen. Looking down at my bare midriff, I saw the large purple bruise at the base of my ribcage. It looked like a blot of ink had stained my skin.

I got to my feet and gave a cursory glance to the other side of the king-sized bed. It was empty. When I'd arrived home – I'd no idea what time, but it was somewhere on the border of late night and early morning – Alice had been asleep on the sofa, fully clothed with her dressing gown over her. I'm not sure whether she'd intended to fall asleep there or she'd been waiting for me to return home. I hadn't woken her, but stumbled up the stairs and somehow managed to undress before collapsing onto the bed.

I moved toward the en-suite and turned on the light. The sudden intrusion of brightness elicited a fresh stab of pain between my eyes. I studied my tired and beaten face in the mirror. I looked every bit as bad as I felt. My eyes were bloodshot and I had big, dark bags under each socket. My face was puffy and pale, and dried blood caked my forehead and one side of my head. I reached up and touched the wet spot just above my eye that was glistening in the light. I winced. The wound was open but it was more of a graze than anything – it wouldn't require stitches, just cleaning up and a plaster. It made me wonder whether it had come from the punch or I'd scraped it as I'd tumbled to the ground like the bouncer had suggested. I couldn't be sure either way.

After a cool, soothing shower I felt noticeably fresher. I got dressed and slowly trudged down the stairs, in two minds as to whether to just walk straight out of the house or at least try to engage with Alice.

As I reached the bottom step, I realised my noise upstairs had already woken her. We lived in an old Victorian terraced house and the worn, creaking floorboards made it impossible to move about discreetly. I stood in the doorway to the lounge. Alice was sitting up on the sofa, the dressing gown still draped over her. Her hair was scruffy, her face a blotchy mess. She looked tired and full of angst. And as I stood there, despite the pain in my gut and the aching in my heart, I realised just how much I still loved her. I really loved her. I had to find a way to forgive her for what she'd done. I just wasn't sure how.

'Ben, what on earth happened to you?'

She got to her feet and came over to me. She reached out with her hand and touched the wound above my eye. I barely reacted to the pain.

'I was mugged,' I said. 'They stole my wallet.'

'Oh, Ben. Have you called the police?'

'No. Not yet.'

'Then you need to. Did they take your phone too?'

'No. It's right here,' I said, tapping my pocket.

Alice frowned at that. 'I'll get you a plaster,' she said.

She rushed off and came back a few moments later. I was still standing by the doorway, not sure what to do or say next. Alice placed the plaster over the wound. When she was finished, she threw her arms around me and burrowed into my chest. Initially I stood motionless, hands by my sides, but then I wrapped my arms around Alice and squeezed her tightly – a natural and unpremeditated response.

'I'm so sorry,' she sobbed. 'You have to believe me.'

I didn't say anything.

'I was really worried last night,' she said. 'I was worried you might not come back to me. I couldn't cope without you.'

When she pulled back I saw the genuine trauma in her eyes. I wanted to hug her again and tell her that everything would be okay. But I didn't. Because I wasn't sure whether I'd be telling the truth.

'I need to go to work,' I said.

'Okay,' Alice said with a disappointed smile. 'I hope we can get through this, Ben. I love you. I love you more than anything.'

'Yeah,' I said, 'I love you too.' Then I turned and left.

The rest of the morning dragged by as I tried to appear useful in the office. In reality, I was about as productive as a stoned monkey. And it wasn't just because of the hangover. I couldn't focus, not on a thing. My brain was all over the place, going over and over the conversation with Alice the night before, the thoughts of her with Fletcher, and the bizarre situation I'd thrown myself into at the strip club. By noon I was wondering whether I should just bite the bullet and call it a day, take half a day's holiday and drag myself back to bed. Or to a pub. Drown my sorrows once more.

But then my phone rang. I picked the mobile up off my desk. Unknown caller. I answered it.

'Is this Ben Stephens?'

The Irish accent and the tone of the voice were unmistakable.

'Yes.'

'This is Callum O'Brady. You remember me, right?'

'Yes,' I said again. I could feel my heart thudding in my chest and my palms getting sweaty. I looked around the office nervously, as though someone might know to whom I was speaking.

'Grand. Well, I have your wallet. Why don't you come around to the club later to collect it?'

'You have my wallet?' I said, my mind in overdrive.

'Yeah, if you're Ben Stephens, I have your wallet.'

'Okay. No, that's great. Thank you,' I said. 'I'll come and get it.'

'I'll be there after eight. Perhaps we can talk some more about that business proposition you have.'

I opened my mouth to speak but he'd already hung up.

CHAPTER 17

In my intoxicated state the previous night, I'd thought O'Brady could help me. But in the cold light of day I was having serious doubts about my drunken judgment – not just in approaching O'Brady, but about what I was approaching him to do.

His sudden change of heart, following his initial outright refusal to engage with me, worried me too. I knew very little then about who O'Brady was. I'd never even met him before. I knew him only by second-hand reputation, hearsay. He was a thug. A criminal. A gangster. He had a reputation for violence and for getting what he wanted.

I'd thought most of what I'd heard was probably embellished make-believe. Playground chatter. People wanting to find a Hollywood baddie on their doorstep just so they could gossip about his notoriety. But something about O'Brady's presence told me that at least part of what I'd heard must have been true. He wasn't a straight-laced businessman, that was for sure.

I just hoped I wasn't already in too deep.

My plan was simple: get the wallet and backtrack out of there as fast as I could.

I finished work at five p.m. on the dot and headed straight to a local real-ale pub not far from the office for some much-needed Dutch courage. Alice had been calling me through the day and had left several voicemails with her in various emotional states, from calm and collected through to full-blown meltdown. I hadn't yet called her back. I was feeling bad about that. I hated the thought of what she'd done – I hated that slimy prick Fletcher too. And yet, as the day had worn on, a gnawing regret had built up in me. I loved Alice, and I knew that while I couldn't excuse what had happened, I could at least sympathise with how hard the last few months had been. Despite what she'd done, I wanted to be with her. I just needed to find a way.

After four pints and some banal conversation, first with the barman and then with another loner at the bar, I was feeling light-headed and had just a sliver of extra confidence, though I was still wracked with nerves. I left the pub and trudged across the grounds of St Philip's cathedral then onwards, past the city-centre shops and over toward the much less respectable area where O'Brady's strip club was located.

Digbeth might have been on the way up once more, but parts of it were still downtrodden and you were only ever one wrong turn away from entering one of the seediest parts of the city. Despite that, I'd never before felt nervous walking the streets there – perhaps because I was usually beered-up. This time, though, my whole body was tense.

I rounded the corner onto Princes Road – a name that was an oxymoron given the decrepit buildings that lined it – and walked as casually as I could up to the entrance to Full Spread. It was five past eight and I doubted it would be open yet, but two bouncers were stationed outside, arms folded, their faces sullen and scowling. I glanced at them both and wracked my blurred memories of the previous evening. I couldn't be sure whether they were the same guys who had so coldly turned me away into the night.

The overgrown doormen, their bodies positioned to cover the closed entrance, barely blinked as I headed right up to them.

'I'm here to see Mr O'Brady,' I said, sounding a lot calmer than I felt.

The men stared at me for a couple of seconds as though I was an imbecile, but then the one on the right, the shorter and older of the two, turned and opened the door for me.

'He's in the office,' he growled.

I nodded and stepped in. As I had thought, the club was yet to open. The inside was fully lit up, the true extent of its dirt and filth and worn-out fittings plainly evident. Two cleaners scuttled about mopping and vacuuming floors. Their efforts were decent, I was sure, but later on, with the lights turned down, nobody would notice the difference.

A solitary barmaid stood in position, getting her area ready for the night ahead. Other than that, there was no-one about and the place was surreally calm and relaxing. I walked up to the barmaid, the same young lady who had been there the night before, I realised.

'I'm here to see –'

'In the office,' she said, pointing over to her right with a sullen pout.

'Sure, thanks,' I said and walked on.

I spotted the door at the far end of the club. In the centre was a small plaque with the words: *Staff only. No exit.* I was a couple of feet from the door when it opened and a woman walked out.

Jaw to the floor, I stared. Her voluptuous and beautifully pert breasts stared right back at me. I couldn't help but let my eyes slide. The only item of clothing she wore was a cheese-wire-thin G-string and a pair of stilettos that made her taller than me. She had a perfectly proportioned body and a silky bronze sunbed tan. But when I finally looked at her face I saw, in the bright lights of the closed club, that it was caked in thick and hastily drawn make-up that made her look unappealing and garish. As with the club interior, I guessed that when the lights went down no-one would notice much, if they were bothered about looking at her face at all.

Without a word, she grabbed my hand and escorted me through the door. We entered a corridor, the white-painted walls and tiled floor a stark contrast to the dark finish of the club. She ushered me into a small, mirrored room, with a plush purple carpet underfoot and an extravagant mock-chandelier overhead casting a warm glow. The only furniture in the room was a leather armchair. She stood me in front of it.

'This is the office?' I said, raising an eyebrow.

'No,' she said, pulling a sultry face and coyly running a finger down my shirt buttons. 'This is a treat. Just for you.'

She slowly began to gyrate in front of me, her hips moving seductively from side to side in a rhythmic fashion to some unheard music. I stood motionless, trying my hardest to keep my eyes off her sumptuous body. But I just couldn't help it. Wherever I sent my gaze she was there, multiple times in the mirrored walls.

She turned around and shook her backside, bobbing it up and down, edging in closer and closer to my crotch. I tried my best to stay calm, relaxed, focused. She straightened up, turned back around, and moved right into me. The smell of her perfume filled my nostrils as she gazed into my eyes. She placed her fingers delicately onto my chin and pushed her bright-red lips, which reminded me of a clown, right up to mine as though she were about to kiss me ...

A step too far. I'd had enough. I was about to shove her back, away from me. But then I hesitated when she took me by surprise – she began to slide up and down, her body and fingers brushing and stroking teasingly all over me. Then her hands began to roam free. No longer the gentle, caressing touch – more deliberate and purposeful.

I quickly realised what was happening.

A treat? Not exactly. She was patting me down. Checking me for any weapons, recording devices or whatever else it was that O'Brady was concerned I might be carrying. An unusual way to do it, for sure, but I'd watched enough TV to understand the focused nature of her hand movements.

She took the phone out of my pocket, gave it a cursory glance – probably checking it wasn't recording – and then stuck it into the thin elastic of her knickers.

She took my keys too and wafted them about, then, satisfied, put them back in my pocket.

'Okay,' she said. 'I think we're done. Mr O'Brady will see you now.'

And with that she backed off, giving me a knowing and unpleasant smile. I was left dumbstruck, my mouth wide open, part of me wanting her to come back and carry on, but a larger part feeling dirty and used and embarrassed.

My eyes followed her across the room to the exit. But when she opened the door, I was quickly brought back to the reality of the situation. There, standing on the other side, was the giant. Elvis.

CHAPTER 18

'This way,' Elvis snapped, indicating off to his right with his head.

I didn't wait to be told twice. I scuttled out of the room and past Elvis, who stood holding out his barrel chest giving me barely enough room to get by.

'Down the end of the corridor,' he said. 'Last door on your right.'

As I walked I looked behind me twice to see whether Elvis was following. He was. My heart was now in my throat. My head was a spinning mess. I cursed myself for getting into such a dangerous position. I thought fleetingly I might not even make it out of there alive.

Was O'Brady capable of murder?

There was little I could do to stop it happening by that point. Even if I turned and fled, would I really get away? I reached the door and Elvis squeezed past me and pushed it open.

Inside the room I immediately spotted O'Brady. He was behind a long and extravagant mahogany desk, casually sitting in an oversized, black leather chair with a tumbler of whisky in his hand. To his left stood another burly man; his name, I would later know, was Mickey Egan. A truly repulsive excuse for a human being.

'Come and sit down,' O'Brady said, indicating the chair in front of his desk.

As I moved over to the chair I felt like a condemned man being marched to his fate. I could feel all six eyes in the room bearing down on me, scrutinising my every move.

'You have my wallet?' I piped up, unsure where else to take the conversation.

'Yeah,' O'Brady said. He took it out of a drawer and held it up for me to see.

'Where did you find it?' I asked.

'Outside,' he said.

He tossed it over to me. I caught it, opened it up and gave the inside a cursory glance. I couldn't remember exactly how much money had been there the night before – maybe as much as a hundred pounds – but there was no cash now. All my cards appeared to be in place.

'It's how it was when I was given it,' O'Brady said, shrugging. I assumed he was referring to the missing cash, which had no doubt been pilfered by whichever one of his men had knocked me out.

'Why?' I asked.

'Why what?'

'Why did you take my wallet?'

'I didn't take your wallet, pal,' O'Brady said tersely. 'I'm doing you a favour here.'

'Sure. Thanks.'

I knew he was lying but there was no point in pushing him. I assumed whatever checks O'Brady had been able to perform on my background from the ID in my wallet had satisfied him; otherwise I wouldn't have been sitting there in his office.

'So what's this proposition you have for me?' O'Brady asked.

I felt my cheeks flush. The fact was the proposition now seemed absurd. Childish. It was an idea born of anger and frustration and alcohol and not even an iota of rational thinking. But I was stuck between a rock and hard place. If I told O'Brady it was nothing, a mistake, that there was no proposition, what would he do to me? At the very least I had to assume I would take something of a pummelling from the giant or his other men. And yet if I went through with it and made the proposition to him, as embarrassing and ludicrous as the prospect by that point seemed to me, I was potentially getting myself into a whole new predicament.

It had to be the better option, though, I thought. I tried my hardest to take my head and my heart back to the previous night. To the anger and hatred I had felt when Alice opened up to me about her infidelity. To the countless scenarios that had played through my mind on an endless loop of her with Craig Fletcher. I had to be able to feel that mad again. It was the only way to make sense of what I was doing.

'There's someone I need you to take care of,' I said.

O'Brady's expression turned to disgust. 'There's what?'

I looked around the room. At Egan stationed off to my right, his cold, menacing eyes staring right through me. At Elvis on the other side, his glare unyielding.

'Take care of someone?' O'Brady said. 'What do you think I am – a nanny?'

'No, that's not what I mean. You know, there's someone I want you to … sort out for me. Beat up.'

O'Brady slammed down his whisky glass. 'Who the hell do you think you are?' he blasted. 'Do you think I'm some sort of lowlife chump who goes around giving people a slap or two to make a living? You little –'

He nodded over to Elvis. I squirmed away but he grabbed me and hauled me to my feet. He twisted my right arm painfully behind my back, pushing it to the point of dislocation. Elvis's other thick arm wrapped around my neck, pinning me in place.

I was a mess. I could barely breathe I was so terrified. I tried not to look at O'Brady, as though that would make him go away, but it was impossible not to look.

My head was bowed but my eyes darted up and down as I waited for whatever was to come next.

O'Brady sat fuming, his face creased with annoyance. I began to seriously doubt that I'd make it out of that room on my feet. A bag seemed more likely.

After a few moments, though, O'Brady managed to wind himself down from his outburst and his face softened somewhat.

'You're a lucky man, Stephens,' he said.

His more placid tone did nothing to alleviate the tension coursing through me, nor did it induce Elvis to relax his grip on me at all. If anything, it seemed to get tighter still.

'It's just as well you have something that interests me,' O'Brady continued. 'Or you'd be out that door already.'

'What do you mean?' I choked out as confusion swept through me.

Elvis's arm around my neck tightened further at my decision to speak up, causing me to cough and splutter and gasp for breath.

'Okay, okay, big man. Just relax there,' O'Brady said. With his words I was given the space to breathe once more, but Elvis's grip on me stayed firm nonetheless. 'Your job. Tell me what you do.'

'I'm a consultant,' was my feeble response.

'Yeah, you told me that. So people pay you to give them crap advice they don't need.'

'Something like that,' I said, managing a wry smile.

'Oh, I know all about that game. I'm sure I could do it myself. Doesn't exactly take much of the grey stuff now, does it?' O'Brady tapped his skull for effect.

'I'm sure many would argue against that,' I rebutted.

'I'm sure they would. But I'm right, aren't I? You go into a business, tell them they're top heavy, overstaffed, that their productivity and profitably is being hampered. The answer? You get them to fire a load of dopes and you take yourself a big, fat cheque in the process. Fecking genius. How people still fall for that bollocks is beyond me.'

I said nothing to O'Brady's scathing comments. I didn't agree with him – he was attacking my professionalism and integrity, after all – but I knew exactly what he meant. He wasn't the first person to say such things, and truth be told, much of the advice I gave out in my role wasn't exactly rocket science. But that's what I was paid to do, and if clients happily bought that service and saw benefit in it then who was I to baulk at it?

'But,' O'Brady said, holding up a finger, 'it's not your advice I need. It's access to your clients.'

'How do you mean?'

'You know what I mean. I'm a businessman, Stephens. And business is all about contacts. I'm looking to branch out. Diversify my interests. You help me, I help you.'

'I'm not sure what you think I can do for you.'

'You'll do whatever I tell you to do,' O'Brady snapped, his face creased with anger. 'But let's not go getting our knickers in a twist. I need information, that's all. Information on your clients. A few introductions. The rest I can do myself.'

'That's it?' I said.

I was surprised by O'Brady's request. I knew that divulging anything other than publicly available data was against just about every privacy and confidentiality law that applied. It was professional suicide. But a few introductions? I could do that. Somehow I doubted that was really all O'Brady was after but stuck in the room with him, what choice did I have but to agree?

'Okay,' I said.

O'Brady nodded and Elvis finally released his grip on me. I slumped down a few inches and nursed my right arm, which was completely numb.

'And that thing you wanted taken care of?' O'Brady said. 'You help me out and you can consider it done. A favour. Payment in advance, if you like.'

'Thanks,' I said, though I realised I had little to be thankful for.

I was about to open my mouth to speak again when something hard crashed into the back of my skull. A searing pain shot through me, stabbing at the front of my brain. I wobbled on my feet, took one lunging step forward and collapsed to the floor.

CHAPTER 19

'Who was it you wanted O'Brady to sort out?' *she asked, her tone flinty.*

However hard she tried to remain impassive as I told her my stories, every now and then I caught a glimpse of what she really thought of me.

'Craig Fletcher,' I said.

'Why?'

'Why? Because he screwed Alice!'

'But she was the one who cheated, not him.'

'Oh, come off it,' I said, shaking my head. 'It's not that simple and you know it. You're married, right?'

I looked over at her left hand, placed on top of the desk. She had two rings on her second finger, one a plain yellow band, the other with a pea-sized, bright-white diamond sticking out of it. It was either a fake or she had a rich husband, as I doubted her own job paid well enough for her to afford such a stone.

She whipped her hand away, under the desk.

'This isn't about me,' she said. 'It's about you.'

'I know that. But you must have been in a situation before when your husband or boyfriend or whatever was being overly friendly with another woman. Or maybe you saw another woman approaching him, flirting with him. I bet you hated her, right? You probably went home that night and had a big bust-up with your husband, didn't you? By the next day you were back on speaking terms again. But that woman? No, she was marked. You hated her. You'd always be wary of her from then on.'

She stared at me but didn't say anything.

'I'm right, aren't I?'

Her lack of response gave the answer.

'But why did you feel the need to go after Fletcher like that?' she said.

'I felt like I had to get my own back on him,' I said. *'I was angry. I needed a release. I had to punish him for what he'd done.'*

'What about Alice? Didn't you feel the need to punish her too?'

'Punish her? You mean beat her up? No. It never even crossed my mind.'

We both paused for a beat.

'So you only blamed Fletcher for what happened?' she said.

'No. Alice wasn't blameless,' I said. *'But I loved her. Fletcher knew she was a married woman. I couldn't let him get away with what he'd done. He had it coming.'*

'Why O'Brady?'

'I didn't know anyone else like that. I didn't even know him really. This was just some brainless, drunken idea. People do all sorts of crazy, irrational things when they're drunk. Maybe I should have just gone around and punched Fletcher in the face myself. Got it over and done with.'

'Why didn't you?'

'I went for what at the time seemed like an easier option. I didn't want the police coming after me, and I really don't think I'm a violent person. And what if I did find Fletcher to give him his just desserts, but he just walloped me back and I was the one scurrying away with my tail between my legs — how would that look? Can you imagine? The man who slept with my wife then later crushed me in a fight that I'd started? I wanted him to get a quick beating from someone he wouldn't know, and that would be that.'

'But you didn't go through with it?'

'No, I didn't. I couldn't. I mean, come on, it's a hare-brained idea — I knew that. I phoned O'Brady the next day and asked him to call it off. He did.'

'He was happy to do that?'

'I think he was angry that I was messing him around, but it really wasn't a big deal to him. One less thing for him to worry about. Beating up Craig Fletcher was never why he called me back to his club. It was his proposition that he was interested in.'

'Your client contacts.'

'Exactly. O'Brady had me right where he wanted. I could practically see the pound signs in his eyes when he first brought up the idea. And I couldn't say no. I was terrified of him and he knew it.'

'But you weren't just giving him introductions, were you?'

'How do you mean?'

'From what I understand, you passed a lot of information to him. You went into business with him.'

'That's not how it was.'

'But you ended up owing him a lot of money.'

'Everyone who deals with O'Brady ends up owing him money. That's just what he does. He's sneaky and vindictive and quite brilliant at manipulation. Isn't that the same as all good businessmen?'

'I'm not so sure you should tarnish every businessperson so viciously.'

'Yeah, well, I say what I see.'

She raised an eyebrow but didn't push me further on the point.

'But over the years, from your relationship with O'Brady you did end up owing him a lot of money. Which was why you took the decision to seek Gemma's help that day when your sister reappeared?'

'Yeah, I did,' I said.

'So tell me about how that worked out. What happened?'

'Well, as you can probably imagine, with someone like O'Brady it really was something of a clusterfuck in the end.'

CHAPTER 20

It's probably worth stating at this point that I hated my job with a passion. I hated the people I worked for and with, I hated the crappy office, I hated the open-plan cubicles with their monotonous grey colour scheme. I hated the clients who always expected the world, who didn't understand their own business as well as I did and who never said thank you, and I hated the work I had to do – the same shit I'd been doing when I was twenty-one years old.

I hadn't always felt like that. At one point I'd been ambitious and hungry for success. Having joined Ellis Associates directly from university, I'd worked up the corporate ladder to a respectable level by my late twenties. If I'd wanted it, if I'd really set my heart on it and given it my all, I would have been a partner in the firm and raking in hundreds of thousands a year for being nothing more than a glorified salesperson.

But just as with marriage my corporate career had encountered its setbacks. The biggest was Rottweiler. I was sure he had been sent to earth to make my life a misery. He was a classic egomaniac who'd been parachuted into the team in which I worked a rung higher than me. That fact alone had caused ire, not just from me but also a number of other project managers in the team who'd been setting their sights on the top.

To add to that, he was the most unpleasant person I'd ever had the misfortune of meeting. Plus he had zero talent. Unless you considered it a talent to be universally hated by those around you.

'Stephens!'

I cringed at the disgusted way in which my name was spoken. His grating voice immediately shook me from my thoughts of the day before. Of Dani turning up out of the blue and questioning me about Alice's murder, dripping vague information of a new killing, quizzing me about the statements I'd given to the police all those year ago. And of me having to come clean, but not quite fully clean, to Gemma about O'Brady and the money I owed him.

Out of the frying pan into the fire, as they say.

I looked up at the snarling face of Rottweiler. 'My office. Now,' he barked.

One or two people at nearby desks glanced in my direction to see the latest victim of his wrath. They could have guessed it was me. Rottweiler had had it in for me ever since joining five years ago. He'd never known me at my best – in the days before Alice was killed, when I was seen as the future of the team. Back then everyone thought I would make it to the top. It was only a matter of time, it seemed. Then Alice was murdered. That threw everything in my life off the rails. I'd never truly recovered my appetite and ambition at work. Scratch that, I'd never truly recovered my appetite in many aspects of life.

When Rottweiler joined the team, my corporate downfall accelerated exponentially. My career wasn't off the rails anymore, it was tied to the tracks and pulverised by train after train of shit and venom and was now left in severed pieces.

No, he had never seen me at my best. Maybe if he had I would have been able to wipe the floor with him and he would have been out the door as quickly as he'd been thrown in.

As it was, even at fifty per cent, even at less, I still outshone him on every project. That was why he hated me so much, I guessed. But over the years his constant barrage of abuse had worn me down to the point where I was entirely disenfranchised. I just didn't care anymore. About the job at least. Him, on the other hand … I hated him with unabated passion.

I got up from my desk and strode confidently behind Rottweiler to his office door. I could tell half the office was following our moves. Some would be sympathetic toward me. Others would be rubbing their hands in glee, enjoying the possible drama that was to come. There were always plenty of sadists in any group of office workers who loved nothing more than to see a colleague suffer in the hope that it forwarded their position.

I ignored all the looks. Each day I was getting nearer to the point of no longer giving a shit about the latest tirade and the repercussions if I didn't bow down to Rottweiler's superiority.

He stormed into his office and plonked his ugly backside down on the chair behind his desk.

'Shut the door,' he said, looking down at some papers.

I did as I was told, trying to keep calm. I knew, deep down, that I was best riding over whatever was to come, but I was on edge. There was so much going on in my life that I wasn't sure I could keep my anger bottled up.

'Where were you yesterday?' he asked, his tone flat.

I looked over at him. His jagged features. His piercing, deep-set eyes behind rectangular glasses. His ruffled grey and brown hair that sat clumsily on his head – a deliberate style for sure, though I couldn't understand why anyone would choose it.

'I was on leave,' I said. 'It was in my diary.'

'Stephens, you can't just skip off for the day whenever you feel like it,' he said, still calm but condescending, a schoolteacher talking to an eight year old. 'That's not how it works here.'

'It's been in my diary for weeks,' I protested. 'It was hardly last minute.'

'But you didn't tell me. You should have made it clear to me on Monday that you were taking the day off.'

'You weren't here on Monday.'

'I have a phone! I have email. Stephens, I'm trying to be nice here. Don't get smart with me.'

'Okay. Is that it?'

'No, that's not it. You left me in the lurch on Sandpiper.'

'Left you in the lurch? You've been on the project with me for six months.'

'But I expected you to be there yesterday to meet with the board. How dare you embarrass me like that?'

'I wasn't there. If you embarrassed yourself, that's your problem.'

Rottweiler pursed his lips. Clearly the meeting wasn't going the way he'd planned. What had he expected? That I'd grovel because I'd spent a day mourning and visiting my dead wife's grave?

Although he was trying to appear calm, authoritative yet in control, I could see the rage building inside him. His cheeks were red. His face was creased. But he didn't say a word, and I was impressed that he kept it in. I'd seen him blow his top many times and I'd felt sure he'd been about to this time. In some ways I'd wanted it. I was up for a fight.

'This is just another minor indiscretion in a long list for you, though, isn't it?'

'Well, I agree it's minor,' I said. 'I'm really not sure what the issue is.'

'That's the problem. You never do see the issue. I'm not sure if that's down to ignorance or incompetence. Either way, it's just not good enough.'

Incompetence? I felt like answering back and reminding him how I'd saved his arse countless times in the past.

'I'm recommending you enter into a performance monitoring plan,' he said, smiling.

I clenched my teeth tightly, feeling a surge of rage and trying my hardest to keep it bottled up like he had done. Being on a PMP basically meant I was on my way out unless I turned things around. I'd be heavily scrutinised for the next six months to make sure my performance was meeting expectations. If not, my time with Ellis Associates was up. And I was positive he would do his damnedest to make sure I failed. Some turnaround for the guy who was being touted as a future partner not so long ago.

In all honesty losing the job wouldn't be the worst thing in the world, given how much I'd fallen out of love with it. But to have it taken away from me by that prick was a big deal. I couldn't let him have the last laugh.

'Is there anything else?' I asked, just wanting to get out of there.

'I've reported this to Whitely already,' he said.

James Whitely. The managing partner.

Rottweiler was now enjoying himself. 'He's aware of the situation. I'm sure you can imagine how disappointed he is.'

I shut my eyes and nodded. That was a stab in the back I really didn't need.

'You should be happy I went with PMP,' he carried on. 'I'd mulled over whether this was a formal disciplinary issue.'

'Disciplinary?' I said, my eyelids springing open. 'Are you crazy? I took a day off to visit my dead wife's grave. It would have been her birthday yesterday.'

'But it's not just that, Stephens,' Rottweiler barked back. 'It's all of your shit that I have to deal with. The constant disappearances. The failed deadlines. The sloppy reporting. And don't think this is just me with an axe to grind. We've had complaints from Sandpiper about your lack of responsiveness lately.'

'So your way of dealing with that is to belittle me and punish me? Don't you ever stop to think about how people feel? About what troubles I might be going through in my life that perhaps I need help with?'

'Stephens, we're talking about your work performance here, not your personal problems. If you need psychological help, I'm not sure I'm the best person to give you advice.'

'Damn right you're not.'

'Okay. I think we're done here,' he said, getting to his feet and pointing to the door.

'Yeah, looks like we are.'

I turned and opened the door and cursed him under my breath as I left the room. Just loud enough so he'd hear it. The f-word was in there. The c-word too. I don't know why I did it. It seemed like a good idea at the time. And I wanted to have the final say.

'What did you just say to me?' Rottweiler boomed. I glanced around to see him jumping up from behind his desk.

I didn't look back again. I carried on walking over to my desk, aware that every eye in the office was now on me.

'Ben Stephens, come back here!'

When I reached my desk, I turned calmly to face him. He was standing outside his office, arms folded, face like thunder. He was fuming. Yet he looked entirely helpless. In a way, I think he knew it too.

I pulled my hand close to my chest and very casually gave him the finger. I heard gasps from my co-workers. I saw Rottweiler's eyes bulge, his mouth open in shock. He was going to explode any second. I stood and waited for it. I'd just signed my own death warrant, but in the moment I didn't care. Everyone held their breath, waiting for the inevitable.

'Ben Stephens! Get in here, now!'

I jumped at the thunderous voice. My insides vibrated and shook and then curdled from the bass growl. All eyes turned to where the order had come from. It wasn't Rottweiler. It had come from the other side of the office. James Whitely.

CHAPTER 21

I kept my head down as I scurried behind Whitely into his office, my tail well and truly between my legs. Biting back at Rottweiler was one thing, but I had more than one reason to want to keep Whitely on my side.

After all, he wasn't just the managing partner, the boss of all bosses. He was also Gemma's dad – my father-in-law.

He strode over to his desk and looked out of the wall-to-wall window at the city. The offices, on the ninth floor of a modern block, had panoramic views, a big selling point whenever clients came to visit. That said, the interior was sparsely but professionally decorated. Rather than luxurious, it was modern and chic according to the designers, who had probably charged an eye-watering fee for their services. If you asked me, it was dull and monotonous and lacking in any creativity.

'I'm sorry, James,' I said, comfortably referring to the big boss by his first name. This was a consultancy in the twenty-first century, after all. In the casual modern office where we worked it was the only way. Except for Rottweiler, who seemed to take some deranged satisfaction from only ever referring to his underlings by their surnames.

Whitely was James to his face at least. Behind his back, he was Boris, a nickname not because of his looks but his ability to come out of any situation unscathed. Teflon had been a lesser-used name for him, but Boris had stuck (no pun intended) due to the fondness of a few of the guys in the office for the film *Snatch*, featuring an impossible-to-kill Russian known as Boris the Blade. In his role of selling numerous often-controversial services to businesses, Whitely had been through the ringer countless times with negative PR campaigns against him and various bouts of litigation. But he'd always come out on top. He was a master at it.

In many ways I admired him, though I'd never wanted to be like him.

'What?' Whitely snapped, turning to face me. 'Oh, yeah, that. Whatever, Ben. I know you've got your problems with him – who doesn't? Just try to not bring the whole office down when you take him on, yeah? It's hardly the way a senior manager should be behaving.'

'Yeah. Sure, of course,' I said, a little dumbstruck that I was apparently being let off so lightly. Rottweiler certainly wouldn't have been happy if he'd been in the room to hear Whitely brush my indiscretion aside like that.

'That's not why I called you in,' he said. 'We'll deal with that separately. Sit down.'

I did as I was told and he sat too.

'I spoke to Gemma last night,' Whitely said.

My heart jumped. I knew she'd made the call. She'd told me so when we'd finally got rid of Dani the day before. Gemma had told me simply that her dad was mulling it over. Well, it looked like whatever he had decided, I was about to find out the answer.

'I have to say,' Whitely continued, 'this is a fine mess you've got yourself into.'

His tone was placid but I could see something close to vindication in his eyes. He didn't feel sorry for me and I doubted he really wanted to help me. He was probably pleased that finally he'd been proved right in thinking that I wasn't good enough for his darling daughter.

'I know,' I said. 'I'm sorry.'

'No, you're not,' Whitely said, his tone as blunt as his words. 'You're never sorry, are you? You hop from one problem to another, dragging everyone else along with you, always on the lookout for the next lump to bail you out.'

I was taken aback by Whitely's sudden, unexpected criticism, but I knew I wasn't really in a position to retort. He was right.

I didn't know exactly what Gemma had told him or what questions he had asked of her, but I knew she wouldn't have mentioned O'Brady. She knew so little about him herself, and letting on to her father that I was indebted to a crook wouldn't have been a winning formula. Regardless, I wasn't about to put my foot in it by giving away to Whitely more than he knew. Not unless I absolutely had to.

'Well, this time the lump is me,' Whitely added. 'But this is the last time. You understand me?'

'Yes,' I said, unable to look him in the eye. 'Thank you.'

'Whatever.'

Whitely opened a desk drawer and grabbed his cheque book. He scribbled in it and then tore out a cheque, which he thrust out to me. I leaned forward and grasped hold of it. Whitely took a couple of seconds and I wondered whether he might be about to have a sudden change of heart. He released his grip and I took the cheque and stared down at the eye-watering figure scrawled on it: one hundred thousand pounds.

'I … I don't know what to say,' I said. I could actually feel a tear in my eye.

'Whatever you've got to say, I don't want to hear it. Don't think for a second I'm doing this for you. You're my daughter's husband and the father of my grandkids, so I have to put up with you one way or another.'

I knew Whitely had never been my biggest fan. Not since Gemma and I had got together at least. At one stage, many years ago, I'd thought he liked me, when I was just a high-flying employee. But as a husband to his beloved daughter, whom I'd met only because he'd employed her as an office assistant, Whitely had always looked down on me with dissatisfaction.

'I'll pay you back,' I said. 'I promise. I'll do everything I can to pay you back as soon as possible.'

'Oh, I know you will,' he said. 'I'm going to break your fucking back to make sure you do. You need to pull your socks up and start working, sonny. Rottweiler wants you out of this place and I have to say, based on recent performance, he's got a point. But you owe me a lot of money now. I'm not going to throw you out and jeopardise that, or spoil the relationship I have with my daughter and grandkids. For some reason she loves you no matter what I do or say. You need to get your act together and make this right.'

'Yes, of course, I will.'

'Go home for the rest of the week,' he said. 'It won't look right to the rest of the team if I don't at least throw you out of here to cool off. '

'Thank you. I really mean it.'

'Just go.'

I took my wallet from my trouser pocket and carefully folded the cheque inside, then walked out of the room. Whitely remained at his desk, not looking up at me. I felt great relief, but it was regret that dominated my mind as I walked through the open space, not making eye contact with the many people I knew were staring at me.

Outside I took a deep breath of cold, fresh air and tried my best to feel upbeat. Could this really be the turning point? Could I finally lay some ghosts to rest and get my life and my relationship with Gemma moving again? I really hoped so.

Yet, deep down, I already knew that was nothing more than a pipe dream. Something would go wrong. It always did.

CHAPTER 22

I didn't want to wait another minute. I didn't know whether O'Brady would even be around, but if he wasn't, I would sit and wait for as long as it took.

I walked the by-then-well-trodden roads to O'Brady's favourite place of business. In the many years I'd known him he'd branched out his interests quite drastically, just as he'd told me he had intended to do when I'd first met him. I'd helped him along the way, giving him the information he needed to set up connections that he could exploit for gain. O'Brady owned bars and restaurants across the Midlands, not to mention a healthy portfolio of apartments and commercial premises that he rented out and a number of businesses that he owned or had stakes in – everything from a cleaning company to a car-parts manufacturer.

O'Brady had made a lot of money on the way. You only had to look at his house, his cars, his clothes and his jewellery to see that. How much of the money he'd made was legitimate it was impossible to know. Yet Full Spread was still his regular hangout, the perfect front for a shady businessman – a largely cash operation was the most straightforward method of laundering ill-gotten money.

The front entrance of the club was locked tight and no bouncers were in sight, so I walked around to the rear of the building to the service entrance, a set of double doors in an eight-foot-tall brick wall topped with barbed wire. I pressed the buzzer on the wall next to the doors and waited. After a few seconds I tried again, and this time I heard a click almost instantly as the doors were unlocked.

The left-hand door swung open and it took me by surprise when I saw O'Brady on the other side.

'You?' he said, a dissatisfied look on his face. 'I was just passing by the back door from the shitter. I thought it might have been one of the girls come to cheer me up.'

'Sorry to disappoint you.'

O'Brady grunted and turned away from me. He walked off and I followed him to the office, my senses on high alert as I scoped out the area, looking for which of his many crew were also in the building. Not that I had any chance against him and his men if they turned on me. Each of them on their own could probably pummel me into the ground without my even inflicting a solitary blow, but it at least made me feel a bit more at ease to know who was about and where they were.

Unfortunately for me it was a full house. As I walked into O'Brady's office I counted six other men already in there. I recognised them all.

'We were just in the middle of a debrief,' O'Brady said, clearly angered about something. Not the start I'd been hoping for. 'We had the boys in blue over here last night – it wasn't pleasant. Some little git was selling coke to the punters. First time it's ever happened in here – or first time the police have cottoned on anyway. I'm convinced the police put him in here so they could sting us, but there's nothing I can do about that now.'

The men all stood motionless. No-one said a word.

'It's not good for business,' O'Brady carried on. 'People come here to have a discreet night out – not to be making statements to the coppers.'

There were a few nods and murmurs of agreement from around the room. It wasn't clear whether O'Brady's comments had been directed to his staff or had been an explanation of the gathering for my benefit.

'You,' O'Brady snapped, pointing a finger at a middle-aged man I knew only as Wrafter. He was O'Brady's head doorman at the club, over six foot with a frame so thick his arms hung at a forty-five degree angle to his body. Even though he was past his physical prime – I guessed he was in his fifties – he wasn't someone you'd want to meet alone in a dark alley.

In O'Brady's presence, though, Wrafter's size and strength were irrelevant – made clear by the sorry look on his face.

O'Brady strode up to Wrafter, took hold of him by the ear and twisted. Wrafter cowered down. It was surreal to watch. The doorman could have quite easily floored the diminutive O'Brady with one fell swoop if he wanted to. He looked like an oversized child being scolded by an angry parent.

O'Brady leaned in close and whispered to Wrafter, 'What do I pay you for?'

'To … to run the door.'

'To run the damn door!' O'Brady blasted. 'Spot on. So why was that little fecker in here in the first place?'

'It was a mistake. It won't happen again.'

'Damn right it won't.'

O'Brady swung back his arm and launched a ferocious backhanded slap across Wrafter's face. He followed up with a downward hook that caught the man on his chin and sent him down onto his knee.

I glanced around the room at the other men. They were all static, unflinching. I guessed they were all thinking the same thing: *I'm just glad it's not me.*

O'Brady thrust up his knee and crashed it into Wrafter's face. The doorman's head snapped back as he tumbled to the floor. It looked like Wrafter had passed out, but O'Brady still wasn't finished. He crowded over the fallen man and then threw a boot down onto Wrafter's face. O'Brady did it again and there was a sickening crack as Wrafter's nose caved in.

Out of the corner of my eye I noticed one of the men – Joey – jump at the brutal sight. Another of them, Colman, had already looked away. The only one still staring intently at the ruthless beating was the detestable Mickey Egan. I could well imagine the delight going through his mind as he watched a fellow human suffering. In fact, I think I noticed the faintest of smiles on his face.

O'Brady had spotted the reaction of his other men too. He launched himself, face snarling, toward Colman – the man who was unable to look. O'Brady threw his arm around Colman's neck and dragged him over to Wrafter.

'Look at him!' O'Brady screamed. 'I want you all to look at him. This is what happens when you mess up. When you don't do your fecking job. Understood?'

All of the men nodded and O'Brady shoved Colman away from him. The relieved look on his face said it all. He knew he'd been let off lightly.

Then O'Brady turned his attention to me. As his eyes caught mine I felt a sudden wave of nausea build in the pit of my stomach.

'Get him out of here,' O'Brady said, his eyes still on me but his hands indicating his fallen doorman.

Two of the other brutes moved over to their battered colleague and dragged his bulky body away, leaving a trail of smeared blood on the office floor.

'So what are you doing here?' O'Brady shouted at me.

'I … I've got your money,' I said, reaching into my pocket for my wallet. My hands were shaking so much that it took me a few seconds to manage the simple feat.

O'Brady raised both eyebrows. I took out the cheque and extended the piece of paper to him. O'Brady frowned and snatched it off me.

'What the hell is this?'

'It's the money,' I said. 'All of it.'

'This isn't money, ye bleedin' tick.'

'It's a cheque.'

'I know what the feck it is. It isn't money.'

I stood, mouth wide open, as the snarling O'Brady began to tear up the paper. My heart sank. I visibly lost a few inches as I slumped down. With each angry tear the sense of dread grew inside me.

O'Brady flicked the remnants of the cheque into my face. I managed not to blink as the pieces of paper fluttered to the floor.

'I want money. Get it? Cash. Something I can use. I don't need a pissing cheque. You know what? I'm sick and tired of your crap. The price just doubled.'

'What! You can't –'

'I can and I just did. Two hundred thousand. But I'm a generous soul and don't you ever think otherwise – I'll give you two weeks. If it's not in front of me by then, the price doubles again and I'll be taking a piece of you and your wifey for my troubles.'

'I …'

'Now piss off!'

O'Brady turned away from me. He was done. Nothing I could say or do was going to change his mind. I looked over to Egan, who was moving toward me. He was a few inches shorter than me, but was thick and muscled with a scarred face and a look in his eyes that screamed violence. I knew a beating was coming, and after just witnessing the bloody fate of Wrafter, I should have turned and ran. Got as far away from there as I could.

I should have. I know that. I'm not sure why I didn't.

Instead I stepped forward, swung back my arm and threw my fist into Egan's ugly face.

CHAPTER 23

I couldn't see a thing out of my right eye. It had swollen up within seconds of the beating I'd taken at the club and was entirely closed. My work shirt was torn and had spatters of red on it. My nose was bloodied and my bottom lip was protruding and fat. I had aches and pains all over my torso – it was very possible that one of my ribs was broken.

I hobbled up to my front door, daggers shooting up my left leg, on which I could barely put any weight. I drew my door key shakily from my trouser pocket and fought hard to fit it into the lock. When I turned the key and the door swung open, I stumbled into the house, somehow managing to stay on my feet.

'Ben!' Gemma gasped.

I groaned when I realised my wife was standing right there in the hallway. On seeing the state I was in, she cupped her hand to her mouth.

'I thought you were at work,' I slurred.

'I finished early. What's happened? Who did this to you?'

'Who do you think?' I said, limping into the lounge where I collapsed on the sofa.

'That O'Brady guy? Jesus, Ben, we have to call the police.'

'No,' I said. 'We really don't.'

'The money,' Gemma said. 'He got the money? At least tell me that. Tell me this can all be over with now.'

'Not exactly,' I said, managing a wry smile. 'Me looking like this isn't his way of saying thank you.'

'But Dad gave you the money?'

'He gave me a cheque. Apparently that's not good enough.'

Gemma's face fell even further. 'So what are we going to do now?'

'Pray.'

Gemma fought hard against the tears. I could see she was filled in equal measure with fear and anger. In the end the latter won out.

'How could you do this to us?' she said.

'Thanks for your concern about my wellbeing.'

'Of course I'm concerned about your wellbeing! But *you've* dragged us all into this. What if they come around and do the same to me and the kids?'

'They won't.'

'You don't know that! I can't believe you could do this to us. You've put us *all* at risk. For what?'

'You're talking like I haven't tried to sort this already. I've done everything I can to make sure this doesn't affect you. To get him off my back.'

'I'm struggling to believe you on that.'

I wanted to argue the point but didn't. I'd come home to rest. To get my head straight. To figure out what the hell to do next. And to get cleaned up and later spend some time with the kids, who were about the only thing in my life that I seemed to have got right. I really didn't need a slanging match over what an idiot I was.

'I need to take a shower, get changed,' I said.

I winced as I tried to get up off the sofa. Gemma stepped over and reached out her hand to me. I was about to turn down the offer of help but she moved forward and hauled me back to my feet.

'You need to be quick. The kids will be back soon.'

'Soon?' I said.

I hadn't expected them back for a couple of hours. It was Wednesday and Harry usually went to an after-school club until Gemma, or occasionally I, finished work. And Chloe was with the childminder on a Wednesday.

'I knew I'd be finishing early today, so Mary is bringing them both straight around when school's finished.'

'Oh, great,' I said.

'Well, nobody was expecting you to come home covered in blood, were they?'

'No. Me included,' I said.

'Come on, let's get you upstairs,' Gemma said, taking my hand. I took the small gesture as a sign of support, though I wasn't really sure if that was the intent.

I scrambled up the stairs as best I could and Gemma helped me strip off my wrecked clothes and then guided me toward the shower. I washed away the blood quickly, and then began to feel my body soothed by the water, its heat encouraging blood to flow into the wounded areas. I would have stayed there, enjoying the sensation, but through the mist I could see Gemma standing on the other side of the screen, towel held out in her hand, waiting for me to emerge.

I turned off the water and stepped out. Gemma placed the towel around my shoulders and gently rubbed my back dry. I finished the job of drying as Gemma inspected my bruised body. She looked at my face, staring into my eyes with sympathy. Then she turned around and opened the cabinet above the sink.

'It just seems to be a lot of bruising,' Gemma said, taking out some cotton-wool balls. 'There're no big cuts, even though you look a real state.'

She handed me a handful of the balls. I wasn't quite sure what she expected me to do with them.

'Your nose,' she said. 'It's still bleeding a bit.'

'Oh,' I said.

I looked in the mirror and dabbed at the blood coming from my nostrils, then decided to just be done with it and stuck a piece of cotton up each one. I looked at Gemma and she shrugged.

I touched my left side, around my ribs, where there was a constant stabbing pain. I resisted the urge to cry out when I hit the most tender spot.

'Is it broken?' Gemma asked.

'No idea. It hurts like hell.'

'You need to go to a doctor.'

'Yeah, maybe. What time is it?' I asked.

Gemma looked at her watch. 'Almost half three,' she said. 'The kids will be here any minute.' The tension on her face and in her voice was unmistakable.

'Right,' I said. 'I need to get dressed.'

I walked back out into the bedroom, but then spotted something over by the dresser that stopped me in my tracks.

'What the hell is that?' I said to Gemma.

She walked over, an uncomfortable look on her face. She looked ... embarrassed.

'What do you think it is?'

I looked at the suitcase, its open lid propped up against the wall. It was half-filled with clothes. My clothes.

'What's going on?'

'I wasn't expecting you back so soon,' Gemma said, hanging her head. 'I was still packing when I heard you at the door.'

'You're throwing me out,' I said. A statement, not a question.

'I was, yes,' Gemma said, unable to look me in the eye.

'But?'

'Well ... I don't know. I wasn't expecting you to come home half-dead, was I?'

'And now that you've seen the state I'm in, you want me to stay?'

'I don't know. Maybe. But the kids? They can't see you like this.'

'So what now then?'

'I didn't want this,' Gemma said, her voice weak and unsure. 'I don't want us to end, Ben, but look at the trouble you've got us into. And it's not just that. You've been moping around for months, barely speaking to me, and when we do speak, we just argue. Neither of us is happy. This has been building for ages. It's heart-breaking to see you in this state and I want to help, but … maybe we just need a break.'

I was lost for words. But really what could I say to that? Everything she said was spot on. And it wasn't that much of a surprise; I'd been feeling her drifting from me for some time. Perhaps if we'd spoken to each other more, we could have tried to work things through sooner. As it was, our silence only seemed to have accelerated what I guessed was inevitable.

Really our separating, even if only in the short term, was a natural next step. But it still hurt to hear Gemma confirm it. I loved her even if it was clear our marriage wasn't working. And the timing of her rejection was all the more painful given the state I was in, not just physically but mentally too.

'This was coming anyway,' she added. 'You have to admit that?'

I huffed but didn't say anything.

'And then you … O'Brady … I can't let our children be part of that. I just can't.'

Anger bubbled to the surface at the mention of my children, my only saving grace. I'd do anything I could to prevent them coming to harm. 'Harry's not yours,' I sneered.

'Don't say that,' Gemma said. I could see the hurt in her eyes.

But I was hurting too, and before I could stop myself I plunged the knife deeper.

'Harry's not yours,' I said. 'He's mine. He's Alice's.'

At the mention of Alice I saw the switch inside Gemma flip. All of a sudden she was seething.

'You don't get to decide what happens to Harry,' I added.

'Piss off, Ben!' Gemma screamed. 'Why would you say that? He's mine and I *do* get to decide. I'm the only one around here who actually gives a damn.'

With that, Gemma started moving in a frenzy, whipping clothes out of drawers and flinging them haphazardly into the case. I stood there motionless, just staring at her, but anger was now taking control of me too.

Gemma zipped the lid and picked up the case, then grunted as she threw the weighty luggage over toward me. It bounced on the bed and smacked into my legs, knocking me back a step.

By that point I was fuming, but I stood my ground, trying not to blow. I knew the situation was only one step from getting out of control. I *wanted* to keep it together. I really did.

'I can't believe I was actually having second thoughts about this,' Gemma ranted, coming back around to my side of the bed. She stood the case up next to me, then started gesticulating irately as she carried on her tirade. 'When you came home and I saw the state you were in, I actually wavered. I wanted to help you. I thought perhaps I was wrong. That we could work through this. That we would be better sticking together. But you know what? Not a chance. It's never going to happen. Not now. I want you gone.'

'You're not stopping me seeing the kids,' I said.

It was all I could think about. My kids. I couldn't lose them. I could see the disappointment in Gemma's eyes. What had she expected? That I would fight back and beg her to change her mind? That I would grovel and tell her how much I loved her and how I couldn't live without her? Even if that had been true, I wouldn't have said it. I was too angry.

'You're not fit to be their dad,' Gemma said. 'Look at you. They can't be part of what you're involved in.'

Gemma put her hand up to her head – exasperation? Confusion? She let out a long sigh as her mood softened from full-on anger.

'Look, maybe when it's over, if it ever does end … maybe things can be different.'

'No. If you throw me out now, I'm never coming back.'

I stood there glaring at Gemma as tears rolled down her cheeks. Without warning she threw her arm back then whipped her palm toward my face. The ferocious slap caught me completely by surprise. I reeled back.

'Don't threaten me, Ben!' Gemma blasted. 'You should be walking out of that door of your own free will. If you had an ounce of decency, you would do it. If not for me then for the kids.'

I was dumbstruck. But it only took me a couple of seconds to regroup. Finally, after months of torment, all of the pressure and tension and anger that had been slowly building and weighing me down more and more each day, came to the fore.

'You stupid –'

My arm pulled back. My fist balled.

Gemma just stood there. She didn't cower or squirm away. I wondered whether she wanted me to hit her. Whether she wanted the excuse.

I lowered my arm. My whole body was shaking.

'You're a coward, Ben,' Gemma said. She stepped aside. 'Just go.'

I picked up the case and left.

CHAPTER 24

'Tell me about the list,' she said.

I frowned. 'It wasn't a list. It wasn't as planned or as thought out as that.'

'You referred to it as a list before.'

'Did I? Well, I meant it figuratively. There was never a piece of paper with words written on it. It was just in my head.'

'Okay. So tell me what was in your head.'

'My head was a mess. Simple as that.'

I wasn't deliberately being vague or obstructive with her. I just wanted to make sure I gave her a straight answer to a straight question.

'After you left the house,' she said, 'when Gemma threw you out, what was going through your head?'

'Regret. Bitterness. Anger.'

'You're an angry person?'

'Is that a question?'

'Do you think it's true?'

'Yes and no.'

'How so?'

'I wasn't always angry. It's something that's built up. And I'm not sure it's subconscious. In many ways I want to be angry. There's a lot to be angry about.'

'So it's your way of coping?'

'Maybe,' I said.

'And can you remember a time before? When you were able to control your anger?'

'I've always been able to control it.'

'Do you really believe that, or do you just not want to admit defeat, that it's finally got the better of you?'

'Maybe. I guess I suppressed my anger for a long time.'

'Why?' she asked.

'I'm not sure. To fit the mould of who people thought I was perhaps. To fit the mould of who I thought I was.'

'Who did people think you were?'

'You know, a loving husband, a dad, a hard-working family man.'

'You're saying that wasn't really you?'

'No, it was me. But … what I'm saying is that there's a certain way you're expected to act based on how other people perceive you.'

'Can you explain that?'

'I'm not just talking about me, we all do this. We pigeonhole every person we ever meet, usually in a matter of minutes. And it's very hard to change that first impression.'

'How does this relate to you and what's happened?'

'What I'm trying to say is that those first impressions aren't always a true reflection of who someone is and what they're capable of. And I guess I was too concerned with living the expectation, of living the life of the person that I thought others saw in me.'

'So what changed?' she said.

'Everything. Alice was the turning point.'

'Her murder?'

'No, before that.'

'Her cheating on you?'

'Probably,' I said. 'It's hard to pinpoint when my outlook changed. There's no single point of reference I can look back to and say, "That's it." You don't always see how people change. It happens so slowly, bit by bit. But then one day you wake up and bam! You realise everything is different.'

'But when Alice first told you of her cheating, that moment seems to be some sort of tipping point from which many of your problems flowed.'

'Yeah, I guess you could say that. But I was still me after that. At least I think I was. I think I was that person all the way up to her murder.'

'So it was her murder that changed you?'

'How could it not? Maybe some of the change had started already, but it was really only coming out the other side of her death that I felt different and I acted differently. After Alice was killed, I was locked in grief. Anger, it wasn't a by-product of that grief, it was more like … it was what came to fill the void left by the sudden absence of happiness and hope. I just didn't know it at first.'

She shifted in her seat. 'We're getting somewhere here,' she said. 'So the anger that you feel sprang up when Alice was murdered, was it anger at you? At her? At having been left on your own with a child?'

'I don't know. It … didn't really come straight away. Or at least I wasn't aware of it.'

'So when did you become aware of this all-consuming anger? There must be a point you can take yourself back to and say, "That was the moment when things really changed for me."'

'Like I say, it was Alice's death.'

'No, I mean after that. Long after you'd finally come out of your grief. When was the moment you woke up and saw that everything had changed? When did you realise you were a different person and know you had to take action?'

'Okay, okay, I know what you're getting at. Yes, I can pinpoint that moment.'

'Tell me.'

'Things really came to a head after that meeting with O'Brady. When he tore up the cheque I gave him and threw it back in my face. I think something inside me snapped.'

'What do you think it was about that moment?'

'I don't know exactly. The violence that I'd just witnessed perhaps. The pressure on me had been there before that, steadily building for years. Alice cheating. Me getting sucked into O'Brady's world. Alice's death. My problems at work. My problems with Gemma, our failing marriage. But that moment in O'Brady's office, as I watched him nearly beat a man to death so coldly … that was the tipping point. I came out of the club that day a different person. And then when Gemma …'

'So that was where the list came from?'

Dark Fragments

'There was no list,' I said again, irritated. 'But it was that moment when I realised I needed to take action – do something drastic to halt my downward spiral. But really, in the end, it all came down to chance.'

CHAPTER 25

I was still fuming as I thudded out of my house, lugging my meagre belongings. I could feel the thunder filling me, sticking in my throat. I had to get away from the house, away from Gemma, before I erupted. I stormed over to my car. Only when I was in the driver's seat, door shut and locked, did I finally let it out.

I yelled, a deep, guttural sound. I yelled so hard it made my head spin and my jaw ache. My voice was hoarse within seconds but I couldn't stop. I started shaking uncontrollably, my fists clenched, my knuckles white, the muscles in my arms and my back and my neck flexed and tight and ready to uncoil.

I thumped on the steering wheel, ignoring the pain that immediately shot through the thin bones in my hand and the stabbing that worsened in my ribs from the beating I'd taken at the strip club. I was past caring. I hit out again and again. When that wasn't enough, I grabbed the wheel and starting pumping up and down as though trying to tear it right off. I bucked back and forth in my seat, my head crashing against the headrest behind me.

When I was finally finished, when my ragged body was spent, I slumped down. My breathing was fast and wheezy, my heart was racing. Sweat droplets formed a continuous mask on my brow. I hung my head down, waiting for a sense of normality to return.

After a few minutes, the fury was still there; I could feel it simmering. For now, though, it was over – I was back in control.

But something felt different.

I pushed the ignition button and enjoyed a moment of satisfaction as the powerful engine of my BMW roared to life. I looked over to the house. Gemma was standing in the bay window of the lounge, arms folded and a dark scowl on her face. She shook her head at me. I just looked away and then I stuck the gearbox into reverse and rolled the car out onto the road.

I drove on for twenty minutes, not entirely sure of my destination, my head brimming with thoughts. I needed somewhere to stay. I had only a small number of close friends in the area but they were all married with kids. I was sure none of them would have wanted me turning up on the doorstep. And the majority of them were from Ellis Associates. I was fast coming to the realisation that it was about time I burned my bridges with that life.

There was my sister, Dani, too. She would surely take me in if I asked. I guessed, based on our last conversation, that she was still living alone – unless she'd shacked up with her latest fling in a whirlwind romance (that was almost certainly doomed for failure) and had simply failed to inform me.

I decided against that idea as well. There would be too many questions from Dani, too much prying. And I was sure that even though she would likely provide me with a roof over my head, my visit wouldn't be entirely welcome. Not given our recent history together. I didn't need that hassle.

Having driven around in circles, never moving more than a couple of miles away from my house, I finally fixed my sights on a small hotel on the Birmingham Road, the main road linking Sutton Coldfield to Birmingham. I would have had many more options if I'd moved further afield into the city, but the hotel was a temporary measure, one way or another. And while Gemma may have kicked me out of my own house, she sure as hell wasn't going to stop me seeing my children; I wanted to be close to them. With my marriage and my job on the rocks, and my life and sanity in the hands of my father-in-law and an Irish mobster, the kids were the only positive thing I had left.

I parked in the small car park that was nothing more than a large tarmacked driveway and carried my case through the entrance toward the reception desk. Having agreed a nightly rate with the receptionist of fifty-five pounds for an unspecified length of stay, I dragged my case up the single flight of stairs to room five. I turned the key in the lock and pushed the door open, then studied the cramped space before me.

It smelled old and worn, and the sparse and aged furniture only complemented the aroma. There was a single bed, the plain white sheets neatly tucked in a turn-down that reminded me of hotels at which I stayed with my parents in the eighties. The patterned carpet and curtains also suggested the decor was the design of someone stuck in the past.

It was somewhere warm and dry to sleep at least. But I didn't want to be in the room any longer than necessary. I left immediately and headed downstairs to look for the bar. Or at least what passed as a bar. I'd seen a more impressive array of drinks in people's houses before. And there wasn't a soul in sight. It appeared, in fact, that the receptionist doubled as a barmaid on the rare occasion that anyone fancied a drink.

I headed out and walked for a good mile or so until I found a decent enough pub in the Wylde Green area of the town. I'd never been in the Shoulder of Mutton but had passed it countless times in the car. It was entirely generic inside, and I was surprised when I entered that the clientele appeared so downtrodden given the relative wealth of the neighbourhood. I guessed on a Wednesday night there weren't that many punters around. Local pubs simply didn't have the draw they'd had a generation before – unless there was an important football match on.

I took a stool at the bar and started to drown my sorrows. And I probably would have stayed there until closing time, or at least until I was rolled out of the door drunk, if something hadn't happened. Actually, it wasn't something, but someone. A face from a long time ago. One I hadn't seen in years, and didn't think I'd ever see again.

This wasn't a person who should have moved me particularly. But with the turmoil that was going on inside me, seeing that face changed everything – my entire way of thinking.

I sat staring, oblivious to everything else around me. Thoughts were coming thick and fast, but few were sticking. My brain was on fire as I tried to grasp where to start, but at the same time I felt an incredible determination and an almost surreal calmness.

Dark Fragments

Gone was the all the pain and sorrow of the last few years. Gone was the misery of losing Alice. Gone was the anger and bitter resentment that had clouded me for so long. I felt alive, as though this was the answer to my many problems.

And then, just like that, I determined what I had to do.

I had a plan.

CHAPTER 26

I wasn't a violent person. But I did *think* about violence. I'd thought for years about all the situations I'd been in where I could have taken action, but didn't. I'm sure that was the same for almost everyone. Yes, it was just daydreaming, but what if the opportunity actually presented itself?

That was where the idea had come from: a lifelong habit of avoiding confrontation and letting people get the better of me.

People like Callum O'Brady, like Whitely, like Rottweiler. And people like Andrew Dove, the man I saw entirely by chance – or was it fate? – in a pub I'd never been to before on a soggy Wednesday night in Sutton Coldfield.

Even twenty years after the event, what he'd done to me still burned strong in my memory as a moment of regret and shame. Like I said: I wasn't a violent person. But I wished I hadn't been so weak so often. My whole life I'd preferred to walk away from my troubles whenever I could rather than face them head on. Over the years my cowardice had caused me more problems than I cared to think about.

When I was a teenager, my dad had led me to believe that it took great strength to walk away from a fight. That it showed character and made me a real man. I reckoned most parents would say that to their children, though. After all, this was my dad who'd tried to reinforce this belief in me, despite his having been quite the fighter in his youth.

The reality is that it takes much more guts to stand up for yourself and to defend yourself against others, knowing that you may end up getting hurt, than it does to run away.

As a young teenager, when I'd walked away after taking a beating from Dove, I'd been ridiculed at school for weeks afterwards. With a black eye and fat lip, I'd had to wear my failure

113

every day like a badge of shame while my enemy was lauded with praise for having wiped the floor with me without a single scratch inflicted upon him. My dad was proud of me for having done the 'decent' thing. Great. Because that made a whole lot of difference to a thirteen-year-old kid.

The truth was, I hadn't walked away from that fight as a show of strength. I'd simply been scared and confused. Dove's sucker punch had taken me completely by surprise.

I'd always been a competitive person, never afraid to fight in a non-physical sense, and even in a physical sense when it came to sports. That had seen me excel at many things, rugby included. My sporting prowess was no match for Dani's; she had far greater athleticism – balance, co-ordination and speed – to back up her winner's attitude. But I was still seen by my peers as one of the top dogs on the rugby field at least.

Teachers and coaches had said I had natural ability, that I was a raw but talented athlete. I was good, but never quite good enough. In later teenage years I was quickly overtaken by those kids who were able to bulk up and become the mountains required in the man's game. But as a determined thirteen year old I'd been an ace on the field.

It was during a training match that it happened. I'd been hurtling around the field for the best part of fifty minutes, tackling here, there and everywhere with ferocity. I'd scored two tries, including one where I'd sprinted a full fifty yards with not one opponent able to get within two yards of me. I was also the kicker and hadn't missed a single attempt in the whole match. It was a training match, sure, and not everyone was giving one hundred per cent, but I took pride in outshining them all.

And that was probably my downfall, because the opposition was clearly becoming disgruntled by my heroic display. So when I went in hard on Dove, tackling him just below the waist and sending him crashing to the ground, that was the last straw.

He immediately swivelled around to sit on top of me, and for the next few seconds, with me lying helpless on the ground, his fists rained down on my face.

I've never known why I didn't hit back. The opportunity was there. I was bigger than he was. Stronger too. But in the moment I panicked. I'd never been in that sort of position before. Rather than even attempt to throw a punch back, my only focus was on dragging myself out from underneath him and escaping the beating.

By the time I finally managed that, a teacher had already darted up to us and pulled us apart. I looked over at Dove and saw a wicked grin on his face. He knew he'd put me back in my place. His look was replicated across the faces of most of his team. Everyone knew it.

The teacher barked instructions but I was sure neither of us took in his words. A friend put his arm around my shoulder and guided me back to the changing rooms.

I looked around on my lonely walk and spotted Dove, still on the field, basking in his teammates' praise. The brave victor. It didn't matter one little bit that I had been the hero during the game. There was only one winner that day in the eyes of everyone on the field, and everyone in the school afterwards.

When I reached the changing rooms I flopped down on the wooden bench and, despite the kindly encouragement from my friend, I cried.

Twenty years had passed since then, and yet thinking about that day still had a powerful effect on me, bringing back raw emotion. Needless to say, Dove and I had never been friends after that. When we'd both left school at eighteen, our separate circles of friends had only become further dispersed into the wider world. After I spotted him in Wylde Green, however, it didn't take me long to track him down.

I guessed his being in the local area meant he still lived there. In the modern world, people leave such a big imprint of their lives in cyberspace (mostly unwittingly), so it took only some brief searches to find that Dove had never made it out of the Midlands. Having attended Aston University, he'd gone on to work for a local accounting firm. His social media profiles showed he lived in the small village of Wishaw, just a few miles away. It wasn't a big place and two quick searches – first in the online phone directory and then on the electoral roll – allowed me to pinpoint his home address.

I scoped out his house. He lived in a newly built executive home – far bigger than the Victorian semi that Gemma and I had splashed out on two years previously. I was immensely proud of our home. It had style and class. Dove's home was almost certainly a lot more expensive than ours, but it was also quite tasteless in my eyes.

Money without class was one of the most vulgar sights to behold, and my impression of who Dove had become was further confirmed by the two large four-by-fours parked in his driveway. With their lowered suspension, giant alloys, sporty trimmings and sparkling paint, I guessed they were used only for showing off, ferrying kids about and doing the daily commute, rather than for any off-road activity. Before I'd even spoken a word to Dove I hated him with renewed vigour.

I watched him come out of his driveway on foot as I sat hunkered down in the front seat of my car, across the road from his house. He walked out of the gates and turned left, back toward the village. He was older and plumper and had less hair, but he certainly hadn't lost any of his arrogance, judging by his cocky swagger.

I watched him in my rear-view mirror. When he was a good distance away, I turned on the engine and swung the car around to follow. When he took a left turn, I sped up to the junction to close the distance, then pulled the car over to the curb and killed the engine. I got out of the car and headed after him on foot, keeping on his tail as he walked to a local pub – the Hare and Hounds – on the main road that bisected the village.

Inside he met with two men I didn't recognise, and spent the rest of the evening working his way through six pints of beer. The pub was comfortably busy with both eaters and drinkers, which allowed me to keep my head down and stay out of sight. I kept a baseball cap pulled low over my face to better my chances of remaining incognito, but I had to assume that if Dove looked over at me, if I caught his eye at the wrong moment, he would recognise me.

But then, he hadn't spotted me the other night in Wylde Green, and really it wouldn't be that big a deal even if he did see me – I doubted he would want to come over and chat. Most likely he would quickly look away and pretend he hadn't noticed me and then spend the rest of the night trying his hardest to not look again.

As it was, I didn't need to worry. The night passed in a haze of beer and drunken chat. The three of them were certainly louder and more raucous than they had been at the start – and Dove was the loudest and brashest of them all – but they all still seemed in control. No-one was falling on the floor, and I presumed, in fact I hoped, that the night would come to a lacklustre end not long after the closing bell rang.

In the intervening time I'd worked through three beers and a shandy myself, and had politely rebuffed the attempts of two locals – whom I took to be regulars – to engage me in lengthy conversation. All in all, I was feeling relaxed and ready.

When the barman signalled last orders, I decided it was time to make myself scarce. I got up from my seat by the bar and kept my head down as I walked out into the cold and blustery night.

A handful of customers loitered in the car park, either smoking or saying their goodbyes, and I decided not to hang around there. I walked away from the pub and took the turning off the main road into much quieter surroundings. Even during the day the village was peaceful, I knew, but at eleven p.m. on a weekday evening it was entirely dead.

I carried on walking. My leg was still stiff and sore from the beating I'd taken the day before and there was a constant stabbing in my ribs, but I blocked the pain out as best I could. The beer I'd drunk at least dimmed the discomfort.

I hid myself in a snicket that ran between two side roads. I knew from the walk to the pub that the narrow alley was a shortcut for Dove to his house. With tall bushes and sporadic trees on both sides, it was unlit. Other than at the two entrances, where light was pushing in from the nearby streetlights, the snicket was virtually pitch black. I stopped behind a large tree trunk and waited.

The tingle of anticipation I felt grew when I heard voices approaching. Two voices. Both male. I stole a glance from behind the tree and saw two men enter the alleyway. In the darkness I couldn't be certain, but neither looked like Dove.

I pulled myself as far around the trunk as I could, out of sight, and held my breath. My body was tense and unmoving as the two men sauntered past. Their intoxicated debate reverberated in my brain for a few seconds until they exited the alley and disappeared into the night.

Just a few seconds later, I heard more footsteps. No voices this time. Again I took a peek – quickly and discreetly. But the solitary man whose footsteps I had heard was much closer than I'd thought. Unlike the previous two men, who had been wrapped up in their heated discussion, this man was alert – probably for the very fact that he was alone.

In the briefest of moments that I'd looked around the tree I'd been sure of two things: it was Dove, and he'd spotted me.

'I can see you hiding there,' Dove slurred.

My heart jumped. But spotting me and recognising me were two very different things. Surely it was too dark for him to have made out who I was?

It didn't matter. If I really was going to do this, now was the best opportunity I would get.

Pushing back any remaining doubts, I darted out from behind the tree. Dove was just three yards away from me and was turning back around to head to the other end of the alley. Whoever he thought I was, he was clearly spooked.

It was only at the last second that he sensed me behind him. His drunken body went to take flight. If he'd been sober, if he'd had the extra element of clarity in his thoughts and actions, he might have been able to react more quickly and make a mad dash to escape. As it was, he had no chance.

I bundled into him, throwing my body right through where he'd been, reminiscent of the clattering tackle that had sparked the fight all those years ago. We tumbled to the ground.

Dove let out a painful shout as my weight slammed down on top of him. The fall alone took the immediate fight from him. I wasted no time.

I threw a succession of blows into Dove's sides as he turned over and tried to fight back. I wormed my way from lying on top to straddling him, pinning his arms. Dove was shouting, calling out, but the words weren't registering in my head.

Once I was in position, it was time for payback. I threw a fist down onto his nose. A sharp pain shot up through my arm but I ignored it and threw another and then another fist down onto his face. Each shot was entirely unimpeded; Dove's face took the full force of my strikes. After the fifth blow he was covered in blood.

At least three wounds had opened up on his face. His eyes were rolling. The fight was already over. A sucker punch – exactly what he'd dealt me.

I was about to deliver one final blow when I heard voices behind me. Shouting. I glanced over my shoulder and saw two men running toward me, the same two who had passed by just seconds before – alerted by Dove's shouts, no doubt.

It was time to go. I jumped up off Dove and went to move into a sprint. But as I pushed away Dove somehow found the strength to grab hold of my ankle. His grip was too weak to stop me and I quickly broke free, but the unexpected obstacle knocked me completely off balance. I stumbled forward then fell toward the ground.

I managed to put out both my hands to help cushion the fall. As I hit the deck my body twisted to the side through its own momentum. I skidded forward, and my right arm and my side scraped across the solid pathway. I winced in pain, then spotted one of the men out of the corner of my eye. He was just a few yards away, bearing down on me. The other, I realised, had stopped to tend to Dove.

I couldn't get caught. Not now. Not at the very first hurdle.

I hauled my aching body back up and limped the first few yards as I ironed out the bumps in my bruised legs. By the time I got to full speed, just as I reached the end of the alleyway, I could hear the rasping breath of the man who had taken chase after me.

I was still in full sprint as I rounded the corner onto the road, my arms and legs pumping. I risked a peek over my shoulder and saw that the man had fallen behind. I didn't let up. I continued to run, my arms and legs moving in a steady, determined rhythm.

Only when I had used up every ounce of energy, when my heart felt like it would explode in my chest, when my lungs ached for air and when my legs felt like immovable lead weights, did I come to an abrupt stop.

I looked behind me once more and smiled. There was no sign of Dove or the other men or anyone else. I was in the clear.

CHAPTER 27

'How did it make you feel,' she asked, 'to have got your revenge on Andrew Dove? To have beaten him so callously?'

'Callously?' I said.

'It was an unprovoked attack.'

'As it was when he beat the crap out of me at school.'

'But you were only thirteen years old then,' she said. 'You were children.'

'So it's okay for kids to hit each other but not for grown men to do it?'

'Well, what do you think? Do you think it's okay for a grown man to punch another man in the face in an unprovoked attack?'

'No. I guess under most circumstances, no, I don't. But this wasn't really unprovoked.'

'Can you explain that?'

'There might have been an intervening period between him smacking me on a rugby field and me getting my own back in a dark alley twenty years later, but the two events are still intrinsically linked. So to answer your specific question, no, it's not okay for a grown man to attack and punch someone in an unprovoked attack, but then I never have.'

She didn't respond to my explanation.

'Coming back to my original question then,' she said, 'how did it make you feel?'

'It's hard to explain. I felt relief. I felt excitement. I felt like a small weight had been taken off my shoulders. It might sound silly to you, but that school-ground incident had played on my mind for the whole of my adult life. I'm not saying it was a defining moment or anything as dramatic as that, but it's one of those big memories in my head that will always be there as a moment of regret. A moment where I wished I'd acted differently.'

'And do you still feel that way now? Do you still have the same regret, or did that dull after you attacked Andrew Dove?'

'It'll never go away. It's like a scar. It may only be a small scar, but that memory will always be with me, a permanent reminder. Taking revenge went a long way to making up for what happened, though it can't change the past. At least some of those memories are less severe and painful now.'

She stared at me intently for a few seconds and I wondered whether she was already finished with her questions, even though there were still ten minutes left on the clock. When she finally broke eye contact, she looked down at the pad in front of her and started scribbling notes, as she did every session. It was strange to imagine my entire life story, all of the ups and the many, many downs of my life, recorded on those few small pieces of paper.

'So what happened after Dove?' she asked.

'I had a plan. At least I thought I did. Maybe not a well-thought-out, fully formulated plan, but an intention at least — to get my own back on them all. But it didn't quite go as smoothly as I'd hoped. Best laid plans and all that. It's the story of my life really. Life has always had a habit of fucking up my good intentions.'

'You think you had good intentions?'

'Yes. In a raw, animalistic sense my intentions were noble. This was retribution. It was justice. It's the way the human race has dealt with indiscretions for thousands of years.'

'Retribution? Is that how you see your actions? As retribution rather than revenge?'

'I'm not sure I see a difference between the two.'

'Well, strictly speaking retribution is a punishment inflicted as vengeance for a wrong or criminal act. It has an element of formality and justness. Revenge, on the other hand, can be very different. Its connotations are much more savage and punitive, and the measures are often more severe and unjust.'

'I'm still not sure there's that much difference. In my eyes, what I delivered — what I intended to deliver at least — was retribution. It was a just punishment that fitted the crime.'

'Intended?'

'Like I said, it didn't quite go as planned.'

'So what went wrong? What happened?'

'It's not what happened but who.'

'*Okay. So* who *happened then?*'
'*Cara Donald happened.*'
'*Who was Cara Donald?*'
'*Cara Donald was one of the biggest mistakes of my life.*'

CHAPTER 28

I've always believed there are some people with whom we were destined to click. Maybe it's something in the DNA, a subconscious reaction to pheromones or something else primal like that. Some people would call it love at first sight. I wouldn't quite go that far, but I'd sympathise with the concept. That was the way it was when Alice and I first met. It was the same with Cara Donald. And I hadn't expected that at all. It took me genuinely by surprise, and my attraction to her led to a cascade of events that I never could have anticipated.

I'd frequented a gym in Brindley Place in Birmingham since as far back as when Alice and I lived in the city. In my twenties I'd been a regular there, going up to six times a week. Even though I'd moved out of the city, I'd kept the membership going and I still enjoyed heading there when I could, usually before or after work, though having two young children had made finding the time harder. I certainly wasn't as fit as I had been in years gone by; my workouts were less frequent and less intense, but I still did my best.

I'd always been a very solitary gym-goer. It wasn't a social occasion for me. I went there alone and I didn't stand around gassing to others while I was there. That said, over the years I'd become familiar with many of the other people I saw. I never spoke to these people, yet I felt I knew a lot about them – their gym customs at least.

It was a Friday morning when I saw Cara Donald. At first my brain registered no surprise. Her face was passingly familiar and I assumed that I'd seen her around the gym before. After a few seconds, though, I did the world's longest double-take as my brain tried to place her. I stared over at her as she headed to a treadmill. She must only have been five foot five or six, but her slim body made her look tall. I could tell from the tight-fitting shorts and vest that clung to her tanned body that she was in perfect shape.

Eventually it clicked. I didn't know her from the gym. Perhaps we'd simply never trained at the same time before, but more likely she was relatively new, which was why we'd only just crossed paths there. I did know her, though.

She'd worked for the same company as Alice, back when we'd first met. She was from the same crowd of people as Craig Fletcher, the man Alice had cheated with. I hadn't seen Cara for something like ten years, but all of a sudden a rush of memories cascaded through my mind.

I'd always been fond of Cara, from a distance at least. She was friendly and kooky, always smiling and laughing. A free spirit. She was incredibly flirtatious too. At least she had been with me. I'd never been quite sure whether she was the same with every guy or she really had liked me. Either way, her flirting had made me feel special, and although nothing had ever come close to happening between us, I'd always been attracted to her. If I'd known her when I was single, I certainly would have tried my luck.

What was I talking about? I *was* single. Gemma had thrown me out, and despite my efforts she'd barely spoken to me since. A week: more than half the time O'Brady had given me to get him two hundred thousand pounds had already passed. Gemma had extricated herself from that problem now. It was clear that neither she nor her father was prepared to help bail me out anymore.

I'd picked the kids up from school twice in the last week, spending some much-needed quality time with them before Gemma came home from work. Each time she'd quickly shooed me out the door on her return, making it clear I wasn't welcome in the house.

It was Gemma's choice to put our marriage on the line like that. I hadn't asked for it. She had. Now I had every right to do whatever I wanted.

I kept an eye on Cara as she pounded on a treadmill for half an hour, keeping myself busy in the weights area. At the end of her run she was red-faced and dripping with sweat, but she looked fantastic still, with her wavy dyed-blond hair and cute face.

She began to walk over from the bank of treadmills to a matted area where medicine balls of various sizes were shelved. I noticed a few other people – both male and female – following her every move. She was just that type of person who caught attention. I got up from the machine I was on and quickly walked over to try to meet her head on.

We reached the mats at the same time and proceeded to do the confused shimmy that happens when two people walk unexpectedly toward each other. I shifted to the left then right, and she mirrored my clumsy attempts to get out of the way.

'Sorry,' I said, laughing, before moving very deliberately back to my left to let her past.

She smiled and looked at me quizzically, as though trying to place my face, but in the end she said nothing of it.

'Did you want one of the balls?' she said through heavy breaths.

Her voice was velvety smooth and she had a Southern Irish twang. Not a strong accent, but enough to make it clear where she was from. For some reason I hadn't remembered that she was from Ireland, but her voice was nonetheless as familiar as it was sweet.

I looked over at the shelf next to us and realised there was just one ball left.

'No, no. You go for it,' I said. 'I'll do some stretching and wait.'

'Thanks,' she said and stepped away to fetch the ball.

I was slightly disappointed that she hadn't recognised me immediately. But then if she was anything like I usually was, she was in the zone and just wanted to concentrate on her workout, not chat and flirt with some guy she may or may not have liked ten years ago.

I hovered for just a couple of minutes until someone else finished, then I took his ball and positioned myself adjacent to

Cara. She was doing some sort of balance pose with the ball, the tips of her toes of one foot on the floor, one hand on the ball, and her other hand and foot in the air. I clumsily started to make up some not-so-elegant poses, which drew questioning glances from the other punters.

'Bloody hell,' I said out loud. 'I really have no clue what I'm supposed to be doing with this thing.'

I noticed a couple of others shake their heads at me, but Cara snickered.

'You're not supposed to laugh at those less fortunate than you,' I said.

'It's not as easy as it looks, is it?'

'It certainly looks a lot easier for you than it feels for me.'

'Maybe you should stick to the weights machines,' she said, and I was quietly impressed that perhaps she'd noticed me earlier after all.

'Yeah. You're probably right,' I said.

I slid off the ball and landed on the floor with a bump, which elicited another laugh from Cara. I got to my feet and put the ball back on the shelf, then walked away from her and the mats without another word.

Whether or not she recognised me, I could tell from the intensity on her face when she was working out that if I tried to start up any other chat with her there, in the gym in the middle of her routine, she would probably cut me off outright. That would be the end of it. The fact I'd managed to make her smile a couple of times, even if she was only being polite, was a good sign.

As I walked away from Cara I tried to think of how I could approach her next. It was childish. Calculated too. Even in my mid-thirties an attractive woman apparently still had the power to make me act like a nervous and irrational boy. But one way or another, I was determined to speak to her again.

I messed around on the weights machines for another five minutes. When I saw Cara finish off and head back toward the changing rooms, I did the same. I guessed she would take longer to get ready than I would, so it wouldn't be too difficult to get showered and dressed and outside before her.

When I was done, I walked out and stood by the gym entrance, looking over toward the elaborate fountain that dominated the main square in Brindley Place. I'd always loved the revamped area by the canals. Even though it was in the middle of a fast-paced city, Brindley Place felt so calm.

Alice and I had regularly strolled through the squares and up and down the canals when we'd lived nearby, frequenting the many bars and restaurants. I still enjoyed taking the kids every now and then, particularly when it was warm, letting them run around by the fountain and seeing them squeal in delight every time a splash of water got them.

I took my phone out of my pocket and held it to my ear and waited. When I spotted Cara coming out of the gym a few minutes later, heading toward me, I began to fake a conversation on the phone, which I promptly ended when she was just a couple of yards away. As I pushed the mobile back into my pocket she made eye contact with me, and before she looked away again I smiled casually at her and nodded. She gave a half-frown and I wondered whether my infantile plan had failed, but then, just as she looked away, she cracked a radiant smile as she sauntered past.

'Good workout?' I asked.

By that point she was a yard past me but she stopped and turned around.

'Yeah. You?'

'If I could figure out what to do with those damn balls, it might have been better.'

She laughed. 'Practice makes perfect.'

'Indeed.'

She went to walk away.

'I know this sounds ridiculous, but don't I know you from somewhere?' I said.

She frowned.

'I don't think so,' she said. 'Maybe you've just seen me in the gym before. I only joined about a month ago, but I'm there all the time.'

I think at that point she probably started doubting my friendly manner, but a second later her features softened again.

'Actually, yeah, you're right,' she said, the look on her face telling me she was now trying to place me. 'You do look familiar. I thought it was just from the gym, but didn't you used to work at Gravesham's? You know, the solicitors?'

'No, but my wife did. Alice. Alice Stephens.'

I saw the spark of recognition in Cara's eyes at my dead wife's name.

'Ah, of course. I'm Cara,' she said. She extended her hand out to me and I gave it a gentle shake. I looked at her quizzically, making her think that I wasn't quite there with her yet. 'Cara Andrews?' she added. 'Ah, you probably knew me as Cara Donald. My married name is Andrews.'

'Yes, you're right,' I said, nodding in a feigned eureka moment, although the mention of a husband made me automatically wary. 'That's it. I think we met a few times at work do's years back.'

'Yeah, we did. I remember now,' she said, giving a warm smile.

I wondered whether she was reminiscing fondly about those flirtatious occasions in the same way I was.

'So you're married now?' I asked.

'Technically yes,' she said, giving a less-than-convincing smile and rubbing her neck. It was a response that enhanced my confidence. I didn't press her on the point but I'd certainly do so another time. 'What about Alice? Did she move on from Gravesham's?'

I hung my head. 'No,' I said. 'Alice died.'

Cara cupped her mouth in horror. 'I'm so sorry,' she said. 'I never knew that. Look at me, I've really put my foot in it this time, haven't I?'

'Don't worry. It's not against the law to talk about it. Plus it was a long time ago and you didn't know. It's fine.'

I noticed her glance down at my left hand. It took me a split second to twig what she was looking at. My wedding ring.

'You're remarried now?' she asked.

'Yeah, I guess,' I said, hanging my head. 'Technically at least,' I added, echoing her own comment.

'I think I know what you mean,' she said.

'Just one of those things.'

She didn't push the subject any further. I noticed that she no longer wore a ring on her wedding finger, though I saw a band of white flesh there that suggested its removal was relatively recent.

'Well, it was nice to bump into you,' I said, not quite sure where to take the conversation next, and aware that if I was too pushy, she'd likely run a mile.

'Yeah. It was,' she said, seeming a little unsure now that I was breaking the conversation off so abruptly. 'You too. And I'm sorry about … you know.'

'Yeah … thanks. Maybe I'll see you around at the gym?'

'Maybe. Hopefully.'

'You can show me what I'm supposed to be doing on those mats, before I injure someone.'

She laughed. 'You bet.'

We exchanged brief goodbyes, then headed our separate ways – me pleasantly impressed with how that first encounter had gone, and Cara with no idea of the life-changing mess she would soon be getting herself into.

CHAPTER 29

I had less than a week to get Callum O'Brady two hundred thousand pounds. There was no way that was going to happen; I'd already come to that realisation. What I needed was to keep him off my back. Although I had a plan to do that, I feared it would be easier said than done. Yet despite the predicament, despite all the problems in my life, the following morning I was feeling more upbeat as a result of my encounter with Cara. Her alluring and optimistic manner, and the potential of what was to come if I pursued her, had lifted my spirits.

It was Saturday and I wanted to see my children. I'd called Gemma several times since I'd last picked the kids up from school. She'd answered more than once, but had quickly fobbed me off with claims of being too busy or unable to talk because she was driving. At the least they were convenient excuses. It was just as likely they were outright lies.

I was completely in the dark as to where I stood with her. I felt I was at a crossroads with no idea which road to take. Should I try to reconcile with Gemma? Did I *want* to? If not for her and my benefit then at least for the kids?

I did love Gemma. She was Chloe's mother. Harry's too, I knew deep down. But I wasn't sure I was *in* love with her. I hated that cliché; I always thought it was ridiculous. But really that described how I felt about Gemma. In a sexual sense our relationship had been cold for some time, despite whatever attempts I had made to reverse that fact. But I loved her.

I missed her. I missed the four of us being together.

That said, I wasn't about to go grovelling back to her. Pride was one of my many faults. Plus, based on her treatment of me since she'd thrown me out, I believed there was a very real chance she would simply laugh in my face and tell me where to go. And *she* was the one who had kicked *me* out. If she wanted me back, shouldn't she be coming to me?

That morning I made up my mind: regardless of what was happening between me and Gemma, I would go around to the house. I desperately wanted to see Harry and Chloe. I hated not seeing them every day, talking to them and hearing about their fun-filled days at school and nursery, where the most traumatic things that happened were that someone pulled their hair or splashed water in their face or – the worst crime of them all – took a chip off their lunch plate. I loved hearing about their playground triumphs and woes alike and remembering how simple and happy life should be.

I drove down my road, turned into the drive of my house and switched off the engine. An awkward sensation coursed through me. This was my home. It had been for years. I'd driven onto the driveway hundreds if not thousands of times before, but this time felt different. This time I felt like an outsider.

I got out of the car and walked up to the front door. The key for the lock was in my pocket. I could have let myself in, yet I chose to ring the doorbell. I wasn't sure why.

When the door was opened, I was completely unprepared for the person who greeted me: Dani.

'What the hell are you doing here?' I said, my tone as sour as the look on my face.

Before my sister could respond, I spotted Chloe and Harry behind her, standing in the kitchen doorway. They beamed when they saw me and came bounding up.

I grabbed them both and lifted them up, one on each arm. They giggled in delight and it instantly softened my mood. I put the kids down and they rushed off back into the kitchen, tittering as they went.

When I looked back at Dani, my brief moment of happiness faded again almost as quickly as it had come.

'So?' I said.

'I came to see you actually,' Dani replied, her voice hard.

'You're not working?' I said, looking her up and down. She was wearing jeans and a low-cut jumper, a far less formal look than the last time I'd seen her.

'It's Saturday. Even DIs get a day off every now and then.'

'Where's Gemma?' I said.

'She just popped upstairs to the loo, I think,' Dani said.

As if on cue I heard the toilet flush upstairs. I shut the door behind me and walked past my sister, not yet sure what to think about her unexpected presence. Whatever the explanation, I didn't like her being in my house without my knowledge one bit.

'If you wanted to see me, you could have called,' I said.

'I could have. But I didn't.'

'And where's your car?'

'In for a service. I took the train. Any other questions? Would you like to know what I had for breakfast? Or how long it's been since I last went to the toilet?'

I turned and glared at her and noticed Gemma coming up behind. On seeing me she kept her expression neutral.

'Hi,' was the best I could muster as Gemma walked past me, into the kitchen.

'I didn't know you were coming,' she said. 'You could have called first.'

'Are you serious?' I said. 'I shouldn't need to call before coming to my own house to see my own wife and children. And anyway, I have been calling you.'

Gemma just tutted in response. We all moved through into the kitchen, where Chloe and Harry were sitting at the table scribbling diligently in colouring books.

'I can see this isn't a great time,' Dani chipped in. 'Maybe we can talk later, Ben. Yeah?'

I was about to agree but Gemma beat me to it. 'Don't be silly,' she said, before turning to me. 'Dani brought the kids these new colouring books.'

Dani smiled and shrugged.

'Thanks, Auntie Danielle,' Harry said on cue.

'You're welcome here any time,' Gemma said to my sister. 'And anyway, as I was saying, I could really do with some help today.'

'Help?' I said. 'What do you mean?'

My wife and sister both turned to me and the look they gave me made me feel as though I'd walked in on something I shouldn't have. It was both surreal and uncomfortable.

'I was just telling Dani that I'd arranged to meet up with the girls for lunch today. She offered to look after Chloe and Harry for a few hours so that I could go.'

I scoffed at her words. This really was beyond ridiculous.

'Did you not think about asking me?'

'I didn't know where you were,' Gemma said, as though it was obvious.

'You might have done if you'd asked me or if you'd answered my calls.'

'It's not a big deal,' Gemma said. 'You weren't here. Dani was.'

'But why *were* you here?' I said to my sister again.

'Don't go getting your knickers in a twist,' Gemma butted in. 'She came to see you. But I asked, on the off chance, whether she could look after the kids, and she was good enough to agree. I was going to have them tag along with me, but I'm sure they'd rather stay here and play.'

My sister looked at me and shrugged again. 'It would be nice to spend a bit of time with them,' she said.

'You're right. It would. That's what I'm here for,' I replied. 'I wanted to take them out for the day.'

'Look, I'll stick around,' Dani said to Gemma. 'Let Ben and I both look after them. You go out and have a good time.'

I shook my head at the situation that was unfolding before me. It was just too bizarre. This was my house. My wife. My children. Yet I felt like a complete stranger. An impostor.

134

Gemma sighed and took a few moments to mull over the proposition.

'Fine,' she said eventually. 'But I need the kids back here by six. We're going over to stay with Granny and Granddad again tonight.'

Granny and Granddad. Again. I cringed at Gemma's words.

That explained why no-one had been home when I'd gone to the house one night in the week to pick up some clothes. I couldn't bear to think about Gemma and her parents sitting together and slagging me off for hours on end. And it wasn't just the Whitely's effect on Gemma I was worried about. I wouldn't have put it past Whitely to slip in some criticisms in front of the kids too. He and his wife had always tolerated me and been largely pleasant toward me – at least I'd always felt that they'd respected me as a good father to their only grandkids. But since my last meeting with Whitely I wasn't so sure anymore. The gloves were off and the situation had changed dramatically. Maybe they would see this as a chance to put the boot in and get rid of me once and for all.

Poisoning Gemma's mind against me was one thing, but would they really have the audacity to do that to my children? For my own sake and sanity, I really hoped not.

'That's great,' Dani said, a big smile on her face. 'I'm really looking forward to spending some time with them.'

I gave her an unimpressed smile. 'Me too.'

'Thanks, Dani,' Gemma said, beaming. 'I really appreciate it.'

My wife gave me no further acknowledgment; she just walked out of the kitchen and back up the stairs. Dani looked at me and smiled unconvincingly.

I didn't like her being there one bit, and I was already wondering exactly what it was she wanted to see me about. For all of her front, her offer to spend time with my children and to help out, I knew that her interest had little to do with her desire to be a good auntie and likely everything to do with her being a detective. And given recent events – Dove, O'Brady – that worried me.

CHAPTER 30

'Would you say that you respect women?'

I scoffed at the question. 'Of course I do.'

'But many of your actions suggest otherwise. You cheating on Alice. The way you were with Gemma – and how you pursued Cara so soon after separating. Your treatment of Dani.'

'My treatment of Dani?'

'Were you jealous of your sister?'

'Jealous of what?'

'As a child. Did you feel jealousy or resentment toward her?'

I thought about the question. I wanted to say no, because I knew where she was going with this – and it was ludicrous, I wanted to claim. But the fact was, this woman had hit on something. And it was something I really didn't want to think about.

'Yes,' I said nonetheless.

'Why?'

'Because Dani was so damn perfect. Everyone thought that.'

'What about your parents?'

'Yes, them too.'

'Do you believe your parents loved Dani more than they loved you?'

I shifted in my seat. I didn't want it to be the case, but what could I say? It was the way I had always felt.

'Have you heard of the Oedipus complex?' she asked.

'No.'

'It's a psychoanalytic theory that at some point children feel sexual desire for the parent of the opposite sex.'

'What are you trying to say?' I asked, feeling genuine revulsion at the thoughts that went through my head at her words.

'It's okay, it's seen as a very natural part of childhood mental development. It's a theory, and not everyone agrees with it. Nevertheless, it's considered important in explaining how humans are socialised, and how children learn to cope and deal with expectation and disappointment. It's also through the Oedipus complex that all sorts of personality traits can be explained – like resentment toward a parent, or even resentment to all members of a sex.'

'You're saying I resent all women because I wanted to sleep with my mother?'

'No, not at all,' she said, and her cheeks blushed slightly at my blunt statement. *'But I am questioning whether your relationship with your mother, and her relationship with Dani, may have had an impact on your attitude toward women in general.'*

I paused for a moment, unsure what to say. More than anything I felt angry at what she was insinuating. Angry that she was breaking down my actions and what was in my mind – who I was – into something so simple and so vulgar.

'I'm not trying to trick you here,' she said. *'I'm just trying to understand how your childhood may have had an impact on your actions in adult life.'*

'Fine. Yes, I did resent Dani,' I said. *'How could I not? My mum and dad adored her; she was the shining star. They loved me too, of course. I had a good upbringing – I said that to you before. But I could never quite live up to their expectations, and I could never quite emulate the brilliance of my sister.'*

'And how did that situation play out when you were children? What was the impact for you?'

'You asked me before whether there was violence in our home. But you asked about the wrong parent. You asked about my dad.'

'And you told me he never hit you. But you're saying your mother did?'

'No, she wasn't violent either. Not really. *But there was one occasion that always sticks in my mind.'*

'Go on,' she said when I didn't immediately continue.

'Dani and I were seven, I think. We were messing around, like kids do. I don't know where the idea came from, but we decided it would be good to start crayoning on the walls. We were inviting some friends over that weekend

for a party and we wanted them to know where to go in the house. So we got a couple of crayons each and started drawing big arrows on the walls – directions to the toilet, the kitchen. I mean, we thought it was a good idea. We weren't setting out to be naughty.'

'And what happened when your parents found out?'

'We'd finished. Dani was somewhere else in the house when Mum saw what we'd done. She completely lost it. She found me in the lounge, crayons by my feet, and she threw herself at me. She grabbed me and hauled me to my feet and slapped me in the face. She was screaming, completely out of control.'

'Were you scared of her?'

'I was petrified. Maybe my memory is clouded now as to exactly what she was like in that moment, but at the time I really thought she might kill me. I didn't know any different. I'd never seen her act like that before and it wouldn't have been that difficult for her to throttle me – I was so small. I thought she might reach out and strangle me to death there and then.'

'But she didn't, of course.'

'No. Dani came to my rescue. She pulled my mum away. Begged her to leave me alone. Dani insisted it was all her idea and that it wasn't my fault. My mum was snarling and shouting, but with Dani's pleading she slowly calmed down. We both got punished that day, but Mum never laid a finger on Dani – not that day or any other.'

'Was that a defining moment in your childhood, do you think? In terms of your relationship with your mum and Dani?'

'Yes, I think it was. Dani saved me from trouble, and not for the last time. I hadn't asked her to. In some ways I didn't want her to. But she did it anyway. It only made her even stronger than me, even more noble and supreme. She saved me from the wrath of my mum, but in many ways, after the event at least, I hated Dani for what she'd done. Why did she feel she had to come to my rescue?'

'Because she loved you. And she knew it wasn't your fault.'

'Yeah, I know. You're right. But that's not how it felt for me. It felt like just another in a long line of incidents that proved how much better Dani was than me.'

'You say it wasn't the last time Dani saved you from trouble. Did that carry on into your adult life?'

'Of course. Dani always felt the need to look after me, I told you that before. But even in adult life, despite what others might think, I don't believe her actions were purely noble. The thing with Dani is that there's nearly always a hidden agenda. Something else happening under the surface that only ever gets brought out when she decides.'

'And that's what happened when she turned up at your house that day?'

'Yes. I hadn't seen her for four years, then all of a sudden she was interested in coming back into our lives and being a good auntie? No, I didn't buy that. Not one bit. I knew it was just a matter of time before she revealed what she really wanted.'

CHAPTER 31

With the kids on their bikes, Dani and I walked the short distance from my house to Sutton Park – an expanse of more than two thousand acres of natural parkland that was one my favourite places to enjoy a leisurely few hours with my family. It was a haven of peace and tranquillity with paths and lakes and woods, a place full of adventure for the kids. I loved it. But with my sister and her as-yet-unspoken agenda accompanying me, I wasn't feeling as positive as usual.

I watched the other families as we meandered along. They all looked so content and carefree. I wondered how I appeared to them. Did they look at me and see just another dad enjoying a relaxing Saturday with his kids? Or could they sense in my face, in my eyes, the difficulties I'd seen in my life?

I was a little surprised that Chloe and Harry hadn't yet said anything to me about my sudden separation from Gemma. I knew they were too young to really understand what had happened, but I thought they'd be full of questions as to where I'd been and when I was coming back home.

Their apparent lack of interest in the situation again led me to question just what they'd been told by Gemma and her undoubtedly acidic parents. But at least the kids were happy to see me and to be in my company. I wanted to make sure that for the next few hours I simply had a good time with them.

The one hindrance to that, however, was Dani. What the hell was she doing there?

'You said you'd come to see me?' I said as we strolled along the pathway, the children storming ahead of us on their bikes and stopping or doubling back every now and then to stay within sight and earshot.

'You always sound so suspicious when you speak to me,' Dani replied.

'Well, it's hard not to be. The last time I saw you all I got was questions about Alice's murder. Your visit was hardly fuelled by you wanting to rekindle our relationship. And I'm guessing this latest visit is probably more of the same.'

'You should be a detective,' she said sarcastically.

'Very funny. So come on, spit it out. Have the police got anywhere on that new murder? A suspect? Anything?'

'Actually there's been some progress, yes.'

I raised an eyebrow. Since her last visit I'd tracked down details of the murder in question on the internet. The victim was a forty-year-old, out-of-work single mother called Hayley Lewis. She'd been found strangled in her home by her teenage son when he returned home from staying with a friend.

The details that had been released to the press were vague and provided no hint of a link to Alice's murder. Nor was there any mention of how the body had been displayed, which I knew from the investigation into Alice's death had suggested a sexual motive to the killing. In fact, without the details Dani had given me previously, nothing I'd read in the public domain would have alerted me to Hayley Lewis's killing being in any way linked to Alice's.

'Are you going to tell me?' I said when it was clear my sister wasn't going to offer up what she knew.

'Yeah, I will do. But that's not all I wanted to talk to you about. What's happened between you and Gemma?'

'That's none of your business.'

'No, maybe not. But I'm interested to hear the story. You're still my brother. I don't like to see you struggling like this.'

'Struggling? You've no idea what I've been struggling with.'

'So tell me.'

'Didn't Gemma fill you in before I interrupted your party?'

'No, she didn't. All she said was that you hadn't been staying there. I'm not sure she'd have told me much more even if I'd asked. Which I didn't, because you turned up.'

'Yeah, of course.'

'What's that supposed to mean?'

'Nothing.'

'So just what is going on with you?' Dani said. 'She's a great mum, you know. And the kids, they're great too.'

'I don't need you telling me that. I know it. But life's not always straightforward.'

'Not for you it's not.'

'We're just taking a break, that's all. I'm sure we'll iron things out.'

'I hope so. Harry and Chloe need you.'

I stopped walking and Dani followed suit. She turned to face me and gave me a questioning look.

'If I needed relationship advice, I certainly wouldn't be coming to you,' I growled.

'Don't be so bloody nonchalant,' Dani said. 'You might think I don't know anything about marriage or relationships and maybe you're right, but that doesn't mean I can't see that you're messing up everything you've got.'

'You know nothing about it,' I snarled and started off again at pace.

'You think?' Dani said as she set off in tow behind me. 'Why can you never be happy with what you've got? You've always got to want more.'

I ignored her. I wasn't interested in a slanging match. If that was all she'd come for then she could forget it. I carried on walking at a measured pace, closing the gap with the kids who were about fifty yards in front.

'Go right,' I shouted out at them. 'Down to the play area.'

Harry turned and waved, acknowledging my instruction, and headed off down the path with Chloe toward the small play area at Town Gate.

I didn't bother to look back around at Dani, but I could hear her footsteps and knew she was only a couple of yards behind. When Harry reached the play area, he swung open the bright-green gate and he and Chloe promptly ditched their bikes and bounded off toward the swings and slides.

When I got to the gate, I picked up the bikes, then moved over to the set of benches on the outside. I knew that whatever the reason Dani was there, she hadn't yet finished having her say, and I didn't want the kids overhearing us if our conversation got heated.

'Look, I'm sorry,' Dani said, holding her hands up when she reached me. 'I was genuinely interested to know why things aren't going well between you two. I don't want to see you unhappy. And I know how much the kids mean to you. You just want them to be happy, and it's not going to be easy for any of you without you there.'

'I know that,' I responded. 'I don't want to talk about it. I've got no idea what's going on in Gemma's head. She told me to leave. I didn't have much choice. Believe me, I'd love to know what she was thinking, but I haven't got a bloody clue.'

'Fair enough,' Dani said. 'I hope you can both work it out. I really do. And you may not believe me when I say this, but I'm here whenever you need to talk.'

'I'll bear that in mind,' I said, feeling more relaxed by her words.

'But that's not what I came to talk about today,' Dani said. 'Although I'm starting to wonder just where all the connecting dots lead to.'

'You've lost me.'

'I'm going to ask you this once and once only.' Now Dani had shifted to her bad cop voice. Even on her day off there was simply no getting away from what she was. 'So I want you to think really hard about what you tell me. Got it?'

'Yeah, got it,' I said.

'I'm here talking to you as a sister. You have to understand that. I'm here to help you if I can, and if you'll let me. But this is your one and only chance.'

'I get the picture,' I said, sounding calm but really I was already filling with dread over what was to come.

'Tell me about Callum O'Brady,' Dani said. 'Tell me about your relationship with him. I want to know everything, and I mean *everything*.'

CHAPTER 32

What was I supposed to do? It was simply impossible for me to come clean to my sister in the way she'd asked. There was too much to tell. The story was too complicated, and too incriminating. No matter what assurances Dani gave me that our conversation was off the record, she was still a policewoman. And O'Brady was a career criminal.

'Why are you asking me about Callum O'Brady?' I said.

'So are you at least admitting that you know of him?'

'Everyone knows about Callum O'Brady.'

'But not everyone is working for him.'

'You think I'm working for him?'

Dani tutted. 'I don't know what I think, to be honest. But I do know that you associating with him can only end one way: with you in big trouble. You must know that.'

I said nothing but I could feel my resolve weakening.

'Come on, Ben. Talk to me.'

'I owe him money.'

I thought I'd be stronger. I thought I'd at least be able to bullshit my own sister. But the fact was that O'Brady terrified me. The burden of dealing with O'Brady on my own was too much to bear. And given recent events, I knew that unless something gave before the fast-approaching deadline he'd given me, then I could very well end up a dead man.

'You owe O'Brady money? How? Gambling?'

I huffed in feigned amusement. 'I wish it was that simple.'

'Is it really that complicated, or do you just not want me to know what you've done?'

Dani was right. It wasn't complicated. The story was really quite simple to tell. The hard part was pushing my pride aside and bringing myself to tell it. And I wasn't sure I was ready to do that. As much as I needed help from somewhere, telling Dani, a detective, my sister … I felt like I still had too much to lose.

'How much do you owe him?' Dani asked.

'Two hundred thousand.'

'Two hundred grand! What the hell, Ben?'

'I know, I know. But have you any idea what O'Brady is like? He sucks people in, chews them up and spits them out. He uses everyone for his own gain, and he always gets the upper hand.'

'Sounds like you really know him.'

I tutted at my sister's flippant comment.

'Can you pay him?' she asked.

'I'm working on that.'

'And then what? You pay him and then it's all over?'

I took a moment to digest Dani's words. She'd hit the nail on the head. The simple fact was that one way or another I'd always be indebted to O'Brady. It was simply too late to change that.

'Callum O'Brady is out of control,' I said with naked fear in my voice.

'I can help you,' Dani said.

'I'm not sure you can.'

'Come on, Ben, listen to yourself. This isn't you. You're just a normal guy. You don't belong in that world.'

'Normal? You really think I'm normal?'

My sister sighed and looked at me, initially with indignation and then with sympathy. Bad cop, good cop. Or was it policewoman and sister? One side of her wanted to grill me, to do what was right by the law, and the other wanted to extend me an olive branch.

'If you're in trouble,' she said, 'I can help you. We can help you.'

'Why are you asking me about O'Brady now?'

'We've been working for years to make some charges stick on him. Everyone knows what he is, but he thinks he's untouchable. Somehow he always slips out from underneath us. But this time we think we can do it.'

'Why this time?'

'Because he's making mistakes.'

'And why have you come to me?'

'Because having someone on the inside will help.'

'You think I'm on the inside?'

'You tell me. You've been surveilled going into his club numerous times over the last few months. Most recently just a few days ago, when it didn't go unnoticed that you came out with blood pouring from your face.'

I felt my cheeks blush with genuine embarrassment. What a ridiculous response. I was in a bind, a life-threatening situation, and my natural reaction on hearing my sister talk about it was to feel shame, as though I were a child who'd been caught having one too many sweets.

'When the surveillance team ID'd you ... I'm sure you can imagine it hasn't gone down lightly with my colleagues. I've been put through the ringer already on this.'

'So you want me to bail you out.'

'Why do you always believe I have an ulterior motive?'

'Because you always do.'

Dani didn't say anything to that.

'How on earth did you get in bed with a man like that?' Dani asked, the disappointment in her voice clear.

'It wasn't out of choice. Believe me.'

'Then tell me what it was.'

'I'm not sure where to start. You said O'Brady's making mistakes. What did you mean?'

'I can't tell you that.'

'If you want my help, maybe you should.'

Dani huffed and looked away. I wasn't sure whether she was play-acting or genuinely thinking through what she was prepared to tell me.

'Do you know Mickey Egan?'

'Yes,' I said with revulsion. 'At least I've met him. I don't know him on a personal level. These people aren't my friends.'

'Well, you were asking me about that new murder. About whether we have any new leads.'

'Yeah,' I said, my brain whirring. 'What are you saying? That you think it's Mickey Egan?'

'Maybe.'

'Maybe?' I said, unable to hide my anger. 'Yes or no – are you telling me you think Mickey Egan killed Alice?'

Dani didn't answer the question for a few seconds. I wished I knew what she was thinking.

'Yes,' she said eventually. 'Yes, I do.'

CHAPTER 33

'Do you know of any reason why Egan would have killed Alice?' Dani asked. 'Or why O'Brady would have had her killed? If you do, Ben, you have to tell me.'

'I can't believe you're even asking me this. If I thought Egan or O'Brady had anything to do with Alice's death then why on earth would I not have said anything to you?'

'Good question,' Dani said. 'But do you think that's possible?'

'Do *I* think it's possible? You're the fucking detective – why don't you tell me?'

The anger in my voice was all too clear. Partly directed at Dani who I now believed was playing games with me, but also at Egan, who I'd always seen as being one chromosome short of a real human being.

'It's a theory we're working on,' Dani said.

'A theory? Do you have evidence?'

'Some.'

'What? What links Mickey Egan to Alice's murder? To the other victim? To the crime scenes?'

'I can't tell you that.'

I let out an exasperated sigh. 'Then what exactly is the point of bringing all this to me if you won't even tell me the whole story? If you're so sure it was Egan then why haven't you arrested him already?'

'It's not that simple. Believe me, we would have done if we could.'

'Because of O'Brady? Is Egan somehow protected?'

'No. Look, the woman who was killed, her name was Hayley Lewis.'

Dani paused and looked over at me, as though trying to gauge whether I knew the name. She must have cottoned on to my reaction.

'You knew her?' she said.

'No, honestly I know nothing about her,' I said, feeling as though I'd been caught out. 'But after you told me about the murder, about how everything was so similar to Alice's death, I did some digging online. So yeah, I knew the name. I've seen what's in the papers. But that's it. I never knew her.'

'No, I didn't think you did. And neither did Mickey Egan, from what I can gather.'

'Then how on earth can you believe it was him? Why would Egan do that?'

Dani just stared at me, and I held her gaze.

'I really don't want to say just yet,' she said eventually. 'Not until we know more.'

Not for the first time, I questioned just how much Dani really knew about Alice's murder that she wasn't letting on to me. I'd always had a sneaking suspicion she hadn't told me everything, but I'd never been able to put my finger on why that was.

I groaned in frustration and was prepared to push Dani further, but the next second I spotted Chloe take a bump when she came off the end of the slide. She burst into tears and I rushed off over to her, as did Harry.

Moments later both kids were hurtling around again, giggling wildly, but the conversation with Dani never restarted. Even though my mind was now swimming with thoughts of Mickey Egan and the two murders, I was happy to just spend the quality time with the children that I needed. As for Dani, she was great over the next few hours, showing herself to be the caring and loving auntie that I'd long ago expected she would be.

We made it back to the house not long after five in the afternoon. Gemma was already back by that point and was in a serious fret about where we'd been. Within minutes Dani made the sensible decision to make an excuse to leave, and promptly she was on her way. I knew she wasn't finished with me, and I wasn't finished with her. Not while she was still holding her cards so close to her chest about what she knew of my wife's murder. And not while O'Brady was still on my back. I'd just have to wait and see what Dani's next move would be.

With her gone, I was left alone to deal with the children and my irate wife. Just the four of us, our family, in our home – a situation we'd been in countless times before, and yet it felt so awkward now.

'Why are you staying at your parents anyway?' I said when Gemma had finally stopped flapping about why we had been out for so long.

'Because I need them,' she said. 'It's been really tough for me these last few days. I hate staying in this house on my own. It's so big and creaky. I never could sleep properly when you weren't around.'

'I bet they're loving all this, aren't they?'

'Meaning what?'

'Meaning they're probably delighted that you've kicked me out.'

'You're such a prick sometimes. Of course they're not happy. They don't want to see any of us unhappy, do they? They're being kind by letting us stay, that's all.'

'Well, there's a far simpler solution,' I said. 'I could come back.'

'That's not going to happen,' Gemma responded without thought.

'Why not? What the hell have I actually done that's so terrible in your eyes?'

'Do you really need to ask that question?'

'Yes, I really do.'

'Maybe if you listened more, if you paid attention to me, then you'd already know the answer to that.'

'Look, I know I haven't been a great husband to you recently, but we can make this work, I promise. I've realised these last days that I really need you, Gemma. I need all of you.'

'Yeah, it's always about *your* needs, isn't it?'

'That's not what I meant at all,' I said, offended.

'It doesn't matter anyway. I've already made up my mind.'

Gemma turned away from me. I probably should have taken that as a signal that the conversation was over. Instead, I moved up to her and gently placed my arms around her waist, then kissed her lightly on the neck.

'Come on, honey,' I said. 'This is silly. Let's just put it behind us.'

Gemma pushed herself out of my grip, spun around and shoved me away from her. I stumbled back two steps and smacked my head on a shelf.

'You don't get to touch me!' she snarled. She walked up to me and pushed me again, but this time, prepared, I held my ground. I could already feel myself becoming enraged, much like I had the last time she'd slapped me, and just like before I wasn't sure how much abuse I could take before I blew.

'Touch you?' I scoffed. 'I gave you a kiss on the cheek. You're my wife!'

'Wife? It doesn't mean I'm your property.'

'What? I mean … Look, I'm sorry, I just thought –'

'I'm not yours anymore. You have to understand that. Can't we at least try to make this work like adults? You can't just waltz in here and expect things to be how they were.'

I had nothing to say in response. Gemma continued to rant at me, but I wasn't really listening. There was nothing I could say or do to rectify the situation. When she finally finished, I opened my mouth to speak, but then movement out of the corner of my eye stopped me in my tracks. We turned to face Chloe. Her face was full of angst and tears were rolling down her cheeks.

'Sweetie, what's wrong?' I said.

I went to kneel down to pick her up, but Gemma barged in front of me and grabbed her. She lifted Chloe up and my daughter buried her head into Gemma's shoulder.

'It's time for you to go,' Gemma said, glaring at me.

I was mad at her, but I realised I was powerless to do anything. Even before Chloe had walked in, I'd been on a hiding to nothing. I hated everything about the situation, and as much as I'd meant what I'd said about missing Gemma, my animosity toward her was growing steadily.

It was time to cut my losses and leave.

I pecked Chloe on the cheek. She didn't respond at all. I walked out of the kitchen and found Harry in the lounge. He was quietly watching TV, but I could tell from the look on his face that he too had heard the argument and that I was likely not in his best books either.

'I'm sorry,' I said to him. I wanted to say more but I really didn't know what to say. 'I enjoyed today, you know.'

'Yeah, me too,' he said without looking up from his programme.

'I'll be back soon. Say hi to Granny and Granddad for me.'

'Sure.'

I kissed him on the cheek and then headed for the door.

CHAPTER 34

'What did you think when your sister revealed that she knew about you and O'Brady?' she asked.

'I was worried. I was suspicious. I was already suspicious about Dani suddenly reappearing – since that first time she turned up at my house, when Gemma and I were in the middle of a panic about O'Brady. I questioned her motives then, certainly. But it also felt so familiar for her to be around again, even though when I did stop to think about why, I was wary. I hadn't seen Dani in years, and whatever ulterior motive she may have had, in many ways it was nice that she was back. More secure.'

'Tell me more about why the two of you had parted for so long.'

'Why do you want to know that?'

'I think it's relevant to what's happened to you. To how you dealt with Alice's death and everything else since.'

'The way I see it is that there's no stronger bond than a blood bond. And the bond between twins is the strongest of them all. I think because of that extreme closeness, any indiscretion is magnified.'

'How do you mean?'

'I've seen it before, not with twins but with family members. My grandma had three brothers who were all very close in age. When I was a kid growing up, I could never tell the difference between any of them; they all looked and acted the same, I thought. They spent the best part of seventy years as the closest of friends, never moving more than a couple of miles from each other, and they did everything together, even in their adult lives. Then, one day, just like that, two of them fell out. The third brother, a bit of a piggy in the middle I suppose, didn't want to side with either of them, but despite his best efforts, the other two just refused to see each other anymore. This went on for years and years and I only found out later what it was all about.'

'What was it?'

Take a guess. You're probably thinking it was money problems or they got into a big fist fight or something like that, right?'

Well, it sounds like it would need to be something serious, yes. But I'm assuming your point is that it wasn't?'

That's my point exactly. One called the other stupid. That was it.'

In what context?'

It shouldn't matter what the context was.'

It probably does have some bearing, though,' she said. 'I can imagine a scenario where someone could say those words with a lot of venom and it could be very hurtful.'

But I don't think it was. From what I understand, it was just a flippant comment, a single remark. The story was that the three of them were sitting in the pub watching football and debating a game that'd just finished. I don't know exactly what led to the comment, but the one brother called the other one stupid. He then refused to back down, and there was no fight or anything, they just went their separate ways at the end of the night. That was the end of it. After that, they didn't speak again for something like ten years. Not until they were brought back together when the third brother died.'

Do you think perhaps there's more to the story than that, though?' she asked. 'Maybe the pub incident was just the culmination of a number of other events and troubles.'

Maybe,' I said. 'And I'm sure with me and Dani that was the case too. There aren't many specific incidents I can really pinpoint, but we're siblings, twins, so of course we fought every now and then. My point is, though, maybe it's the closeness that makes those seemingly small events so much more powerful and hurtful.'

You feel like your sister hurt you? Or was it the other way around?'

It was probably both. Alice and Dani were best friends. That's how I met Alice in the first place. I think that was always an awkward dynamic for all three of us. It tested our loyalties in different ways.'

Did you feel Dani was more loyal to Alice than she was to you? Is that what you're saying?'

In some ways, yes. In others, no.'

'And what was the impact of that?'

'*At times it made it hard to properly voice my opinion to either of them. It always felt like I was up against two people rather than one.*'

'*How did Alice's death affect your relationship with Dani? You still saw each other after that?*'

'*We did to start with. But we were both grieving. Alice's death affected us both.*'

'*So that was the reason you stopped seeing Dani? Because of Alice's murder?*'

'*It wasn't just that. Things were difficult for a long time. First Alice was killed. Then, two years later, my dad died of a heart attack while he was out doing the gardening, three days short of his sixty-fifth birthday. The year after that, Mum passed too. Those three deaths of immediate family members so close together turned my whole world upside down. Dani's too. It changed us both. Just look at what's happened since.*'

'*I imagine such a traumatic time may under other circumstances have brought two siblings closer together, though,*' she said. '*Why wasn't that the case for the two of you?*'

'*You're right. It should have done. In the aftermath of Alice's death and then my parents', that was exactly the case with Gemma. I was closer to her at that point than I'd ever been before, or since, maybe for that very reason – the trauma brought us closer together.*'

'*Was that it then? Your sister felt left out because you had Gemma and she had no-one? I think you said Dani was never good friends with Gemma?*'

'*No, I don't think that was it. I think Mum was the big turning point.*'

'*In what way?*'

'*She was all on her own by the time she was diagnosed. Her deterioration was so rapid that no-one was really sure what to do. I think in the end both Dani and I felt a certain amount of bitterness and anger toward each other. Dani felt that I didn't support Mum enough in her final weeks.*'

'*Did she say that to you?*'

'*No. But I could tell.*'

'*And what do you think?*'

'*Looking back, maybe I could have done more, but I had a wife and two kids to look after as well. And in those last few weeks I felt as though*

Mum pushed me out, as though I wasn't needed or wanted anymore. Mum was so delirious by the end; the dementia that set in had taken such a toll that she no longer recognised me. She often thought I was my dad. Other times she thought I was a doctor or even just a stranger. It was me, her only son, sitting next to her, but she would talk away about me – in the third person – complaining that I never came to see her anymore. She was so unfeeling and bitter in the things she said about me. I've never felt so hurt, even though I know, or at least I hope, she didn't really mean it.'

'Why did that have an effect on your relationship with Dani?'

'I don't know. It's hard to explain. I know it wasn't Dani's fault, but it brought home how much more fond of Dani my mum was compared to me.'

'Did you ever discuss it with her?'

'Who?'

'Dani.'

'No. Never.'

'You just went your separate ways?'

'Yeah. After Mum passed we spoke briefly a few times to arrange the funeral. The last time I saw Dani before the day she turned up at my house was when I hugged her and left her by my mother's grave.'

The woman shifted in her seat and paused for a few seconds before she asked the next question. I didn't know why, but I felt like she was skirting around something rather than just coming out and asking me directly what she wanted to know.

'Do you think those intervening years would have been different for you if Dani had been around?'

'Undoubtedly. But there's nothing I can do about that now.'

'Do you think your life would still have turned out like this?'

'That's impossible for me to know.'

'What did Dani's reappearance mean for what you had planned? This plan of retribution you had thought out. Your sister's a police officer and she'd already confronted you about Callum O'Brady.'

'I knew I hadn't heard the last from Dani on O'Brady. She'd barely even laid the foundation by that point. But, naively, I felt like I was one step ahead. I was already thinking about how I could get my own back on O'Brady.

The two-week deadline he'd given me was nearly up, and there was simply no way I could find the money he wanted in time.'

'So what was your plan?'

'Initially? Initially my plan was to ward off O'Brady. To buy myself some more time.'

'Did that work?'

'Yes, but not how I'd anticipated.'

'How so?'

'I said I thought I was one step ahead of my sister. But the truth was, I was already way behind. I just didn't know it until it was already too late.'

CHAPTER 35

Three days had passed since the first meeting with Cara. I'd been back to the gym the previous day but she wasn't around. There was a balance I had to find. I wanted to play it cool, but at the same time I was intent on bumping into her again. With Gemma insistent that she didn't want me and making it difficult for me to see the children, I needed some positivity in my life. Cara seemed like my best option for that.

This time I was in luck. It was Monday evening and I'd rightly assumed she would be there post-work. We gave each other a cursory smile and hello in the gym but otherwise didn't speak. After we both finished our separate workouts, I quickly changed and made my way outside to wait for her, determined this time to make the moment count.

As I stood waiting, I felt my phone vibrating in my pocket. I took it out and looked at the screen. A mobile number I didn't recognise. I debated whether or not to answer. Usually I just ignored calls unless I knew for certain who was on the other end. And even when I did know the caller sometimes I didn't answer. I've just never liked talking on phones. Something about not knowing what the other person was doing, the lack of visual or other cues, made a phone conversation too stilted and awkward. If the call was important, the person would leave a message – that was my theory. This time, though, curiosity got the better of me. Immediately I regretted the decision.

'Where are you?' Dani asked.

'Hello, sister.'

'No games, Ben. Where are you?'

'Dani, I'm busy,' I said. 'What do you want?'

'I want you to tell me what you were doing last Thursday night.'

'What are you talking about?'

'I'm talking about Andrew Dove.'

Everything around me seemed to go deathly silent. I could almost imagine all the other people in the busy square staring over at me, waiting for my response to Dani's blunt statement.

'What?' I said, trying to sound genuinely confused by the name.

'Oh, come off it. You know who. I'm not an idiot. I remember who Andrew Dove is. I remember what he did to you.'

'Of course you do. I remember it too. My point is, why on earth are you bringing his name up? What does he have to do with anything?'

'Okay, so we're going to play it like that, are we?'

'Play what like what?'

Dani let out a long sigh. 'Last Thursday night Andrew Dove was beaten up not far from his home and hospitalised.'

'Wow. That's terrible. I'd like to say I'm shocked, but you know, I don't really know him and I never liked what I knew of him, so I'm not really that moved right now by your revelation.'

'Oh, I'm sure you're not.'

'But I still don't know why you brought this up. This is what you wanted to talk to me about?'

Dani began to laugh. I knew she was just mocking me, but I let her get it out.

'Good one, Ben,' she said. 'Seriously, that's some great acting you've got going on there.'

'Okay, enough now,' I snapped. 'What the hell do you want?'

'It's time to stop playing about. I know it was you. You need to tell me what happened.'

I didn't know how Dani knew, but even if it was just to get her off my back so I could get back to looking out for Cara, I decided it was best to admit to what I had done.

Apparently Dove had ended up in hospital with a broken rib and nose and a cracked eye socket. When Dani reeled off the list of injuries that I'd inflicted, I was strangely impressed with myself. I'd never thought I had that in me. And as far as I was concerned, Dove deserved it. It was retribution.

I was relieved to hear that Dove had no idea who had attacked him. He'd told the police that he'd seen little of the attacker. His description of a dark-clothed male of unspecified race and age included nothing unique to identify me. So my problem wasn't Dove, it seemed, but instead a random witness sighting – not of the attack but of me lurking around Dove's house in my car.

The witness had come forward to the police after hearing of Dove's attack and told officers she'd seen a black BMW coupé 'acting suspiciously'. Such a vague description would have been written off as nonsense or at best coincidence by the police if it hadn't been for my sister. Dove's name in the police report had caught her attention, and the description of a car that was identical to mine had told her all she needed to know. The fact that Gemma had confirmed she had no idea where I was that night only cemented Dani's suspicions.

I could have pleaded ignorance, argued that the evidence was circumstantial at best. I certainly would have done if it had been anyone other than Dani talking to me. But even before Dani confirmed it, I felt like she had my back.

'So what are you going to do?' I asked.

'Nothing,' Dani said.

'You're not going to have me arrested?'

'No.'

'Why?'

'I don't know what's going on with you. I know there's a lot I'm not seeing, and I don't know exactly how or why Dove fits into all that … but I hope this is it now. Done.'

'I was just angry,' I said, trying to sound less on edge, hoping it would get Dani to lay off me. 'I needed someone to vent it on. Dove fitted the bill. He deserved it.'

'I know he did. Don't forget what he did to me too. I hate him just as much as you.'

I wouldn't ever forget. Dove and Dani had been an item for all of two minutes when they were fifteen. But Dove had been a true arsehole, badmouthing her around the school, making up sordid stories – at least I hoped they were just stories – about what my sister would and wouldn't do for him.

I'd been hell bent on punishing Dove myself for that. The only reason I didn't was because of Dani. Not because she warded me off, but because she got to Dove first. Made him pay in her own unique way. In the end Dove was the butt of jokes the school over. He never regained his reputation.

Somehow Dani always managed to come out on top of any situation.

'But what he did to you was years ago, Ben,' Dani said. 'So this is it. Like I said, I don't know what's going with you, but it ends here. No more. I'll let you off this one.'

'Thank you,' I said.

'If someone else puts the pieces together, though, or if a witness comes forward and makes it clear it was you out there, you're on your own. I can only protect you so far. You understand that?'

'Of course. Thank you. Is that likely?'

'Who knows? No-one is particularly excited about Dove. He was drunk, nothing was stolen and he's not seriously injured. I think, to be honest, it'll get written up as a drunken assault, and unless someone else comes forward with further information it'll go away quietly.'

'I hope so.'

'Me too. But I'm not letting you off this one for free.'

'Why did I not doubt that?' I said. 'Spit it out, Dani. What's the condition?'

'O'Brady. You have to help us. I'm helping you on this one, Ben. But you have to help us too.'

I shut my eyes and gritted my teeth. For just a fleeting second I'd genuinely thought that Dani was helping me out as a sister. That she could see my life was a shambles, that Dove was such a small element and she could overlook my misdemeanour even though it went against her professionalism. But no, that wasn't Dani. I began to wonder whether her colleagues were already aware that it was me who had beaten up Dove. Perhaps they were even listening in on the conversation we were having, waiting for me to agree to help catch O'Brady. I wouldn't have been at all surprised if that was the case.

'I've got to go,' I said, trying to hold back my growing irritation.

But my words weren't just a means to end the conversation. Off to my right I'd spotted Cara coming out of the gym doors.

I heard Dani ranting as I pulled the phone away from my ear, but I wasn't listening. I pressed the button to end the call and tried to regain my composure as Cara approached, a warm smile on her face.

CHAPTER 36

I pushed the phone into my pocket and turned toward Cara.

'Hi,' I said, giving a less-than-convincing smile, the conversation with Dani still reverberating in my mind.

'Everything okay?' she asked, immediately picking up on my mood.

'Ah, it's not his fault, I guess,' I said, thinking on my feet. 'I was supposed to be having a night out, but it looks like it's just been cancelled.'

'Bummer.'

'It is. With the kids, it's so hard making arrangements.'

'You've got kids?'

'Yeah. Two.'

'They live with you?'

'I don't know,' I said, frowning at my unusual answer. Cara's look matched my own but she didn't probe further. 'It's all being sorted out still. They're with their mum at the moment. I don't know what will happen. Anyway, all my friends have kids now too. Impossible finding a convenient time to go out.'

'I bet.'

'You don't have kids?'

'No,' she said, looking away from me. I got the impression it was a sore subject for her.

'I guess I'm out for the night now, though,' I joked. 'I've got nowhere better to go, so I may as well make the most of it.'

Cara laughed. 'Yeah, you should.'

'You can join me if you like,' I said, trying to make it sound like a casual invitation. 'I haven't been out around here for ages. You can show me where all the cool kids go.'

'Oh, I'm not so sure I'm one of the cool kids these days either. I'm as old as you are.'

'You reckon?'

'I'm flattered you think otherwise, though.'

She went silent and began to look uncomfortable. I didn't know whether she was trying to think of what to say to get away from me, or she was actually considering my proposition.

'Don't worry,' I said. 'I shouldn't have asked. I was only messing around. I'm just disappointed I'm not going to be getting out for once, that's all.'

'No, no,' Cara protested. 'Don't be silly. I'm not offended. Actually I don't have any plans tonight. I'd only be sitting around on my own at home too. We could get a quick drink if you want?'

'Yeah?'

'Yeah. Why not? Seems a shame for you to go home so soon.'

Home? What home? I thought, but all I said was, 'Okay, great. Let's do it.'

Cara beamed me a smile, which I reciprocated, helping to wash away the aggravation I was feeling toward Dani and most other people in my life. We headed to a bar around the corner from the gym, overlooking the canals. I bought a round of drinks: a pint of overpriced European lager for myself and a large glass of white wine for Cara. Even though it was a Monday the bar was busy with post-work drinkers, but we managed to find a table. Within a half hour or so people were already starting to filter out, clearly not wanting to let their hair down so early in the working week.

A part of me felt guilty for how I'd very deliberately crafted the situation with Cara. Yet as time wore on, that feeling was well and truly sidelined. I was amazed at how comfortable and relaxed conversation was with her. We just clicked. We talked about anything and everything, from the mundane to the profound. It wasn't like me at all. I'm not a particularly shy person; I'm just not that talkative. Not so with Cara.

It wasn't even that we had much in common – our lives were really quite different. But she was warm and friendly, engaging and endearing. She was also pretty in a girl-next-door kind of way. I was strongly attracted to her. Not just lust – it was more than that, more solid. The only way I can describe it is that it felt like the first time Alice and I met. I felt a certain bitterness toward myself for comparing anyone to Alice. But as the night wore on, as the drinks went down, that bitterness faded as I quickly fell for Cara Andrews.

When the clock wound toward eleven p.m., we were both worse for wear from the countless drinks we'd consumed and becoming increasingly animated and flirtatious. We'd moved bars and were sitting on a bench next to each other, our shoulders and legs brushing, our faces just a few inches apart. Every time we turned to speak to each other I'd gaze into her eyes for just a second longer than necessary, and on many occasions she'd do the same. More than once I'd thought about leaning over to kiss her.

The closing bell sounded and I suggested we head out. We both stood up, wobbling and giggling, and moved toward the exit. Cara fell into me drunkenly. I put my arm around her to steady her and felt a jolt of warmth and satisfaction.

We stumbled outside and stopped. I let go of Cara and looked at her longingly.

'I had a good time,' I said to her. 'I really mean that.'

'You're going already?' Cara said.

'You're not?'

'One for the road, do you think?' she said, giving me what I took to be a seductive look.

'Why not?' I said without even a moment's contemplation.

'Great. This way, follow me.'

Cara grabbed my hand and ushered me away. She took me to a late-night bar that was just coming to life as the pubs around it began to close up for the night. I'd never been there before. We walked in to a thumping baseline that made my brain shake and my insides curdle, and I quickly felt out of my comfort zone. I'd never considered myself timid, but it had been a long time since I'd been to anything that resembled a nightclub. The fact that I was at least ten years older than the vast majority of the other punters made me feel further alienated.

Cara seemed oblivious. She pulled me through the crowds of people over to the packed bar. There didn't seem to be a formal dancefloor anywhere, but nevertheless people were gyrating and pulsing to the ear-splitting music.

'It's busy,' I shouted over at Cara.

'It always is. Even during the week. Because it's new, I guess. And there aren't many proper clubs open on a Monday.'

After five minutes without any luck getting to the bar, I decided to get my elbows out and I nudged and pushed my way to the front. It did the trick and I finally got served, but my efforts hadn't gone unnoticed. As I moved back from the crowd to Cara, drinks in hand, I was shoved in the back and I stumbled forward, Cara's sticky red cocktail overspilling down my arm.

I turned around to a group of four guffawing men – though I'd use the term "men" loosely, they could well have been in their late teens. They were all smiling and laughing at me, but then one of them, the shortest of the group with a t-shirt that looked two sizes too small stretched over his fat-free torso, began to stare at me coldly. I mouthed an obscenity at him, then turned around and headed to Cara, whose face was tinged with just a hint of anxiety.

'What was that?' she asked, her voice and manner making her appear far less intoxicated than the bubbly, giggly person I'd entered the bar with minutes earlier.

'Nothing,' I said, turning around to the group to see the man still giving me the evil eye. 'It was nothing.'

Cara seemed to relax again, but I couldn't let it go. The group of lads had riled me. It was the drink, I'm certain of that. But it was also Gemma and O'Brady and Dani and Whitely and Rottweiler and Dove – basically my life.

I'd held my shit together for so long, but it was becoming an impossible task to keep everything locked up inside. Quite simply, I wasn't sure I *wanted* to keep it all locked inside anymore.

We found two seats and I tried to let the night move on. But I just couldn't. Cara was talking to me but I was barely concentrating. The blaring music certainly didn't help. Cara's words washed over me as I kept my eyes fixed steadily on the group at the bar.

When I finally looked over at Cara, I could see disappointment on her face. She wasn't an imbecile. She could tell I wasn't listening to a word she was saying. I was annoyed at myself for having spoiled the mood, but my head was on fire. The pounding baseline, the alcohol coursing through my bloodstream and my chaotic thoughts were making me feel delirious and detached from reality.

No matter how hard I tried, there was only one thing on my mind.

'Ben ... Ben?'

I looked over at Cara again, fighting hard to bring myself back around. I was about to offer an apology, however disingenuous, but then I saw movement out of the corner of my eye that grabbed my full attention.

I got to my feet.

'I'm just going to the toilet,' I said to Cara without looking at her, my eyes focused on the man from the bar.

I dodged and pushed my way past the other drinkers over to the toilets, the thumping music enhancing my growing focus.

The man who'd shoved me in the back was right in front of me, oblivious to my presence, as we headed into the packed gents'. The stench of urine and vomit stuck in my nostrils the second I walked in. The urinals were crammed with men relieving their bladders, but the man I was focused on walked right past, over toward the bank of four cubicles.

The first two doors were locked shut. The third was open and the man took a step in. Just as he began to turn to shut the door I lurched forward, barging in through the open door.

I grabbed him by the back of his neck and shoved him forward. I reached back and locked the door with my free hand, then flung the man's head against the side panel of the cubicle.

There was a loud crack as his head made contact with the wall. At least it appeared loud to me, but with the din of the music from the bar and the many raucous voices in the toilets it was probably nothing.

The cubicle walls shuddered and the man groaned. Without giving him a chance to react, I crashed his head on the wall again, then threw my fist into his side once. Twice. He cried out in pain and I pushed him forward. He fell to his knees.

I thrust his head down, into the foul toilet bowl that was filled with urine and shit and dirtied paper. The man squirmed and bucked but it was no use. Something had taken over me. It would have taken the strength of ten men to ward me off.

My face was creased, my whole body, every muscle and sinew, tensed and primed. I held firm, pushing his face into the disgusting water, hearing him gargle and shout and choke.

I lifted his head out of the bowl. He initially cried out again, but barely a second later he began retching violently. Watery vomit spewed from his mouth. Much of it went straight into the bowl, but some also sprayed and splashed out over the sides, over the back wall and down his front, onto his legs.

My free arm lifted up to cover my nose and mouth, blocking out the putrid smell. For a few seconds I had to fight the urge to retch. My headed started to spin. Then a sliver of strength creeping into the man's movements brought me back to reality.

I shoved his face forward and there was a gruesome crack as his forehead collided with the porcelain rim of the toilet bowl. I let go and he slumped to the floor, landing in a pile of his own vomit.

He was moaning. His body was twitching. There was a large, bloody gash on his forehead. I stepped back, my eyes firmly fixed on him. There was no sign of the fighting look he'd given me at the bar.

I reached back and unlocked the door, then stepped out into the open. Two men were standing outside, waiting for a free cubicle. I gave them a drunken smile and slurred my words.

'I wouldn't go in there, lads. My mate's just puked his guts up all over. I'm off to get someone to help lift him out.'

One of them nodded. The other just turned away. Neither seemed particularly bothered by what I'd said. I strode out of the toilet and back over to Cara, whose face was now sullen and sour. I was too wired to really care.

'Come on,' I said, holding my hand out to her. 'I'm shattered. The drink's gone to my head. I think we should probably call it a night.'

'Yeah,' she said. 'I think you're probably right.'

CHAPTER 37

I was rudely awakened by the incessant buzzing of my mobile phone on the bedside table. I only managed to open my eyes for a few seconds before the stabbing in my head became too severe. I quickly shut them, and after a moment the phone stopped. I was already drifting off again when the noisy vibration started up a second time. I reached over and grabbed the phone and only opened my eyes when the mobile was in front of my face. I stared at the number and in an instant became alert.

My memory of the alcohol-fuelled evening was hazy, but as I answered the call and put the phone to my ear, it was the rotten smell of urine and faeces and vomit, still stuck in my nostrils, that brought a sudden clarity.

What the hell had I done last night?

But beating up some random guy in a bar toilet was really the least of my worries, I quickly realised.

'You hadn't forgotten about me, had you?' Callum O'Brady said.

'No, of course not.'

'Good. Glad to hear it. This is just a friendly reminder. Your time is nearly up. I'm going to be needing that money.'

'Yeah, about that. Perhaps we should meet up.'

'So you've got it?'

'No. But I do need to talk to you.'

'I hope you're not blowing me off.'

'No, I'm not. We need to talk.'

'Fine. Come and meet me at the club later. I'll be there all night.'

'I was thinking somewhere more … neutral.'

'And why's that?' O'Brady snapped.

'Last time I was at the club I took a beating. I'm not really in the mood for more of the same.'

'A beating? You punched my man Mickey in the face. What did you expect?'

'Yeah, well, I'd like to avoid being pulverised this time.'

'Okay, fine. I'm being nice to you here, Stephens. I hope you're going to return the favour. Tell me where and when.'

Three hours, two pints of water and four paracetamols later, I was feeling almost human as I headed into central Birmingham.

It hadn't escaped me that the two-week deadline O'Brady had given me would be up in twenty-four hours and so far I'd made no headway in getting the two hundred thousand pounds needed to keep him off my back. I was somewhat surprised that O'Brady and his cronies hadn't badgered me daily for the money following the beating I'd taken in his strip club a few days previously. But his call had brought the immediacy of the situation back to the forefront of my mind.

There was simply no way I was going to get that money before the deadline. I'd known that all along. But there would have been no point in letting O'Brady know that fact any earlier. Why sign my own death warrant?

Now, with the deadline looming, I needed two things. More time and to keep him at bay. That was what I hoped to get from our next meeting. But more importantly, I needed a plan to get O'Brady off my back for good. Dani had offered me a potential way out. Actually the last time I'd spoken to her it had been more of a threat. Would helping the police really achieve my aim, though? I wanted to get revenge on O'Brady, but incriminating myself in the process wasn't the most appealing option.

It was an option, though.

But first things first: I needed to meet with O'Brady.

I'd managed to get him to agree to meet me outside the Bullring Shopping Centre in the heart of Birmingham. Probably one of the busiest spots in the entire city. I was amazed he agreed, but he did. I arrived at five minutes to twelve. We were due to meet on the hour and I was pleased to see he wasn't there yet, giving me the chance to settle in. I walked down the restaurant-lined thoroughfare separating the two halves of the shopping centre and parked myself by the glass wall looking out over St Martin's Church below.

Off to my right was the space-age Selfridges store, its contours and thousands of packed aluminium discs making the outside of the building look like the scales of a snake. I stared at the striking façade for a few seconds, reminiscing. It was impressive, certainly, but what I hated about the Bullring was the crowds. In fact I detested the endless droves of shoppers slowly meandering and cramming onto the escalators so much that I hadn't been there shopping for a number of years.

Its bustling nature was exactly why I had chosen it for the meet with O'Brady, though.

It wasn't just the crowds that I had to keep me company, either. CCTV cameras lined both the interior and exterior of the Bullring. There was no way O'Brady was going to try anything stupid when he was so exposed.

Was there?

It was two minutes past twelve when I spotted O'Brady. As usual, he had a small troop with him: Elvis and Mickey Egan – the man I'd punched in the face a few days ago. The man my sister believed killed my wife and Hayley Lewis.

Egan's pointed features and beady eyes reminded me of a great white shark. He was a true predator. Even before they spotted me there was an angry snarl on his face – a permanent fixture that exposed his jagged and misshapen teeth.

Elvis and Egan were unsightly together. Unnerving. Even out in the open, with crowds of people walking around me in every direction and the CCTV cameras overhead, I was shaking as the three approached me. The conversation I'd had with Dani about Egan reverberated in my mind.

O'Brady was red-cheeked and breathing heavily by the time he made it up the few steps from the church to where I was standing.

'Stephens,' he said as he came to a stop a couple of yards from me. No offer of handshake. 'This is a funny place for a business meeting if you ask me.'

'You walked here?'

'Yeah. We were at the club. Thought we'd get a bit of fresh air for a change. Supposed to do you good or something like that.'

'That's the theory.'

'If you ask me, exercise is overrated. My boys here have all the muscle I'll ever need, and if you're talking about cardio, you can't beat a good ol' humpathon.'

I resisted rolling my eyes at O'Brady's pathetic banter and forced myself to instead laugh in acknowledgement.

'So why have you brought me out here?' O'Brady asked. 'I don't see you carrying anything for me, so I'm presuming it's not good news.'

I assumed O'Brady was referring to the fact that I clearly didn't have two hundred thousand pounds in cash on me.

'I have a proposition for you,' I said.

'Really? Seem to remember you saying that to me at least once before. Someone you want me to take care of again?'

O'Brady laughed at his own quip and his goons followed suit. This time I didn't pander to him.

'I think you'll find my propositions have generally worked out pretty well for you.'

'*Generally?* What use is *generally?* That means whatever you've got to say is nothing more than a gamble. I don't like gambling, because no matter how good the odds are there's always that chance of it going balls up. I only back dead certs and you don't get those without a fix.'

'You could say anything in life is a gamble. Every business deal you've ever entered into had a chance of failure. But you've shown you've got a knack for picking the right ones. You are a gambler, I'd say. A very good one.'

O'Brady raised an eyebrow at my flattery but didn't respond. I sensed, though, that he was quietly impressed with my off-the-cuff response.

'Why don't we take a walk?' I suggested to O'Brady. 'Without your friends.'

'And why's that?' O'Brady asked, a suspicious look on his face.

'We're out in the open here. There're police crawling around, cameras everywhere. These two are hardly inconspicuous, following you around like they do.'

'What's that supposed to mean?' Egan spat. I guessed he probably didn't understand the meaning of inconspicuous and his only response was offence.

O'Brady shot him a glare and Egan immediately backed down.

'Come on, then,' O'Brady said. 'You lead the way.'

'And what are we supposed to do?' Elvis said, sounding lost.

'I don't care,' O'Brady said. 'Go and buy your wife some knickers or something. Nothing too fancy, though. She's not that good looking.'

Elvis grunted and O'Brady gestured for me to get moving. We moved off toward the doors to the West Mall.

'So tell me about this proposition,' O'Brady said. 'It had better be good.'

'It's going to be,' I said. 'But first, I need to make something clear.'

'And what's that?'

'The two hundred thousand. I can't do it. I just can't. Not in the timeframe you gave me.'

I heard O'Brady sigh and I looked over and saw the angry look on his face. This was exactly why I'd wanted to give him the message in a public place. If we'd been back at the strip club, that one statement from me would probably have been the end of the conversation. And that would have meant only one thing. As it was, out in the open, I felt I had a chance to actually discuss the situation properly. Or so I hoped.

'This isn't exactly music to my ears,' O'Brady growled.

'I know, and I'm sorry. But I just don't have that kind of money.'

'Two weeks ago you brought me a cheque for a hundred grand. So what's happened?'

'A lot. There's no chance of me getting that now. It was from my father-in-law. But because of this whole mess I'll never get help from him again. My wife's kicked me out, you know.'

O'Brady laughed and I had to clench my fists tightly, my nails digging into the palms of my hands, to keep a calm exterior.

'Your wife's kicked you out? Seriously, you have no balls at all, have you?'

'I love her,' I said. 'And this mess is already ruining my life.'

'Your marriage issues really aren't my problem.'

'Well, in a way they are. She wouldn't have thrown me out if it wasn't for you.'

O'Brady stopped walking and I followed suit and turned to look at him. His face was creased with indignation.

'Don't forget who you're speaking to,' he snarled. 'We might be out in public now, but you keep that tongue of yours in check. You can't stay out here forever.'

I held my hand up in apology. 'I'm not trying to offend you,' I said. 'I'm really not. I'm just telling you how it is. I can't get that money. Not in the timeframe you've given me. The only possible way to get my hands on that sort of cash is through our house, but that could take weeks to arrange. I'm not trying to duck out of this, I just need you to understand.'

'That's what all this is?' O'Brady spat. 'A sob story to get you more time? This is your bloody proposition?'

'No, no, not at all. That's my point. If you want that money, I can get it, but you'd have to wait. I'd get it to you, you have my word, but I'd need more time. *But* ... my proposition is something else entirely. You know I've always come up trumps in the past. All the leads and information you've had from me over the years – this is bigger than any of that. If you give me the chance, I can make you way more than two hundred thousand.'

O'Brady gave me a long, hard stare. I held my ground and stared right back. I knew my words were appealing to his greed, but not his vindictive side. I just had to hope that greed would win out. At least for now.

'Okay,' he said eventually. 'I'm open to the suggestion. I'll hear you out, so go for it. Convince me.'

I'm not sure whether O'Brady noticed the relief that washed over me. I tried not to let it show. But inwardly I was delighted. Because he'd just opened the door for me, and I was stepping right through with everything I'd got.

The fact was, there wasn't a proposition. It was entirely bogus. I had no connections anymore. Whitely would never let me set foot in Ellis Associates again and that was my one real source of potential business for O'Brady. But just as I'd hoped, O'Brady was lured by my talk of money, and whatever he thought of me, it was true that I'd come up trumps for him plenty of times in the past.

The trap was set. There was still a way to go, but one way or another, I was going to make O'Brady pay for the trouble he'd caused me.

CHAPTER 38

After leaving the Bullring I headed back across the city centre toward where my car was parked at Snowhill station. I was halfway across the grounds of St Philip's Cathedral when my phone buzzed in my pocket. I lifted it out and looked at the caller ID. Dani. The last thing I needed.

'What do you want?' I said.

'Did you have a good meeting?' Dani asked, entirely calm and collected.

'Meeting?'

'With Callum O'Brady. How did it go?'

I stopped walking. Thoughts flashed through my brain. How did Dani know?

'Look over to your right.'

I looked over and spotted two policemen walking in through the gates at the edge of the square. They were regular beat bobbies with bright jackets and tall hats. It wasn't unusual to see police milling around in the city centre. But these two weren't just there on the off chance. They were heading toward me.

'Look over to your left,' my sister said.

I did as I was told. A policewoman and policeman were walking in my direction. By that point adrenaline was surging through my body. I started to think of escape routes. There were six gated entrances to the square. Two were already blocked, but as I quickly scanned around I noticed at least two in my line of sight that I could head to.

'Don't run,' Dani said, as though reading my mind.

She was probably right. If I ran, where would I go? And what exactly would I be running from?

'What's going on?' I said.

'Move forward,' Dani responded.

I took a step forward. Then another. Then another. From my new position I could now see one of the other entrances up ahead. There was no sign of any police by that one.

'On the bench, to the left of the gate.'

My eyes shot from the open entrance to the bench a few yards from it. There sat Dani.

'Come over,' she said. 'We need to talk.'

I deliberated for only a few seconds. Running away simply wasn't an option. Filled with nerves, I walked over to my sister and sat down on the bench. I looked around and noticed the four police officers were still nearby, trying to make it look as though they were just out on their normal business.

'Why did you feel the need to bring your chums?' I asked.

'They're for your protection as much as anything else.'

'My protection? What are you protecting me from?'

'Do you really need to ask that? When are you going to realise that this isn't a game? You're getting yourself in some serious shit here.'

'If you'd taken any notice of me for the past four years, you'd realise I've been in the shit for a long time.'

'How very heartfelt.'

'No, not really. It's rather convenient that you're finally interested in my predicament at the point where it can help your damn career.'

'Think what you will. This issue is bigger than you and me.'

'So what do you want?'

'Tell me about what just happened between you and Callum O'Brady.'

'How did you know?'

'Because we do our jobs. O'Brady is under constant surveillance now. I told you that already.'

'Yeah. Maybe you did.'

'So what was it about?'

'Money.'

Dani waited to see if I would add to my frank statement. I didn't.

'Let me set the scene for you here,' Dani said. 'If you were anyone but my brother, we wouldn't be having this conversation right now. You'd already be arrested and banged up.'

'For what?'

'Andrew Dove for starters.'

I hung my head, embarrassed. But I was also angry with Dani, who was cornering me, and with myself for having been so stupid as to give her the space to do so.

'So what now?' I said.

'You tell me. You could start by explaining what's happening with you and O'Brady.'

'I told you, I owe him money.'

'But I want to know how and why.'

'It's hard to explain.'

'No, it's not. What's difficult is you getting over yourself and doing the decent thing by coming clean.'

I sighed. 'My life is shit, Dani. It's always been shit. Ever since … you know.'

'Alice.'

I saw the emotion in Dani's face as she said the name.

'Yeah,' I said. 'I don't know. Probably before that too. It's just me. I attract misery.'

'You've got a wife and two great kids. You've got a nice house and an expensive car. You *had* a good job. A lot of people would say you've had more than your fair share of positives in life.'

'That's not how it works, though, is it? Material accumulation doesn't make for a happy life. Come on, Dani, you know how much I've suffered over the years.'

'Fine. Yeah, I do.'

'I didn't want any of this.'

'Maybe not. But you've found yourself in this position. Whatever the reason for that and whoever you think is to blame, it's *you* in this mess in the here and now.'

'Do you really think Egan killed Alice?' I said, gritting my teeth at the hatred I felt toward that vile piece of scum.

'We're still working on that. Egan's link to Hayley Lewis is strong. If we crack one case, we're hoping it can help us crack the other.'

'Are you going to tell me what that link is?'

'No, not yet. But we think we'll get there. But O'Brady? He's something else. We need help.'

'Help. You mean you need me to snitch on O'Brady. Put my life on the line for you.'

'You've got a choice,' Dani said. 'You either help us or you don't. I'm sure you can figure out the consequences of choosing one over the other.'

'Help you do what exactly?'

'Help us get O'Brady. Help us put that bastard behind bars.'

'And if I don't?'

'Then there's nothing more I can do to help you. And in all likelihood, you'll end up going down with him.'

CHAPTER 39

I was sitting in an interview room at West Midlands police headquarters. I was exhausted. I looked at my watch. It was five fifteen in the afternoon. I'd been in the room since eight that morning and had only been out three times for brief toilet breaks.

Technically, I was there of my own accord – a courtesy because of Dani's efforts, or so she said. But that apparently didn't make the process any less burdensome, and I was still being treated with what felt like contempt.

Perhaps that was just how detectives dealt with everybody all of the time. They were so used to dealing with criminals, to interviewing and interrogating, that they forgot how to interact like normal human beings.

Dani had warned me it would be like that, so I had at least been somewhat prepared. I'd tried to play the whole situation coolly, but the gruelling process was tiresome nonetheless.

I'd been taken directly from the bench by St Philip's Cathedral over to the police headquarters, just a few hundred yards away. I hadn't been arrested at any point, but I'd had quite the escort and I felt almost like a condemned man walking down the corridors of death row as I was shepherded by my sister and her colleagues through the busy city centre.

I'd spent the rest of that day being interviewed before spending the night back at the hotel in Sutton Coldfield. First thing in the morning I'd returned for another full day of endless questions about my life and everything in it – seemingly the only things I didn't need to disclose were the number of shits I took a day and my favourite sexual position. Of course, what they really wanted to know about, and what they relentlessly grilled me on, was my relationship with Callum O'Brady.

Dani had quite quickly been removed from the process of interviewing me, though I knew she was doing everything she could to remain involved in the wider operation. Following an initial briefing from Dani and one of her underlings, I'd been thrown straight in front of a superintendent and chief inspector from the Criminal Investigation Department.

Completely out of my depth, I'd immediately demanded that I be given immunity before I opened up with what I knew about O'Brady. There was little point in going ahead with the plan to ensnare O'Brady if I was simply exposing myself to prosecution. I'd not reckoned on the force with which the CID officers would object to that request, however.

Quite quickly I became the focus of their ire, and they issued numerous threats about what would happen if I didn't co-operate now that they knew I was involved in O'Brady's criminal life. I was told, assuredly, that I would be given immunity only if they deemed it appropriate based on the information I had to offer and the extent of any criminal behaviour I had been involved in. Plus, in any case it wouldn't be their decision but that of the Crown Prosecution Service. If I didn't talk at all, though, there would be no chance of immunity, and they promised me they would get to the bottom of O'Brady's dealings with or without me.

Really I wasn't left with much of an option other than to talk. And so it began: two days of gruelling interviews.

I'd never been in a police station before in my life, yet the interview rooms I'd been in over the two days felt strangely familiar from the myriad TV shows and movies I'd seen over the years.

The room I was in now was nondescript, with a large mirror covering one wall that I could only assume was one-way glass, allowing others to observe the conversation. Within the room there was nothing save for a simple wooden table, three metal chairs and a flickering overhead strip-light that emitted a persistent and annoying low-key hum.

The officers had left the room some thirty minutes previously to consider what we had talked over in the last two hours. I wondered with whom they were now discussing their findings on the other side of the mirror.

I didn't know too much about police ranks, but I assumed from the imposing manner and wrinkled face of Superintendent Jackson that he was a fairly senior officer. At least I expected there weren't too many above him within his division of CID.

Chief Inspector Marsh carried an air of authority about her too. I guessed she was in her late thirties; she had a tough face with piercing green irises and hair tied back so tightly it stretched the skin around her eyes and made her look stern.

I sat in quiet contemplation for a further fifteen minutes before I heard the deadbolt of the interview room being unlocked. Strange, I thought. I hadn't remembered them locking me in before. It made me feel uncomfortable. Jackson and Marsh walked back into the room and sat down on the chairs on the other side of the table from me.

Marsh put two bundles of papers onto the table and pushed them across to me.

'What are these?' I asked.

'What you asked for,' Jackson said. 'Immunity.'

I quickly scanned the documents in the first bundle, confirming that, at least in principle, they were what they were purported to be.

'We've had to jump through some pretty big hoops with the CPS to get them to agree to this,' Jackson continued, 'and the judge who signed it wasn't exactly keen on the idea, believe me. It's taken a lot of persuasion to get to this.'

'Thank you,' I said.

'It also ties you in to helping us,' he continued. 'You're our witness now and we need your help until O'Brady is convicted. That means you need to see this through, and if you decide to walk away before this is over then the deal is off.'

'Understood.'

'Take it away, make sure you're comfortable. Consult your lawyer, whatever. It does what it says: protects you from prosecution over anything you've disclosed to us thus far, and anything you might become involved in as a direct consequence of this operation. What it doesn't do is protect you for anything you haven't told us about that we deem worthy of further action.'

'Well, I've told you everything you need to know,' I said, not even batting an eyelid at my false assurance.

'Yeah, I'm sure you have,' said Marsh sarcastically.

'And this one?' I asked, holding up the other, smaller bundle of paper.

'A disclaimer,' Jackson said with a wry smile. 'Should anything go wrong.'

'What could go wrong?' I joked with obvious nerves in my voice.

'Clearly we're not covered for anything that happens as a result of police negligence,' Jackson said, 'but we can't protect you from every outcome. You get that, right?'

'Yeah, I get that. What you're trying to say is that if O'Brady finds out what I'm doing and decides to skin me alive, the police will wash their hands of it.'

'Well, I'm pretty sure we'd want to speak to him about that,' Marsh said. 'Skinning people alive is against the law.'

'But my family wouldn't be able to sue you for it,' I said.

'Not unless it was our negligence that caused it or failed to prevent it.'

'And exactly how often do these types of operation go wrong?' I asked, turning my attention back to Jackson.

'Every now and then,' he said. 'But the success of it is down to you as much as it is us.'

'That makes me feel much better.'

'What we're offering you is as good as anyone in your position could hope for. We don't want you to get hurt, of course we don't, but we can't prepare for every eventuality.'

'Have you got a pen?' I asked.

Jackson hesitated, then fished in his jacket pocket and handed over a black ballpoint. As I took it Marsh threw her hand out onto the table, over the documents.

'Aren't you going to take those away to consider them first?'

I pulled the documents out from under her hand. 'You're still recording, right?'

'Actually no, we're not recording this conversation. But you have two officers in the room to witness it and two more behind that screen.'

'Well, that's good enough for me,' I said and promptly signed my name on the last sheet of paper in each bundle. 'As long as these documents are what you've told me they are then what do I have to worry about?'

The officers both eyed me suspiciously but didn't otherwise argue with my rashness. I pushed the signed papers back toward Marsh.

'So what next?' I asked.

'Next you meet with O'Brady,' Jackson said.

'And do what?'

'And play it cool. We don't need to get results each and every time. We need you to move closer to him. Find out more about what he's been up to and what he's planning. You can't expect to get the silver bullet straight off.'

'So I'm going to have to do this more than once?'

'Wasn't that obvious?'

'I don't know. I've never been a police informant before.'

'It could take a lot more than one time.'

'And Egan?'

'What about Mickey Egan?'

'Is this going to help get what you need to convict him too?'

'If we can then yes.'

'And are you going to tell me exactly what you know about Egan and what you need on him to be able to do that?'

'A confession always works nicely,' Marsh said.

'But this investigation is specifically into Callum O'Brady,' Jackson said. 'I understand your sister may have disclosed more to you than she should have done about Mickey Egan, but that's a completely different matter. This isn't a simple murder investigation. This is an investigation into an entire criminal network of which O'Brady is the head.'

I felt embarrassed all of a sudden at the thought that I'd put Dani in the shit. She'd told me details about Hayley Lewis's murder in confidence. But then it was a big deal to me. It related to the murder of my wife after all. I thought about pushing the subject further. Just like with Dani, these two were so tight-lipped about what they did and didn't know. I guessed that was their prerogative, though. I wasn't one of them. I was just an asset they would use to get what they wanted. I'd only ever be told what they wanted me to know.

'How do I do it then?' I said. 'Do I wear a wire?'

'A wire? You've been watching too much telly.'

'What then?'

This time it was Marsh who reached inside her jacket. Her hand came out clutching a Blackberry mobile phone, the type that first popularised the email-led device in the noughties. Way out of date compared to modern handsets. No touchscreen or apps or mobile internet anywhere in sight. She placed it on the table.

'Cutting-edge technology?' I said. 'You want me to email him?'

Nobody laughed.

'We're not GCHQ,' Jackson said, picking the phone up and turning it over in his hands. 'It does what it needs to do. It's a listening device, a regular handset that's been upgraded somewhat. The bugging is within the phone's software.'

'But I need to use the phone?' I said. 'In O'Brady's presence?'

'No, not at all. We can monitor the phone's usage, see incoming and outgoing calls, texts, et cetera, but we can also remotely activate the phone's microphone, which has been enhanced so that we can listen in to whatever's happening around the phone. You wouldn't be able to make or receive any other calls while we're doing that, but anyone who opened up the phone while it was recording would be none the wiser.'

'Sounds straightforward,' I said.

'Obviously it'll work better when the phone's out in the open. But I'll let you figure that one out.'

'Yeah, thanks for that.' I took the phone off the table. 'So that's it? We're done now?'

'We're done. Contact us when you know your plans. We need to make sure we have feet on the ground nearby wherever you're going. Just in case.'

'Just in case?'

'Well, we wouldn't want you getting yourself hurt, would we?'

'No,' I agreed. 'We certainly would not.'

But I knew that when dealing with a man like O'Brady, my chances of that were slim to none.

CHAPTER 40

By the time Jackson and Marsh were satisfied enough to let me go, it was nearly six p.m. My head was swimming with thoughts. Could I really help to bring down O'Brady? Or was I just setting myself up for a fall? A large part of me was still trying to figure out a much more rudimental form of retribution against O'Brady, much like I'd dished out to Dove. But the prospect was hardly filling me with confidence, especially now that Dani and her colleagues seemed to be scrutinising my every move.

And then there was Egan. What was it that the police had that linked him to the murders of Alice and to Hayley Lewis? I had to find out more about that.

What I knew with absolute certainty was that I needed something to take my mind off Callum O'Brady and Mickey Egan. I hadn't seen the children since coming home from the park on Saturday. It was now Wednesday and I was missing them like crazy. But with the police and the interviewing I'd simply had no chance. I called Gemma on leaving the police headquarters, and she actually answered the phone, but only to tell me they were at Whitely's house. I knew I was anything but welcome there, so it looked like I'd have to wait to see Harry and Chloe.

I'd been texting Cara through the day and had managed to repair most of the damage I'd done the last time we met. Initially her messages back to me had been cold and blunt, but I'd apologised profusely, blaming my changed behaviour in the Karma Bar on alcohol and lack of sleep and the fact I rarely got a chance to go out anymore. I was a social retard – for want of a better word – or something like that.

The back and forth texting had done the trick. I'd managed to persuade Cara to meet me again, though she had already arranged a quiet drink with a friend straight from work so she couldn't see me until eight p.m. That was fine. It gave me enough time to head to the hotel to rest and collect my thoughts before meeting her.

The whole world seemed to return to some semblance of normality when we were out together. With everything else that was going on in my life, her presence was exactly what I needed to keep grounded. I needed someone like Cara to help me keep sight of who I really was. She brought out the best in me.

We agreed to meet in central Birmingham again, it being convenient for her given she lived and worked there. As with our first date, we quickly settled into each other's company. We went to a newly opened tapas bar and ate and drank our way through several rounds. As ten o'clock approached we were both giggly and tipsy, though we'd certainly had nowhere near as much alcohol as the first time we went out together. Cara was a little bit wary of me, it seemed, following my odd behaviour at the Karma Bar, not that it spoiled the night at all.

We were partway through our fifth drink when Cara's phone began to vibrate and emit an ear-piercing racket. She glanced at the phone, then at me, an apologetic look on her face. I wasn't sure whether she was apologising for the ghastly sound or the unexpected interruption.

Cara picked up the phone, got up from the table and went outside to take the call. Two minutes later, she stormed back into the bar, her face creased in an unforgiving glower.

'What's the matter?' I asked as she thumped herself down on the seat.

'Oh, nothing,' she said, shaking her head.

'Tell me,' I said, reaching out and putting my hand on hers.

She looked up at me but didn't say anything.

'I'm a good listener,' I said. 'I generally forget half of what I'm told anyway, so go for it. Rant away if you want.'

She smiled but it quickly faded again.

'Seriously. Try me.'

'It was my husband,' she said.

'Oh,' was all I could manage.

'He's drunk. He wanted to chat. Wanted to tell me how much he loves and misses me.'

In a way I could sympathise with him, given that my wife had thrown me out.

'You still love him?' I said.

'I really don't know. But it'll never work now. I've filed for divorce already. He's making everything harder than it needs to be. He's refusing to sign the papers, convinced that I'll suddenly wake up one morning and want him back. What he's actually doing is pushing me further away.'

'Love makes us do all sorts of crazy shit,' I said.

'Well, he's certainly crazy. He also has zero ability to do anything for anyone other than himself. It never ceases to amaze me how selfish and insensitive some people can be.'

'Oh, believe me,' I said, trying to sound jolly, 'I know all about that. Kids are just about the most insensitive beings on this planet. You should hear some of the things my three year old comes out with. She really knows how to cut my heart in two.'

Cara laughed. 'Yeah, I can imagine. I love them at that age. I have nieces. I've wanted kids my whole life.'

'What's stopping you?' I said.

Cara gave me a blank look and I wondered whether I'd overstepped the mark.

'Just one of those things,' she said eventually. 'It wasn't through lack of trying. I've been pregnant but … it's just never worked out.'

I didn't seek clarification, but I could only presume she'd had a miscarriage, maybe more than one. The hurt in her eyes, I knew the look well. I wondered how much bearing those troubles had had on Cara's break-up.

'I'm sorry,' I said. 'It must be hard for you.'

'It is,' she said. 'But I'm convinced it'll happen for me one day.'

'Of course it will.'

Cara rolled her eyes and I wasn't sure whether it was at my comment or her thinking of her husband.

'Well, that's really blown the mood,' Cara remarked, trying to sound brighter.

'Hasn't it just,' I said. I reached into my pocket and took out my wallet and opened it to show Cara the passport-sized pictures I kept of Harry and Chloe.

Cara beamed a smile as wide as her face. 'They're beautiful. She looks just like you.'

'You think? I always thought she was prettier than me.'

Cara laughed. 'Don't do yourself down.'

'You think I'm pretty?' I joked.

'Oh, very. A bit of make-up would spruce you right up.'

'I'm flattered. You're not so bad yourself.'

'Not so bad? Wow, it's no wonder you're single.'

We both laughed and I put the pictures away. With the ambience restored, we settled back into the night. It was gone eleven when we finally talked ourselves into leaving. Before we got to our feet, we found ourselves caught in a moment, neither of us saying a word, both of us staring intently into each other's eyes. I wondered whether I should make a move, but just as I was building up the courage, Cara looked down at her watch.

'Have you seen the time? I was only coming out for a quick drink!'

'Well, it was quite a quick drink, followed by another ten quick drinks afterwards.'

'Is that how many we've had?'

'No, not quite. I can still think straight. Just about.'

'Come on, why don't we get out of here?'

I stood up and held my arm out to her, and she grabbed it and hauled herself upright, bundling into me and giggling.

'Yep, you've definitely had enough,' I said.

She hit my arm playfully and we moved off toward the exit. Outside, we both stopped and waited to see what would happen next. After how the last date had ended I wasn't sure she'd be offering one for the road, yet I really didn't want the night to end there and then. I was infatuated with Cara and it wasn't just the drink making me feel that way.

'You live just around the corner?' I asked.

'Yeah, five minutes' walk.'

'I'll walk you back. Not sure you'd make it on your own.'

'Oh, you're hilarious,' Cara said. 'Go on then. But no funny business.'

I held my hands up in defence. 'I wouldn't dream of it.'

We walked through the city and along the dark and virtually deserted canal towpath toward the block of flats where she lived. When we reached the door to the building, Cara began to fumble in her bag, looking for the key. She took out a plastic card and held it up against a panel on the wall and the door clicked open.

'I guess this is it,' I said.

'I guess it is.'

'I had a great time, Cara.'

I pulled the door open for her.

'It was good,' she said, looking up at me. 'We'll definitely do it again.'

'I'd like that.'

'Can't wait … Goodnight then.'

'Night.'

We stood in awkward silence for just a split-second and then Cara moved toward me and craned her neck to reach up to me. I guessed she was just trying to give me a friendly kiss on the cheek, and I leaned in to do the same, but she took me completely by surprise when she planted a lingering kiss on my lips. I stood stunned, my eyes wide with shock.

She moved away, laughing. 'Are you always so stiff and awkward when you kiss a girl?'

'No ... I ... er ... not at all –'

'Okay, let's try that again then.'

Cara came back and this time I didn't hesitate. Our lips parted and we wrapped our arms around each other, squeezing each other tightly as the passion of the kiss grew.

I was holding the door open with my leg and Cara stepped backward, into the building, taking me with her. We sidestepped, the kiss becoming more frantic and clumsy, our hands roaming over each other's bodies.

We passed the lift and fell through a door into the stairwell, where we stopped for a minute and got our embrace back under some sort of control. But the power of lust and temptation washing through our intoxicated bodies was too much. We shimmied backward and Cara half-stumbled over the bottom step, falling down onto her back, with me following on top of her.

For the first time our lips parted and I stared into her eyes, seeing the fiery thirst of desire. She leaned forward and lightly bit my bottom lip, and then we began to kiss again, even more frantically than before.

Her hands moved down and began to unbuckle my belt. Then she pulled down her leggings and panties and I whipped down my jeans. We both let out an excited murmur as I gently pushed inside her and we began to clumsily but fervently have sex right there on the stairs.

Our bodies bucked and jolted in ecstasy for a few seconds when we both came just a couple of minutes later. Then we lay there, completely still and uncomfortably silent.

I kissed her on the cheek, then got to my feet and began to pull up my boxer shorts and jeans.

'I'm sorry,' I said, barely able to look her in the eyes.

'What for?' she said, getting to her feet and looking more than a little annoyed by my reaction.

'That shouldn't have happened. I mean ...' I trailed off. I had been about to say I was married. But did I really owe any loyalty to Gemma? And Cara certainly didn't to her husband.

'I wanted it to happen,' Cara said.

'Are you sure you're going to feel like that in the morning?'

'I didn't fuck you because I'm drunk,' she blasted. 'I did it because I wanted to. And I thought you wanted to.'

'I did. I mean … I'm just …'

I stopped digging and shut my mouth, moved over to her and grabbed her with both arms.

'I did want to,' I said, before planting my lips back on hers. 'And I'm glad we did.'

When I moved my face away I saw the look of annoyance dissipating.

'I want to see you again,' I said. 'I really mean that. I really like you.'

'I want that too,' she said coyly.

With the awkward moment all but forgotten, we embraced and kissed one last time before we said goodbye. I watched longingly as Cara climbed up the stairs toward her apartment. But as she moved out of sight my positivity quickly evaporated and a feeling of remorse filled me. Not because of what we'd just done, but because I was absolutely certain that bringing Cara into my unsettled world could only end badly for her.

Though I could never have anticipated quite how badly events would soon spiral out of control.

CHAPTER 41

'Did you see Cara again?' she asked.

'Of course,' I said.

'You mentioned you felt remorse. About what exactly?'

'It's hard to explain. There was some guilt, certainly. I don't know why, but I felt I had this ulterior motive for wanting to be with her, as though I was trying to get back at Gemma. But that wasn't true at all, because I really did like Cara. I knew from the first time we spoke that there was a connection between us.'

'Wasn't it just lust, for both of you?'

'No,' I said. 'Absolutely not. I genuinely liked her. Having sex with her in that stairwell … it wasn't a mistake exactly because we both wanted it, but it wasn't what I'd intended either.'

'What had you intended?'

'I enjoyed her company that night, and I think she enjoyed mine too. I felt so natural with her. It would have been a perfectly good night even if it had ended without a single kiss. What happened … it was her as much as me. Her more than me, in fact.'

'What did that tell you about her?'

'That she was unhappy. That she was grateful that someone other than that no-good husband of hers was giving her attention. And that she liked me.'

'When did you see her next?'

'A couple of nights after that.'

'Did you sleep with her again?'

'No. Not that night anyway. Like I said, it wasn't about that. Well, no, it was – I mean, part of it was. I just wanted to see her. Whenever I was with her I felt happy and positive, which was a relief given everything else that was happening.'

'What about Gemma? Did you feel guilty for having betrayed your wife?'

'I didn't betray her,' I said with absolute conviction.

'You had sex with another woman.'

'Gemma threw me out.'

'But you were still married, and at one point you said you wanted to get back together with her.'

'I don't know what I wanted. But either way, it was Gemma's decision to kick me out. If she hadn't done that then I probably would never have met Cara.'

'That sounds like a convenient excuse.'

'It's anything but.'

'What would you have felt if Gemma had done the same? If she had sex with another man at that time?'

'I probably would have found the man and ripped his balls off, but I'm not sure I was exactly in a good state of mind overall.'

She paused for a beat to write down what I'd said.

'I was being facetious,' I said.

She looked up. 'I know. My point was, though, that you must have known Gemma would have been seriously hurt by your infidelity, and yet you're claiming you felt no kind of guilt?'

'I didn't sleep with Cara to get revenge on Gemma. Me and Cara … just happened.'

'Except you very deliberately crafted the moment with Cara to enable you to go out with her. You said so yourself. I'm not sure I'd say that it just happened.'

'But there was nothing sinister about that. I just liked Cara and wanted to get to know her. And it was never intended as revenge against Gemma. You have to understand that Gemma and I had been on the rocks for a long time. I loved her – as the mother of Chloe … and Harry, I truly loved her. But as a partner, it was clear to both us that it wasn't working. There was just nothing there anymore. For the security of the kids, sure, some part of me wanted to be back with her, but that was the only reason.'

'You're just talking about sexual attraction, though, aren't you?' she countered. 'That's all you were lacking with Gemma and all that you found with Cara.'

'You make it sound sleazy, but really there's nothing wrong with that, is there?'

'Would you say lust is a strong basis for a relationship?'

'Sexual attraction is how the human species has mated and reproduced for thousands of years. Without that attraction in a relationship it's hard to keep it going. You may think that sounds childish or selfish, or like I'm a sex-crazed imbecile who has no control over his libido, but that's just not it. I liked Cara. I had real feelings for her, which I'd only ever felt before with Alice. I really wanted to be with her.'

'You never felt like that about Gemma? Even at the start?'

'With Gemma it was different. Yes, when we first got together I fancied her, I really did. She's beautiful, and my lust for her led to our affair, which ultimately, some time after Alice's death, led to our marriage. But after that lust wore off, the feelings just weren't there like they were for Alice. The relationship was empty.'

'But you meeting Cara is quite reminiscent of you first meeting Gemma – when you cheated on Alice. You've suggested that Alice was the perfect partner for you, but the picture you've painted of your relationship with her was that it was far from rosy in the end.'

'Of course it was far from rosy. She slept with another man.'

'And you slept with another woman, Gemma.'

'But I wanted it to work with Alice, I really did. I put everything I could into making that marriage work.'

'And was it working?'

'We were still married when she was killed, so I'd say it had been.'

'But was it really working?'

'Our relationship was perfect,' I said. 'But that kind of pure happiness can never last. It's impossible. Life is too complex. We weathered the storms, we did our best, but you're right: in the end our best wasn't enough.'

CHAPTER 42

My relationship with Alice had never quite recovered following her betrayal. Although the marriage had carried on and we'd brought Harry into the world, her infidelity was always there in the background.

Plus there was Gemma. Would my life have panned out differently if Gemma hadn't come along? Maybe, but it's impossible to know. The affair with Gemma was a mistake. My relationship with her wasn't planned, and I hadn't slept with her purely out of spite, even though I know that's why my guard was down when we first started our affair.

So why her? Well, Gemma was, quite simply, a stunner. Yes, later our relationship had its troubles, and I don't think either of us could have predicted where those first passionate encounters would lead, but I'll happily admit that what first attracted me to Gemma was that she was drop-dead gorgeous. And maybe just another small part of it was the fact that she was Whitely's daughter.

From her very first day in the office Gemma had caused quite the stir. Whitely had brought her in part-time as an office assistant, a general dogsbody who ran errands. It was essentially a bogus position and it was clear to everyone that the job only existed because Whitely wanted it to. Yet no-one thought any less of Gemma because of it. She was charming and happy and people liked her being around. Everyone was drawn to Gemma. I was. And just look at the trouble that got me into.

My life with Alice was going through so much change when Gemma and I first got together. The change had started some months before that. Though neither of us had known it at the time, Alice had been pregnant with Harry when she'd slept with Craig Fletcher.

When we'd subsequently found out that she was expecting, just a few weeks after her coming clean to me, it was a shock to say the least. It should have been a happy moment – for both of us. Instead my immediate response was to be left wondering what could have been. My life, our lives together, had so very nearly been flawless. If only she'd known of her pregnancy beforehand, she would never have found herself pushed to Fletcher in the first place.

Harry should have saved us, should have brought us closer together once more. If anything, he pushed us further apart. As well-behaved as Harry was, as much as I loved him then and now, in the end he represented just another further wedge between me and Alice.

My relationship with Alice came to a head when I arrived home from work one evening, a little after six. Harry was having an uncharacteristic tantrum. My immediate thought was that the mournful look on Alice's face was because of the trouble he was causing.

Harry was lying on her lap, his face a deep red, his eyes squeezed shut. His whole body was writhing and bucking and he was screaming so hard his voice had grown hoarse. I expected Alice to bung him over to me the minute I walked through the door so she could leave the room to have a breather. That was her usual approach on the odd occasion that Harry lost control and when Alice was fraught and at a loss as to what to do with him.

This time, however, she clung on to him even more tightly and she turned her body away from me, barely acknowledging my entrance.

'Come on, give him to me,' I said, walking up to her and holding my hands out.

'No,' Alice snapped. 'I'm fine. I can handle it.'

Her forthright tone knocked me back, but I assumed it was Harry's behaviour that was stressing her out.

I ignored her words and reached out and pulled Harry away from her. She resisted for a second, but then let go. I cradled Harry in my arms, gentling swinging him back and forth, and within seconds his cries had died down and he opened his eyes and stared at me intently. I gazed back and felt that immense sense of pride that only a parent knows.

When I looked back over at Alice, she was glowering. My first guess was that she was jealous and somewhat perturbed by Harry's sudden comedown. It's a natural reaction that every parent and grandparent knows: that moment when the baby you've been so lovingly trying to settle suddenly goes silent the second someone else takes him off your hands.

But it wasn't that at all, I soon realised.

'Who is she?' Alice blurted out.

My heart jumped in my chest and I immediately guessed what the vague question meant. I tried my best not to let my inner reaction show.

'What?'

'No bullshit. I know. Please, just do the decent thing. Tell me who she is.'

I hung my head and looked at Harry. He was still staring at me, but it seemed his features had hardened and he too was now giving me a suspicious and disappointed look.

'Her name's Gemma.'

Silence. No-one spoke. Not even a murmur.

'Her name's Gemma?' Alice said. 'That's it? That's your confession?'

'I don't know what else you want me to say.'

I looked back up at Alice. I saw only anger and contempt in her eyes. No pain or sorrow. It was disconcerting.

'I'm sorry, Alice. I'm so sorry.'

'Who is she?' Alice said.

'She's no-one. She works at the office.'

'She's no-one? Then why the hell are you sleeping with her?'

'There's really no good answer I can give to that,' I said.

Alice stood up. I cowered away slightly, a direct response to the intent I saw in her eyes. I expected her to stride up and belt me in the face. Instead she held out her arms.

'Give him to me,' she said.

I handed Harry to her.

'It's his bedtime,' she said, and then she turned and left the room and thudded up the stairs.

The altercation had been brief, but nonetheless it left me feeling wounded. If anything, I would have felt more at ease if we'd got into an all-out slanging match. All I could think was that Alice was containing herself while she put Harry to bed and that soon she would let rip on me.

For the next half hour I sat solemnly in the kitchen while Alice was upstairs reading to Harry. I tried to think of all the things I should say when she returned. The reassurances of how I still loved her and wanted to be with her. They were all true, but I couldn't get any of the words into the right order and nothing I could think of saying sounded genuine even to me.

When Alice finally came into the kitchen her look of anger was gone, replaced with abject disappointment. We both looked at each other for a good while in absolute silence.

'I'll leave if you want me to,' I said, looking away from her.

'No, you bloody won't,' Alice said. 'You're not leaving me to look after our baby on my own. We're a family.'

'I didn't say I wanted to. I thought maybe that was what you were thinking.'

'I'm not going to pretend that I'm not devastated by this. I mean, after everything we've been through. I really never thought you could do something like this.'

'Well, I guess now you know how I felt,' I chipped in, and immediately regretted it.

'You arsehole,' Alice said. 'Is that all this is? You getting your own back on me? You thought what I did gave you free reign to sleep with whoever the hell you wanted?'

'That's not what I thought at all,' I said. 'Not even close. I didn't want this.'

'Of course you didn't. That's why you slept with another woman. Then slept with her again. And again.'

I said nothing to that. I had no idea how Alice had found out and it really didn't matter. But she clearly knew that my affair with Gemma wasn't a simple one-night stand like hers had been.

'Are you still seeing her?' she said.

'Yes.'

'Do you love her?'

I hesitated. 'No. I love *you*.'

For the first time, Alice's resolve seemed to break and her eyes began to well up with tears. She quickly regained her composure, though.

'Like I said, I can leave if you want me to.'

'That's not what I want,' she said, putting her hand to her head. 'What I want is to turn back the clock. To put everything back how it was. I know I messed up, and I'll never forgive myself for that, but I'm not going to pretend that knowing you've been with someone else hasn't crushed me.'

'I'm sorry.'

'I know I don't deserve anything more than this,' Alice continued. 'I just want to move forward now. Let's try to make things right. We've both messed up. But if we want it, we can make things work. I still believe that. I still love you.'

I was dumbstruck. Was this really the extent of my punishment? I was dubious as to just how much truth was in what she was saying, and yet I felt exactly the same as she did.

'I want us to keep going,' Alice said. 'We've both made mistakes, but we have to put them behind us now. For the sake of all of us. I don't want our family torn apart because of our own selfishness and stupidity.'

'We'll get through this,' I assured her.

'I hope so. But one thing, Ben. Tell me it's over. That you'll never see her again. You have to promise me that. I don't care why you did it or who she is. If you love me, you'll finish it.'

'I will.'

'Promise me?'

'I promise,' I said without even thinking.

And in the moment, I really meant it.

CHAPTER 43

I had sex with Gemma the very next day. After the conversation with Alice, I had wanted to do the right thing and break off the affair with Gemma. I truly had every intention of doing just that. But the simple fact was that Gemma was a master manipulator. She knew how to get what she wanted. And for whatever reason, she'd decided that she wanted me.

I'd arranged to go around to Gemma's apartment. I'd rehearsed what to say. I was to keep it short and to the point. I liked her, we'd had fun, but it was over. My marriage to Alice was too important to jeopardise any further. I had Harry to think of too. The stability of the family. I guessed Gemma would be hurt and angry by my decision, that she'd probably claim I'd used her for sex and that I was a low-life scumbag. I was happy with that prospect. It would at least mean that the affair was over and I could get on with rebuilding my marriage with Alice.

In the end, I didn't even get the well-practised words out. Gemma pounced on me the second she opened her apartment door. I was an idiot. I was a sucker. Gemma knew my weakness. I couldn't resist her when she was in the mood like that.

Over the next few months I tried again and again to break it off with Gemma. At one point I even managed to get out some of those pre-planned words. I told Gemma how much I loved Alice, how I could never leave my wife. Gemma was hurt by my words, but somehow she won out. She just wasn't prepared to let me go. To give up on me. It was like she saw it as a game and revelled in the power she had over me.

Ultimately she claimed to love me. She claimed that *she* couldn't live without *me*.

I believed her. I wanted to believe her. There was so much I enjoyed about the time I spent with Gemma compared to my still-stuttering marriage to Alice. No matter how hard I tried to rekindle what we'd lost, our relationship never truly recovered. Part of that was due to Harry, I realised. As much as we both loved him, nothing changes a relationship like a baby. No matter how much we both wanted our marriage to be like it had been in the past, that could never happen.

Another part of the problem was Dani. My own sister. When she found about my affair with Gemma ...

I'd always felt close to Dani, but all of a sudden it was like I was a marked man. I hadn't just let Alice down, I'd let Dani down, and our parents too. Once again I was the disappointment of the family, though now it was Dani who was at the head, driving that thought.

Despite my best intentions to keep my marriage working, it felt as if Dani was set on tearing me and Alice apart, day by day. And Dani was an expert at getting what she wanted.

I counted myself unfortunate that my bank of memories was filled with far more devastatingly bad days than sublimely happy days. Few of those bad days had Alice in them. Even after everything, I still considered her to be the love of my life. Yet there were *some* bad days with her.

In fact, there were some very bad days.

'You lied to me,' Alice said.

She was sitting on the edge of our bed. I was standing across the room.

'I'm sorry,' I said. There were simply no other words.

'It's too late now,' she said, sounding entirely matter of fact.

'I still love you,' I said.

I wanted her to say the words back. She didn't.

'I want you to move out,' she said.

I looked down at my feet. Her response was inevitable. I'd blown it. I should have broken it off with Gemma. I'd had the chance, I just hadn't had the strength – or was it the desire? – to see it through.

But even then, in that moment, I still wanted Alice. I wanted her to want me to stay.

'What about what you told me before?' I said. 'That you didn't want me to go. That you wanted us to stay together as a family.'

'You promised me you would stop seeing her.'

'I tried. You have to believe me.'

'I'm struggling to see that.'

'Give me another chance. Please. Just one more chance. I can't live without you, Alice. And think about Harry, about what this would do to him.'

'Don't you dare bring him into this,' Alice growled. 'Harry is not your excuse for neglecting and hurting me like this.'

'I still love you, and I know you feel the same for me.'

'But that's where you're wrong, Ben.'

She stared at me and I saw a look in her eyes that I'd never seen before. It sent a shiver right through me.

'What?'

'I don't love you,' she said. 'Not anymore.'

'I don't believe you.'

'I want a divorce. I want you gone, out of my life.'

I tried to speak but no words came out, just garbled sounds.

'You can't be serious?' I said eventually.

'I'm absolutely serious. It's over. And nothing you can do now is going to stop that.'

'But ... why?'

'Why? If you really need to ask that question then you're a lot dumber than I thought.'

'I'll finish it. I promise I will.'

'It's not about *her*,' Alice said, the last word emphasised with extreme bitterness. 'It's you, Ben. I don't love *you* anymore.'

'But ...'

'I don't love you anymore,' Alice repeated.

'Is this because of Dani?' I said, feeling anger rise. 'Has she put you up to this?'

Alice's lack of response said it all.

'Just get out!' she screamed.

By that point I was as livid as I was upset. My whole world had just been shattered. Alice's manner, her self-satisfied tone, was too much to take. And knowing my own sister - someone who should have been looking out for *me* - had been gunning for this outcome ...

'I'm not going anywhere,' I said.

CHAPTER 44

What stopped you breaking it off with Gemma?' she asked.

'I was weak,' I said. 'There's no good excuse. I was attracted to Gemma. We had great sex together.'

'So that's all it was, sex?'

'No. I mean ... it's so difficult to explain. It was more than that. But you have to realise I met Gemma when Alice was pregnant. Then when the baby came ... you know.'

'So you and Alice weren't having sex. Is that what you're trying to say?'

'We were ... but it just wasn't the same. She'd gone through a hell of an ordeal with Harry. She was recovering from a major operation. Even when she'd healed physically, she'd lost a lot of confidence, not just in the way she looked but in herself. Plus there was her cheating. Things were rocky.'

'And that had all affected your sex life?'

'Of course it had. And our cheating aside, I'm sure that's the same for many couples who have kids. Having a baby is stressful. There was little time for us to be intimate with each other, even if we'd wanted it. But I still loved her. I still wanted to be with her. Our sex life wasn't the same as it had been, but so what? Marriage is more than sex.'

'That's a convincing statement, but you were having an affair. So did you have feelings for Gemma at that point?'

'I don't know. Of course there was lust. Ultimately I thought there was love too. I married Gemma for all the right reasons. But looking back, the love was never there. I mistook my sexual attraction to Gemma and her attraction to me for love.'

'What about Gemma? At the start, what was her motivation do you think?'

'I never felt there was anything particularly sinister about Gemma's behaviour. She wasn't having the affair with me in order to wreck my marriage

or to hurt Alice. She wanted to be with me. And that was nice for me. Everybody likes to be wanted. Everybody wants to be loved.'

'So why do you think it went wrong with Gemma?'

'There are countless reasons. Really, it was never right, no matter how much I wanted it to be. I couldn't pretend forever. In the end I realised there was just nothing there with Gemma. Not on my part at least. I simply didn't love her the way I'd loved Alice.'

'And what about Cara Andrews?'

'What about her?'

'How would you describe your attraction to her?'

'I said before, it was natural. I liked her in so many different ways.'

'So you're saying you had genuine feelings for her, that it was more than just lust?'

'I think so. I think in another life I could have loved Cara. But we never got that far. We only saw each other a few more times.'

'What happened?'

'It went badly wrong. For both of us. Though she suffered far more than I did.'

'Tell me about it.'

'It started with Callum O'Brady. The sting operation. From there, everything turned to shit.'

CHAPTER 45

With my sister and Jackson and Marsh on my back wanting to keep the plans for the sting with O'Brady moving, my life was fast approaching a crossroads from which there would be no going back.

I hadn't seen my children for days. Gemma had decided to simply ignore each and every call I made and message I sent. Unsure of where life would soon be taking me, I decided to take matters into my own hands and go to the house. It was nearly seven p.m. and Harry and Chloe wouldn't be far off getting ready for bed. If I was quick, I might get a chance to see them for a few minutes and read them a story or two – a once menial task that had taken on huge significance now that it was no longer part of my routine.

That was assuming Gemma would even let me in. It was clear our marriage was heading only in one direction. And with Cara on the scene, I wasn't about to beg Gemma to take me back into her bed. Regardless, one thing I knew for sure was that she damn well wasn't going to stop me seeing my children.

I was already turning into the driveway when I realised my plan may not be quite as simple as I'd hoped, though. Parked up on the gravel was the gleaming bright-blue Bentley Continental GT that belonged to Gemma's dad. I'd always thought it was a vulgar excuse for a sports car, a statement of wealth and nothing else. It suited the arrogant Whitely perfectly.

I could have called it quits there and then. It would have been the most sensible option. Instead I cut off the engine, got out of the car and strode up to the front door.

As I reached the door my hand was in my pocket, grasping for my keys. In the end I decided against that approach. I reached up and rang the bell, then gave three loud knocks.

A few seconds later Whitely opened the door.

'What are you doing here?' he said, looking me up and down with disdain.

'I've had a rough day, James. I just want to see the kids for a few minutes.'

'You can't just come around whenever you feel like it.'

'Says who? It's my house.'

'Says me.'

I stood and stared at Whitely, and he stood and glared right back. He folded his arms and moved forward, blocking the entrance.

'You're not welcome here,' he snarled.

'This is none of your business,' I barked back. 'I want to see my children.'

'You have to get through me if you want to come in.'

'Oh, believe me, I'd love to knock you down, you smarmy prick.' I could see shock on Whitely's face. It was probably years since anyone had challenged him like that; he was so used to the world bending to his will. 'But I didn't come here for a fight.'

Just then I spotted Gemma and her mum, Irene, coming into view behind Whitely.

'What's going on?' Gemma said, striding up, exasperation in her voice.

I shook my head. It was all too much. The Whitely clan, all banding together against me. What point was there in standing and fighting it?

'I just came to say goodnight to the kids,' I said as calmly as I could, a complete contrast to how I was really feeling. 'Your dad would rather have a boxing match with me, though, I think.'

Gemma gave Whitely a questioning look. He just shrugged. She pushed him out of the way and put herself between me and him.

'You should tell me if you're coming,' she said.

'If you answered your phone that would be a bit easier.'

'Look, Chloe's already in bed,' Gemma said. 'She's not been well, a stomach bug. Harry's shattered. It's not a great time, Ben.'

'You can't keep me away from them forever. They need me. They need their dad.'

'Okay. But not tonight.'

'Fine,' I said after a few moments. 'I'm not going to cause a scene just to please you lot.'

'What are you talking about?' Gemma said.

'It doesn't matter. I'll come back another time.'

'Wait,' Gemma said.

I raised an eyebrow as Gemma darted back off inside. I looked over at Whitely and saw a knowing look in his glistening eyes. Gemma came back a few moments later with a brown envelope in her hand. She pushed it out toward me.

'What's this?' I said, taking the envelope, my eyes fixed on her.

Gemma said nothing. I lifted the flap on the end of the envelope and pulled out the sheath of white papers by just a few inches. That was all I needed to determine what they were.

'It's for the best,' Gemma said. 'You must agree with that? I want to end this properly, amicably. I hope we can do that.'

I stared back at Gemma, so many confusing thoughts crashing through my brain. Was a divorce really that much of a surprise? No. But it still hurt. And it made me mad with rage, particularly given the unpleasant smirk that was plastered on Whitely's face.

I pushed the papers back into the envelope, then turned and headed away. I looked back over my shoulder as I reached my car. Gemma and Whitely were still standing in the doorway. As I opened the door to the BMW and got in, they finally moved away and shut the front door. I had already started the engine and shoved the gearstick into reverse when I paused. With the engine idling, I looked up at the house. Our house. My house.

I took a few seconds to think. My brain was in such disarray. I couldn't think straight. Why couldn't I just be happy? Why couldn't my life be normal?

It was too late, I realised, for that to ever be the case.

I stepped out of the car, leaving the engine running, and looked at the windows of the house. No sign of Gemma or Whitely or Irene or the kids. I stepped over to the edge of the gravel drive where there was a line of loose yellow bricks – a handful of spares from when we'd had the driveway and front wall redone. I'd intended to bed them into the ground to create a better border between the gravel and small front lawn – one of many DIY jobs in the house that would never be completed, at least not by me.

As I took a brick in each hand, I felt calm. Absent was the raw anger and hatred that had filled me when I knocked down Dove, and when I smashed a stranger's face against a toilet bowl. Even though I knew it was those same emotions now driving me on, I felt entirely relaxed. It was a strange feeling. A nice feeling.

I moved toward the Bentley and swung back my right arm, then brought the brick crashing down onto the windscreen. The glass cracked and sank inwards a number of inches. I pulled back on the brick but it was firmly wedged in the ruptured mess.

The windscreen hadn't smashed into pieces – it was designed not to – but the damage was certainly done. I arced back my left arm and swung the other brick against the driver's window. That one did smash. Hundreds, maybe thousands of small square chunks of safety glass crashed down onto the ground and all over the driver's seat. I let out an amused grunt as I looked back over at the house. Gemma was just coming into view in the lounge window, a shocked look on her face. I smiled at her and she dashed off out of view – to tell Whitely what I'd done, no doubt.

I lifted my heel and brought the sole of my shoe down onto the driver's wing mirror, severing it with ease. It fell to the ground and rolled to a stop at my feet.

The front door opened. Whitely stood there, aghast, eyes fixed on his beloved car. I expected him to jump into a rage and throw himself toward me. Part of me wanted it. But he just stood there looking absolutely numb, as though he'd just been told that someone close to him had died.

I moved back to my car, got in and backed up onto the road. I glanced over at Whitely. He was still standing inside the house, but his eyes were on me now. The look of outrage, of hatred, on his face was a true picture. I beamed at him and lifted my hand to wave, just as I pushed my foot down on the accelerator. As I shot off into the distance, I knew with absolute certainty that I'd reached a turning point. Hell, I'd gone right past the damn thing. There was no going back.

Fuck Whitely. Fuck Gemma. Fuck Dani and O'Brady and Egan. Fuck them all.

It was time to make every one of them pay.

CHAPTER 46

I couldn't stand the thought of Gemma coming out on top, her and Whitely both. But they would have to wait. The man I was going to see deserved every bit of wrath that was now begging to come out of me. If I could only find a way.

I hadn't seen Callum O'Brady since our rendezvous in the Bullring shopping centre nearly a week before. I'd spoken to him twice on the phone since then and I could tell he was getting edgy. The original deadline for the two hundred thousand pounds had expired, and he was increasingly coming to the conclusion that my evasiveness since our last meeting was down to me looking for ways to buy more time without delivering anything of value in return.

He was right to think that. Buying time was exactly what I had been doing. As much as I hated O'Brady and wanted to see him suffer, I also knew exactly how dangerous he was. And with me in bed with Jackson and Marsh, I was playing a deadly game.

I walked through the streets of Digbeth over to the Full Spread, feeling the nerves build inside me. Back on O'Brady's home turf, the last thing I wanted was to be starting on the back foot, yet given the tone of our recent conversations, it seemed inevitable. I'd tried as best I could to get O'Brady away from this place, but having done me the 'favour', as he put it, of granting me some leeway by not demanding the money, he outright refused my suggestion of meeting on neutral territory.

Meeting O'Brady on his hallowed turf was exactly what the police wanted me to do, even if it was without doubt the least safe option for me. O'Brady was far more likely to be himself there, which only increased the chances that he would incriminate himself.

My biggest problem was that the police had so far been entirely unsuccessful in getting any sort of surveillance inside the club. Which made my role, from the police's point of view, all the more vital; from my point of view it was all the more dangerous.

As I rounded the final corner onto the dirty back street where the club was located, I spotted the car straightaway. It was a battered old Ford Mondeo. Bumps and scratches marked its pale-blue body and large bubbled clumps of orange rust were visible around the wheel arches and along the edges of nearly every metal panel.

The car certainly wasn't out of place parked in the grotty street, but the two occupants, trying their best to look inconspicuous, certainly were. Police officers. Sergeants from CID. I'd been led to believe there were six officers in total stationed near the club: a precaution should the meeting take a turn for the worse. I hadn't seen the others, but these two couldn't have looked more like policemen if they'd tried. Maybe it was just because I was on the lookout for them, though. I hoped that was the case. If O'Brady or his men rumbled the officers then all bets were off.

I approached the main entrance to the club. It was a few minutes past eight in the evening and no bouncers were stationed outside, but I could see the padlocks were off the battered steel double-doors so I guessed someone was inside. I knocked loudly on the doors and waited.

A few seconds later I heard various deadbolts being turned. One of the doors swung open to reveal a woman. Her form cut a stark contrast to the gloomy darkness of the club beyond. I didn't recognise her. Not that I was a regular, but I'd seen a number of the dancers before and was familiar with their faces, the bar staff too. This woman was tall and plump and dressed in jeans and a plain jumper. She just looked … ordinary.

'I'm here to see –'

'I know, I know,' she said, moving aside to let me in. 'Come in. He's been waiting for you.'

I smiled at her and walked past her into the club. Inside the main lights were on but dimmed. It was dark, not as dark as when the punters were in but dark enough to hide the major cracks and warts of the interior.

I spotted a gaggle of people over on the platform area. They were standing, chatting happily. Among them was O'Brady, with some of his trusted comrades, but also a number of the dancers – although they had more clothes on than I'd ever seen before. That wasn't exactly a difficult feat to accomplish, I guessed.

As I approached, the conversations died down. All eyes turned to me and O'Brady stepped forward from the crowd.

'You're late,' he said.

I stopped, confused, and looked at my watch. 'It's eight,' I said.

'Exactly.'

'We agreed to meet at eight?'

'No. *You* said eight. I said six.'

'But we agreed on eight, I thought?'

I tried not to show it but I was already rattled. Was this just O'Brady's way of quickly gaining the upper hand, putting me on the back foot, or had I really messed up?

'Well, you're here now. And it's a good thing for you too. I was just about to send some boys out after you. I don't like people playing games with me, and you seem intent on that lately.'

'I'm sorry. I'm not playing games.'

'You'd better not be. Or I'm going to finish you for good.'

I nodded in acknowledgement of O'Brady's words and put my hand in my jeans pocket where the Blackberry phone was located, running my fingers over it as though it were a comforter. I wondered whether O'Brady's threat of violence had been heard, although I knew such a vague statement on its own was of little use to the police.

'Is this a bad time?' I asked, indicating the crowd of people behind.

'Yeah, it is,' O'Brady responded. 'We're doing auditions for a new club. You wouldn't believe how many girls have come forward for this new gig. Auditions are the only way. Not a bad way to spend an evening, though, eh?'

'I guess not.'

'My old woman looks after it.' O'Brady indicated over to the lady who'd let me into the club.

'Your wife?' I asked, looking over at her. I knew O'Brady was married, but I'd never met his wife before or even heard him talk of her much. She was nothing like I expected. I guessed he would have some trophy wife to hang off his arm.

'Yeah. My wife,' O'Brady said, looking at me suspiciously as though my surprised tone had offended him. 'She's got a great eye for the girls. Can tell the ones that'll get the punters drooling better than any fella can. Plus, she knows which ones'll get along with the others and which ones'll forever start cat fights. I like to keep a happy ship here.'

'Of course,' I said, turning my attention back to O'Brady.

'Well, you're here now, so come on.'

I followed O'Brady, presuming he was heading to the office. As we entered the bright corridor I saw Mickey Egan coming out of one of the storerooms. He gave me a knowing look, and as my eyes moved down I saw his hands, his arms, all the way up to his elbows, were smeared with thick red liquid.

Blood.

O'Brady turned to me. He must have seen the shocked look on my face. In fact, he probably enjoyed seeing it.

'Any luck?' O'Brady said to Egan.

'All sorted,' Egan responded. 'Just going to get cleaned up.'

By that point my pulse and my breathing were out of control. I wasn't far off an all-out panic attack. Egan moved to the side as we walked past him. Beyond the fear that consumed me, I had a strong feeling of contempt for Egan. Dani thought he was capable of murder. Unfortunately for me, it sure looked that way.

I reached inside my pocket to the phone again. I was in way over my head now. All of the thoughts of violence and revenge and retribution that had been swimming around inside my head were washed away in an instant. I was terrified. I just wanted to get out of there. Alive. And in one piece.

'Problems?' I asked, surprising myself by being so forward.

'Not anymore,' was O'Brady's chilling response.

CHAPTER 47

I risked a peek as we passed the storeroom from which Egan had just emerged, but I saw nothing. The door, bloody fingerprints on it, was ajar an inch or two, but I could see nothing of whatever horrors lay beyond.

We headed into O'Brady's office, and as I turned to shut the door I realised Elvis had followed us in, which only added to my anxiety.

'You said you're doing auditions,' I said. 'For a new club?'

'Yeah. You hadn't heard?' O'Brady said as he sat down at his desk. He indicated for me to sit opposite. I did.

'No, I hadn't.'

O'Brady tutted. 'That's why you'll never amount to anything, Stephens. Your mind's too closed to what's going on around you. It's been all over the local press. The biggest, most exclusive dancing club in the West Midlands.'

'I don't get much time to read the papers.'

''Course not. Too busy being an everyday gom.'

'A what?'

'An idiot. A fool. That's what you are. You don't get anything in life without working yer arse off. That's why you've got nothing. You're lazy.'

'I've got a decent job. A nice house,' I said, my blunt, defensive tone completely at odds with how I was feeling. 'Wife, kids too. I may not be a wannabe business mogul like you, but I'm happy with my lot.'

'Job? You're suspended. Ah, did you think I wouldn't know about that? I know people. I talk to people. Your house? It's all on debt. Your wife? She hates your guts, I heard, has thrown you out.

Shame, she's a pretty lady that one. She'll not be on her own for long.'

I clenched my fists but didn't rise to the challenge. For whatever reason, O'Brady was trying to rile me and I had to try to stay on track. I held O'Brady's stare but didn't say a word. After a few moments he smiled and looked away.

'Business mogul?' O'Brady said. 'That's quite a compliment actually. People talk about the luck o' the Irish, but I got here through hard work and nothing else.'

'You've certainly done well for yourself.'

'Quite a change for the Irishman around here since I first came, you know. Back in the seventies we ran large parts of this city. Whole areas were Irish. You'd walk into your local boozer and they'd be doing IRA collections. It was like a little home from home.'

'A lot's changed,' I said.

'Damn right. Once the Pakis came they started crowding in on us. Now it's the bleeding Poles, taking over what were our areas.'

'Well, the Irish were just immigrants too,' I countered.

O'Brady gave me a deathly stare. 'I hate that word. Anyway, that wasn't my point. It was the bombs that changed it for us.'

He was referring, I knew, to the pub bombings in central Birmingham in 1974 that killed twenty-one people and injured nearly two hundred. The IRA were widely believed to have carried out the atrocity, though they had never officially claimed responsibility.

'Before that the Irish had a lot of support in this city,' O'Brady said. 'People liked us. But the bombs changed all that. All of a sudden every Irishman was marked. We were driven out. Many went home. Others moved areas, breaking up the power we once had. Some of us stayed. I stayed. I saw an opportunity.'

O'Brady paused and looked at me. I wasn't sure whether he wanted me to say something, congratulate him maybe. I didn't.

'My point is, I'm a businessman. I always have been. You can save all that politics nonsense. I came here to make money and that's why I'm still here now.'

'And that's why I'm here too,' I said. 'To talk business.'

'Good. You know, I'm not happy with you playing me, stringing me along. So this is your last chance. Tell me what you're going to do for me.'

The door behind me opened and in walked Egan. My gaze fell down to his arms, which he'd done a lazy job of cleaning. Although they were now dry, they were still stained red. I felt a surge of bile in my throat as I thought about just what barbarity lay in that storeroom.

'You're done?' O'Brady queried.

'The others are finishing off. I thought you might want me in here. To help out.'

Egan glared over at me and I quickly looked away, back at O'Brady.

I shuffled in my seat. My thoughts were all over the place. All of the prep that I'd gone through with Jackson and Marsh and my sister seemed so distant, and irreconcilable with the position in which I found myself.

I had to do something. Ultimately I reacted on pure survival instinct. Fuck the sting operation. I just wanted to get out of there alive.

'The thing is,' I said, 'the situation's changed a bit since we last spoke.'

O'Brady raised an eyebrow, a look of disgust on his face.

'Changed how?'

With my heart drumming in my chest, I reached into my pocket and took out the Blackberry and put it down on O'Brady's desk.

'What's that?' O'Brady said, his tone edgy, nervous. Rare for him.

'It's a phone.'

'I can see that. But what's the fecking point you're trying to make?'

'It's a bugged phone.'

O'Brady stared at me. I could tell he was raging. 'Bugged? Bugged by who?'

'The police,' I said, my gaze fixed on O'Brady. 'They're listening to this conversation right now.'

There was absolute silence for a few seconds.

'The police?' Brady said, looking somewhat dumbstruck.

'Yeah.'

'And why would the police be listening in to our conversation on your phone?'

'Because I'm working for them.'

CHAPTER 48

Everyone in the room held their breath as they waited for O'Brady to respond. Elvis and Egan both moved forward and crowded around the desk. Their unwavering focus was on the inanimate object that lay there, as though they were waiting for the phone to perform some sort of magic trick.

O'Brady said nothing, but he indicated frantically to Elvis to go outside. Elvis shot off. I guessed he'd been sent to gather some of the other goons and go and see whether there was any heat outside the club.

O'Brady, Egan and I sat in silence for a minute. I wondered what the police's response would be. Would the standby units spring an attack and come crashing into the club? Or would they scarper? Perhaps they would just remain in place while they waited to see what would develop.

When Elvis returned less than a minute later, his face ashen, he simply nodded at O'Brady. I took that to mean he'd spotted at least one of the unmarked vehicles. In a way, that gave me a little comfort. While I would have much preferred an unlikely rescue mission, I knew it was the last thing the police would do. They had no right to barge into the club when they as yet had no evidence that anything was untoward. But at least they were still somewhere out there.

Would that be enough to stop O'Brady killing me?

O'Brady signalled for me to get up and I did. He followed suit. He indicated to Elvis and the phone, and then drew a finger across his neck, which made me wince. Elvis nodded and picked up the phone, then hurried away out of sight.

O'Brady nodded to me and walked out of the office, turning right to head to the fire exit. He pushed down on the release bar and flung the door open. It swung one hundred and eighty degrees and crashed against the wall before springing back and almost taking me out.

Egan and two other men, who'd come scuttling down the corridor after us, followed us outside. O'Brady stopped when he was a few metres away from the club building, near to the barbed-wire-topped wall that ran along the perimeter of the yard. He turned to face me.

'Anything else on you?' he asked.

'No,' I said.

He signalled to his men. One of them grabbed me from behind. The other patted me down, then stripped off my clothes, checking in pockets and creases for any sign of other phones or bugging equipment.

Within seconds I was left standing in the cool air in nothing but my boxer shorts. I was shaking violently, though it wasn't from cold. It was from fear.

But surely O'Brady wouldn't attack me there, in the yard, knowing the police were nearby and without first knowing my explanation? At least I hoped that was true. It was the only basis for me having come clean.

When the goon was satisfied, he picked up the pile of clothes and looked to O'Brady for further instruction.

'Nothing?' O'Brady questioned. The man shook his head. 'Fine. Take the stuff inside.'

O'Brady looked me over with contempt. I could tell his mind was buzzing. Mine was too. Of all the stupid, dangerous things I'd ever done in my life, this definitely came out on top.

'Inside,' O'Brady said to Egan.

Before I knew it Mickey Egan had seized hold of me and he began dragging me back toward the club, my heels scraping painfully across the tarmac. He hauled me into the office and shoved me down onto the chair. His thick arm wrapped around my neck, choking me and pinning me in place.

O'Brady came into the room and walked around in front of me. There was a sinister look on his face. But I could also see that he was deep in thought. He didn't know quite how to react to the situation.

He nodded to someone behind that I couldn't see, then turned his attention back on me.

'Talk to me,' O'Brady said.

It was unusual to see him so guarded with his words. Just moments before he'd been spouting off, and now he could barely string three words together.

Egan released his grip on me just enough to let me speak, though my voice still sounded choked and hoarse.

'The police approached me. It wasn't my fault. There was nothing I could do.'

O'Brady glared at me for a good while. I wondered what he was thinking. Could he see the walls caving in on him or was he only pondering violence?

'What have you told the police?'

'Some things,' I said vaguely. If O'Brady was going to be tight lipped then it was only right that I did the same. Blurting out details of what I'd told the police would likely frighten him and make him even more lethal. 'Not everything.'

'Some things?'

'They can't hear this conversation now,' I said. 'You have to believe me on that. The phone was the bug.'

'You're sure about that?'

'Yes!'

Just then Elvis came back into sight. He handed something to O'Brady. Something small, metallic. Shiny.

Cable-cutters.

'We're going to play a little game,' O'Brady said with menace. He moved over to me and leaned down. 'It's called twenty questions. You know how it works?'

'Please! Don't do this.'

'Each question is a chance for you to tell me the truth. You give me an answer I don't like …'

O'Brady held up the cutters and brought the handles together. The blades slid over each other with an ominous scraping sound. A wave of nausea ran through me.

'You don't have to do this!' I cried out.

'First question,' O'Brady said, moving closer. Elvis kneeled down next to him and pinned my wrists to the chair arms. No matter how much I squirmed and struggled, there was no chance of me fighting him and Egan off. 'What did you tell the police about me?'

'What? … I …' I stammered, trying to think of what to say. It wasn't that I intended to hold back, just that the question was so open I really didn't know where to start.

'Not good enough,' O'Brady said.

He took the forefinger of my left hand in his grip and opened the blades of the cutters. He moved them over my finger, right down at the knuckle.

'No!' I screamed. 'Wait. No. Please.'

O'Brady looked up at me. The cutters were in position. The blades were already nicking my skin and I could feel blood dripping down.

'The reason I told you,' I said, 'is that the police have someone on the inside.'

O'Brady squinted. He held firm with the cutters.

'Surveillance,' I said. 'Not me. They've got surveillance on you. I don't know for how long. Maybe in the club too. An inside man.'

O'Brady's face changed. He moved the cutters away from my hand and I let out a long sigh of relief. Though I knew I was far from in the clear. I hadn't quashed any of O'Brady's hostility toward me. I'd simply put doubt in his mind as to what the police knew.

'There's been surveillance on me for years,' O'Brady said. 'That's a way of life. It's not a problem. And in the club? No chance. I have this place swept every week. I know what I'm doing.'

O'Brady's confidence never faltered and my body slumped. But O'Brady wasn't finished.

'They can't hear what's going on in here,' he said. 'I can absolutely guarantee you that. I can do whatever I want. You can beg and scream all you want. No-one will hear you.'

I began to whimper.

'But that other thing you said – an inside man. Tell me more.'

O'Brady nodded to Egan and he finally let go of my neck. My head dropped forward and I coughed and spluttered as I tried to get my breathing under control. When I'd taken a second longer to recover than O'Brady was happy with, I felt a sharp tug on my hair. Egan lifted my head so I was eyeball to eyeball with O'Brady.

'Talk,' O'Brady said.

'I'm in a lot of shit,' I said. 'The police have enough to put me away. Or so they say.'

'For what?'

'Nothing to do with you,' I said. 'My own mess.'

'And yet you're causing problems for me.'

'They already know all about me and you. They know everything. Far too much to have come from a few foot patrols following you around the place.'

'Who is it?'

'I don't know.'

'But they did tell you there's a mole in my crew?'

'They alluded to it, yes. It's the only explanation.'

O'Brady stood tall and stepped away. He turned and put his hands on his hips. No-one in the room said a word for what seemed like an eternity.

'The police want me to help them,' I said. 'Help them put you away.'

'So why aren't you?'

'Because you terrify me,' I admitted. 'You always have done. Look at the position I'm in. The police think they have a hold over me, but that'll never take away the fear of what you might do to me. I had no choice but to agree to what they said; it was the only way to stop them locking me up. But I don't trust them. And I know they've got someone else working against you.'

O'Brady turned and looked at me. He kneeled back down and pushed his face close to mine.

'I'm going to let you go,' he whispered into my ear. 'You're right: I can't touch you in here. Not when the police know where you are, and not while there might be a rat somewhere.'

'Thank you,' I said, and I meant it.

'Don't thank me. I'm never going to forget this. I don't care how long it takes me, I'm going to make this right. As long as I'm still walking this earth, I'm going to be watching you. Waiting. I'm going to find that mole, and I'm going to kill him. And when this has all blown over, and believe me when I say that it will, I'm going to come for you too. Until that day, Ben Stephens, you're nothing but a dead man walking. Now go.'

CHAPTER 49

I was thrown out of the back exit into the street wearing only my underwear. Literally, thrown. Two men hauled me up and tossed me in the air, and I landed with a painful thump on the pavement outside, badly grazing my hip and my elbow and my shoulder. My clothes were tossed out after me and I clumsily dressed myself as tears rolled down my face.

I knew in that moment that it was the end of my life as I knew it. Given the road ahead, I knew at best I'd end up behind bars, and at worst my body would be cut into pieces and I'd be dispatched across the country.

After realising I was stranded outside the club, with no help coming for me from the police, I headed away on foot. I wandered aimlessly around the city centre as I tried to make sense of what to do next. It was gone ten p.m. when I walked into the hotel back in Sutton Coldfield.

I uttered a cursory greeting to the receptionist as I headed toward the staircase. She mumbled in return. I came to the door to my room, unlocked it and pushed it open. I entered, then turned around to close the door, but jumped in shock when a hand pushed past me and slammed the door shut.

Before I knew it my right arm had been grabbed and twisted back and upwards, behind my back, and I was thrust forward up against the door, my cheek smacking into the wood panel. I grimaced and let out a surprised shriek.

With all the thoughts that had been running through my mind of O'Brady and his death threat, it was only natural to leap to an immediate conclusion as to what was happening.

But the voice I heard speak told me otherwise.

'What the hell do you think you're playing at?' Dani hissed.

My mind relaxed just a touch on hearing her voice, but my body remained stiff as she kept me in the painful hold.

'So?'

'I'm sorry,' I said through gritted teeth.

'Jackson wants to throw you straight into a cell. He's not the kind of man to piss about with. With everything you've told us about you and O'Brady, I'm not sure I'm that far away from agreeing with him. You're really determined to throw your life away, aren't you?'

'You're hurting me,' I said, trying to squirm out of the hold, or at least reduce the pressure. It felt like my arm was about to snap.

I could well imagine Dani was loving the moment. She was already superior to me in almost every facet of life, but I'd always at least been bigger and – I believed – stronger than her. Yet here I was entirely at her mercy, her unrelenting grip giving me no room for manoeuvre.

Eventually Dani let go and shoved me painfully in the back. I winced again and immediately clutched my sore arm. I turned to Dani, who was glaring at me.

'It was the only way,' I said to her.

'The only way to what? You're going to have to explain that one to me. I've just spent the best part of two hours getting Jackson to climb down off the wall. He wants blood. Your blood. If it wasn't for me, you'd be locked up already. I've saved you once again.'

'It's not what you think. I just … in the club, I couldn't go through with it. There's no way O'Brady was going to just open up to me and give you what you need.'

'You were told that. Jackson and Marsh made it clear that it could take time.'

'And every time I went in there I would have been putting myself on the line.'

'It was what you were offered. What you agreed to. You're not in a position to make up the rules here.'

'I know that. But sitting in that club, it just became too real. I was scared. Do you know what I saw today? His man, Mickey Egan, arms covered in blood.'

'Whose blood?'

'I don't know! That's not the point. But these are mad men. O'Brady was going to start cutting my fingers off with a set of fucking cutters! Come on, Dani.'

I saw her expression change slightly but she was still angry.

'I hear what you're saying,' she said, 'but we need real, tangible evidence. That was the whole point of the bug, to get that evidence. Not just for O'Brady, but maybe for Egan too. You want to get him, don't you? If he really is the man who killed Alice?'

'Of course I do! But I'm just not sure … I can.'

'That's simply not good enough, Ben.'

'And what about your inside man?' I said.

Dani glared at me but didn't respond.

'I know there is one. There has to be. I just don't know who.'

Still Dani didn't say a word. The look on her face was answer enough.

'O'Brady's going to find who it is,' I said. 'He's going to kill him. You need to get your man out, whoever he is.'

'You let me handle that.'

'Who is it?'

'I can't tell you.'

'Why not? How do you expect me to help if I don't know half of what's going on? The same with Alice and Hayley Lewis. I know you're not telling me everything.'

'Telling you won't help you.'

'How do you know? I know more about O'Brady than you ever will. I can still help you to catch him. Maybe Egan too.'

'I don't see how.'

'If you want to catch O'Brady in the act, this is your golden opportunity. You need to up your surveillance. Pull all the strings you can. I know O'Brady. He's going to do everything to find your man. This could be your chance.'

'You want us to catch O'Brady in the act of doing what? Killing our informant?'

The scathing way in which Dani spoke riled me, but I held it in.

'If you stay close, it won't come to that,' I said. 'And you might get more. O'Brady hates my guts, but I can still be useful to him. If I can get back on the inside, plead with him that I'll keep him informed of the police's operation, who knows what I'll find?'

'You think O'Brady will ever trust you again?' Dani said.

'Who knows? Maybe. Probably not. If I had something useful to give him, it might still happen. I could feed him disinformation. Help you snare him while he tries to track down your guy.'

'You don't get to decide what we do,' Dani said. 'You're a witness only because we agreed to it. You've admitted to being complicit in his activities. You do what we tell you, or there's nobody to protect you.'

'Fine. It was just a thought. I'm trying to help.'

'You're doing a pretty crappy job so far.'

'Just do your job, Dani. This is your chance to catch O'Brady at his worst.'

Dani huffed and took a few moments to think. When she next spoke her voice was calmer, as though she was coming around to what I'd said. Or at the least she was resigned to the fact that, with me having blown the previous plan, it was the only option currently available.

'Maybe,' she said. 'Maybe it is an opportunity. I just hope we can stop him before it's too late.'

CHAPTER 50

'Did Dani ever tell you what crimes the police believed O'Brady had committed?' she asked.

'No. They would only ever talk in open-ended terms to me. Extortion, fraud, corruption, money-laundering. They gave me few specific details. Maybe they didn't trust me enough.'

'How about violent crimes? Murder? You suggested how scared you were of O'Brady – had you ever witnessed firsthand that he was capable of such an act?'

'Murder? No, I'd never witnessed that. Did I believe he was capable of it? Yes. Maybe not always, maybe not in the early days.'

'So when you first went to see O'Brady, when you wanted him to beat up Craig Fletcher, you didn't then see someone capable of killing?'

'I'm not sure what you're getting at.'

'I'm just trying to understand your relationship with him. What you saw in him, and whether that perception changed over time. How you came to be so fearful of him.'

'I never liked O'Brady. I never respected him or looked up to him or anything like that. And if I'd thought O'Brady was a psychotic killer, I'd never have approached him. When I first met him, I thought he was a thug, a gang leader.'

'And did that perception change?'

'I guess so. Over the years I heard things. I saw things too. O'Brady was capable of violence. I mean, just look at the times he'd had me beaten up.'

'And murder?'

'I never saw him kill anyone, but I heard that he had. O'Brady was definitely changing. He seemed more dangerous.'

'Can you explain that?'

'The police, the sting operation they wanted me to be involved in, that put me in a dangerous position with O'Brady. Then there was the other

informant, the inside man I was sure the police had. O'Brady could tell his days were numbered. He was becoming more deadly, almost desperate, out of control. I think that was why I was so scared.'

'So when O'Brady made the threat to you, that one day he would come for you, you believed that?'

'Absolutely.'

'That day in the club, did you ever find out what Egan had been doing? Why he had blood covering his arms?'

'No. But if you ask me the same question for Egan, did I think he was capable of murder, the answer is yes.'

'But you never saw him —'

'I didn't need to see him doing it to know what he was capable of.'

'After Dani confronted you in your hotel, what happened next?'

The next few days were a struggle. I didn't feel safe anymore. The police refused me any kind of protection, said they had no direct evidence that there was a threat to my wellbeing. O'Brady's threat was simply my word, which they didn't feel was sufficiently reliable, given form.'

'So what did you do?'

'Nothing for two or three days. I holed up in my hotel. I didn't know what to do. I wanted to see my children, I wanted to see Cara, but ... it's hard to explain, it felt like my life was over.'

'Were you in contact with O'Brady at all during those days?'

'No. I was in contact with Dani and Marsh — we were trying to figure out a way to get me back on the inside with O'Brady so they could get what they needed. They said it was the only way to stop him. We all had ideas, but the issue was trying to find something that wouldn't result in my immediate death.'

I smiled at my sarcastic words. She didn't smile back.

'But you never did?' she said. 'Find a way back in with O'Brady?'

'No. It's not like this went on for weeks or anything like that, just a couple of days.'

'And then what?'

The kids were off limits. Gemma was refusing to let me see them. I think she realised I was in serious trouble — maybe Dani had even told her some of what was happening. I knew that distancing myself from them at that point in time was probably best for all of us. Which left only one other person I wanted to see.'

'*Cara?*'

'*Yes.*'

CHAPTER 51

Eventually, despite being scared out of my skin at leaving the confines of the hotel, I bit the bullet and agreed to meet with Cara. We'd been bombarding each other with texts and I wanted to at least try to appear like a normal human being to her. We made plans to stay at her apartment that night – I didn't want to take her back to the rundown hotel that was passing for my home.

After grabbing a quick meal, we headed out past the Jewellery Quarter toward Hockley, to a bar Cara had recommended.

'So where are we going?' I asked as we ambled by a gleaming glass block of new-build apartments, one of many in the redeveloped area.

'It's supposed to be really cool,' she said. 'I used to go there all the time when I first moved over from Ireland. My uncle owned it. I worked there on and off too. Just helping out.'

I raised an eyebrow. I'd noticed a passing unease with her a few times during our dates. Even though her marriage was all but over – just waiting for a signature on a piece of paper, as was mine – I still sensed that she was wary of who might be watching us, people who knew her from her old life. And I guess I was exactly the same. I hadn't told anyone about my relationship with Cara.

It wasn't a surprise, then, when Cara had suggested we head to a bar that was out of the main city centre and further from where she lived. But a place that was owned by her uncle? That went against the grain.

'So this place is kind of a home from home for you then?' I said. 'You'll know all the regulars.'

'I wouldn't think so,' she said. 'This area is completely different now. It was just a down-to-earth pub back then. Full of Irish. Just a drinkers' pub. My uncle sold it and moved back home a few years ago when my aunt died. I haven't been back to it since, but I heard it got bought out recently and it's supposed to be really busy again. It's all different, though. It's some trendy lounge bar now, or whatever they call them.'

'Yeah, going for a night out was certainly a lot simpler when the two choices were pub and club.'

And she was right about the pub – it certainly wasn't an old local anymore. Although there was a decent selection of real ales on the taps, the modernist interior with mood lighting, bare brick and swathes of oak took away any sense of what it might have once been.

The clientele, largely twenty-something hipsters with carefully coiffed hair, tanned skin and designer clothes – both men and women alike – perfectly complemented the flash interior. What was most eye-opening, though, was the prices.

'Four ninety-five for a pint!' I choked when the barman handed me my paltry change. He just shrugged. I turned to Cara and handed her the glass of wine that had cost nearly twice as much again.

Cara rolled her eyes at me. 'Yeah, but I'm worth it.'

'I'll remind you of that later,' I said.

With all the tables and chairs taken we perched in a small alcove and steadily worked our way through a couple of rounds of drinks as we people-watched, chatted and flirted. I could feel Cara becoming more loose and easy with me as time wore on, and as the expensive alcohol worked its way through my veins, my fiery lust for Cara began to grow.

'Why did you come here?' I asked.

'This bar?'

'No, I meant why did you leave Ireland?'

'No reason in particular. I love it back home but I wanted to try something different. My brother had moved to London and wouldn't stop raving about it. I wanted to get out there too, live somewhere new, but I didn't want to follow directly in his footsteps. My aunt and uncle lived here and were happy to put me up while I looked for work. I'm not sure I ever intended to stay so long but I loved it. And then I met Dean.'

'And the rest is history,' I added.

'Yeah,' Cara said, before letting out a long sigh.

We both went quiet for a few moments and for the first time in the evening there was a genuine awkwardness between the two of us. I was trying to think of something funny to say, a quirky remark to get her mind back on track, but as I looked away from her, over to the other side of the bar, a familiar face caught my attention.

Shit.

I quickly looked away and down at my drink.

'Is something wrong?' Cara asked.

I smiled and shook my head. 'No, nothing.'

Cara turned to where I had been looking. I looked over again. It was a crowded bar, but all of a sudden everything around me became a blur. Except, that is, for the hard and ugly face of Mickey Egan. His being there surely wasn't a coincidence.

I grabbed Cara's arm to pull her attention back to me. Just as I did so, Egan's stare fixed on me and I froze.

'Who is it?' Cara asked, the anxious look on her face surely mirroring mine.

'Nobody,' I said.

'The bald guy, with the wonky nose? That's who you were looking at?' she said. She quickly turned her head to look over again and then back at me. 'The one who's now staring over at us? Both him and his buddy, in fact.'

I cursed, and as much as I wanted to resist, I just couldn't help but take another split-second glance. Sure enough, the man Egan was with, who'd had his back to me before, had now turned too. Dani Coonan. Another of the O'Brady clan.

'You know them?' Cara queried.

'Yeah.'

'What's the big deal?' she said, sounding way more relaxed than I was. 'Are you ashamed to be out with me or something?'

'No, no, it's not that. They're not friends. Far from it.'

'Then why is it an issue?'

'I think we should probably go,' I said.

'Seriously? What's the matter with you? Who are they?'

'I'll explain later. Come on, we really should go. Let's get back to yours. I've got a busy night planned for you.'

I tried to give Cara a relaxed, playful look, but I could tell from her response that I hadn't really pulled it off. Seeing Egan and Coonan, their dark scowls when they registered me, had shaken me.

Even if bumping into them really was just by chance, I was absolutely certain that following my antics at the Full Spread I was a marked man one way or another. Unless something gave, O'Brady would only tolerate my existence as long as he was still looking for his mole. And even if I really did have some breathing space, the last thing I wanted was to be running into his goons in the meantime. O'Brady would be punishing each and every one of them as he rattled through the ranks to find the informant. I was likely about as popular as a floating turd.

I looked over at the two men one more time, then took hold of Cara's hand. 'Please?'

She looked at me quizzically but relented, and we moved away from our spot. I chaperoned her out into the street, managing to refrain from looking over at Egan and Coonan as we went.

Once outside, we set off back toward the city at pace. Cara struggled to keep up with me as she hobbled along on her three-inch heels. We'd made it only a few yards when I heard a booming voice behind me.

'Stephens!'

It was Egan. And he did not sound happy.

CHAPTER 52

'Stephens, you piece of shit! Stop right there.'

Of course I didn't. I just kept going, though I could sense that Cara was falling behind me. I half-turned and slowed my pace just a little to let her catch up, then grabbed her arm and pulled her along with me. As I was turned I spotted Coonan and Egan about twenty yards behind. They were running.

'Fuck,' I uttered.

'What the hell is going on?' Cara pleaded.

I didn't answer. I didn't know what to say. We just had to get away from them. I knew if I went into an all-out run, I could lose those two lumps. But what about Cara? I assumed Egan and Coonan had no idea who she was, so they may well ignore her and carry on after me. But I couldn't just leave her and take that risk.

I couldn't. Could I?

I was still debating the option when a sharp tug on my arm brought me to an abrupt stop. I turned and looked down and saw Cara crumpled on the ground. I tried to haul her up, but she whipped her arm away and cradled her ankle. I saw that the heel of her shoe had snapped. She shouted out in pain as she tried to stand.

It was now or never. I looked back toward Egan and Coonan, just ten yards away.

'Cara, come on. We have to go.'

'Go where? Why?'

If I was going to run, leave her there, I had only a couple of seconds left to do it.

'Please,' I begged, holding out my hand to her.

I looked at Cara and noticed the tears in her eyes, then looked back up at Egan and Coonan.

I wanted to leave her. But I couldn't.

A second later, the choice was taken away from me.

'What do you want?' I said to Egan when he was almost within touching distance, my hands up in surrender.

He took no notice. Without breaking stride, Egan bundled into me and shoved me hard. I stumbled backward, lost my footing and tumbled to the ground. My elbow and then the back of my head smacked painfully on the pavement, taking the brunt of the fall. I cringed in pain and my vision spun wildly. Before I knew it, Coonan had grabbed me and was hauling me back to my feet.

'What did you do that for?!' Cara screamed at Egan.

Her feisty character was one of the things that attracted me to her. She was a fighter and I loved that. But on this occasion she really should have kept her mouth shut. She should have taken the opportunity to get out of there. And what she did next only confirmed her fate.

Egan had his back to her when she launched herself toward him. She lashed out with her fists, smacking him on his back, his neck and his head. Egan barely flinched. He was shorter than me, I guessed five nine or five ten, but he was thick and muscular and probably more than twice the weight of Cara. He turned around and grabbed both of her wrists, then arched his head back before delivering a head-butt right onto the crown of Cara's nose.

Blood immediately streamed down Cara's face and onto the ground. The blow had the desired effect of subduing her attack. Luckily for her, Egan hadn't put his all into butt. If he had, it would have been game over for Cara right there and then.

'Up there,' Egan said to Coonan, pointing over toward an alley that led behind the terraced buildings of the main street we were on.

'Leave her out of this,' I pleaded. 'Please. Just let her go.'

Neither of them responded.

Coonan began to pull me. I tried to resist, digging my heels into the ground. I took a weak swipe at him with my free arm. It caught Coonan on the back of the head. He stopped and turned, snarling, and delivered a fist to my stomach that caused me to double over in pain.

Without giving me a second to recover, Coonan then twisted my arm around behind my back until the shoulder and elbow joints were strained to bursting. He began to pull me toward the alleyway.

Egan dragged Cara along too by the arms. She cried and called out, but it was no use. We were both helpless.

They pulled us along the deserted street and then down into the dingy alley. Industrial waste bins lined one side and the stench of rotten food came and went as we were taken down into the bowels of the alley.

'Here,' Egan said, letting go of Cara and pushing her away from him. She stumbled into the brick wall behind her. Coonan released his grip on me and flung me toward Cara.

I grabbed her. Held her. Her head was bowed and she was sobbing. I looked over at Egan and Coonan and saw hatred in their eyes, but also twisted amusement at the sight that lay before them.

'Leave her out of this,' I said to them. 'Whatever this is about, she's got nothing to do with it.'

'She's with you,' Egan said, a wicked smile on his face. 'She's part of this.'

I let go of Cara and moved in front of her, trying to shield her from the two thugs. It was one last show of strength, though really I knew I had little chance of fighting back against whatever attack was coming.

'Does O'Brady know about this?' I queried, my tone defiant.

'O'Brady?' Coonan scoffed. 'You think he gives a shit about you?'

'No, maybe not me personally. But he might not be happy if you beat up his business partner. You could lose him a lot of money.'

'O'Brady knows we're here,' Egan said. 'He sent us to follow you.'

'You've caused a lot of trouble for a lot of people with your lies,' Coonan snarled. 'O'Brady's giving everyone grief because of you. There's no informant. Just you. The truth will come out sooner or later.'

'There is! I swear there is. I'll help you find who it is.'

'No chance,' Egan said. 'It's time for a little payback.'

He took a step forward. I readied myself. I wasn't going down without a fight.

'Stop!' Cara screamed. And for just a second she had everyone's attention. 'This is crazy. Whatever you're about to do, just think about it.'

'You shouldn't be with him,' Egan spat. 'You're one of us.'

'What are you talking about?'

'You're one of us,' Coonan said. 'Irish. You should stick with your own.'

Something inside me snapped.

I launched myself at Coonan, catching him completely by surprise. I smacked into him and we collapsed to the ground.

My mind took me back to the attack on Dove, where I'd floored my foe in much the same way and then happily delivered blow after blow, completely in charge.

For just a second I thought I had the better of Coonan too. But although I'd had the element of surprise, Coonan was quite a different prospect.

As I wrestled for control, Coonan spun around, out of the hold, and somehow got back on top, wrapped an arm around my neck and squeezed it like a vice. I was lying flat, Coonan pinning me down with his weight. I clawed at him, trying to escape the hold. It was no use.

Coonan delivered a fist to my nose with his free hand. The shockwave spiralled out across my whole body as my head went into a daze.

Dark Fragments

I heard Cara screaming. The distant sound brought a sliver of clarity back. Coonan laughed and pulled me around to face her.

She was grappling with Egan, lashing out at him again with everything she had. At first Egan took it in his stride, an arrogant look on his face. But Cara's attack was relentless. She was fighting with pure desperation.

Egan's demeanour soon turned. He reached into his jacket and pulled out a long knife. The blade glistened even in the dull light. When he thrust it up onto Cara's neck, her hopeless fight suddenly waned.

'Yeah, that's right,' he said. 'Nothing like cold, hard steel to show who's in charge.'

'Let her go!' I shouted. Egan didn't flinch.

Before I knew it Coonan had thumped me twice, hard, in the kidneys. The searing pain in my sides caused my whole body to stiffen.

Egan leaned in close to Cara. 'I said you shouldn't be with someone like him,' he whispered. 'Just look at the mess he's got you into.'

Cara's eyes met mine. I didn't know what to do or say.

'Please,' was the only word I managed. I wasn't even sure to whom it was directed.

Perhaps I should have made sure it was to Cara. Maybe it would have prevented what happened next. She turned to face Egan, pursed her lips and spat in his face.

The look of shock and disgust on Egan's face ... it was the last show of strength he would allow her.

Egan punched Cara hard in the face. Her head snapped back. The blow split her lip to add to her already bloodied nose. He smacked his knee into her stomach twice in quick succession. Cara doubled over.

With her head still bowed, Egan thrust an uppercut onto her jaw. Cara's eyes rolled and her head wobbled loosely as Egan spun her around and pinned her up against the wall.

'No!' I shouted out.

I tried to buck and squirm, tried to throw Coonan off, but it was no use. Every time I found the strength to fight back, I was quickly subdued by Coonan's fist or by the tightening of his vice-like grip around my neck.

Cara began screaming and sobbing as Egan lifted her skirt and used the knife to snip off her lacy knickers. He then sliced through her blouse, before pinning her head against the wall using the knuckle of his fist, which he ground into her neck.

With his other hand Egan clumsily undid his trousers, then he thrust himself toward Cara, who let out a harrowing scream. I tried once more to fight back, but there was nothing I could do.

I shut my eyes and willed it all to be over. Willed Egan to leave her alone. To not go through with it.

My wish wasn't granted.

'You shouldn't be with him,' Egan purred into Cara's ear as he aggressively thrust his hips back and forth. 'You need a real man.'

'Jesus, Mickey,' Coonan said, revulsion in his voice.

'Shut it!' Egan boomed.

'Just get it over with. We need to get out of here.'

'Stop him,' I pleaded to Coonan, my voice weak. It was the only chance I had left. Coonan was the only one who could help her now. 'Please stop him.'

But no help came.

When Egan was done, he shoved Cara away from him, discarding her like a piece of filth. She fell to the ground and curled up into a ball.

Egan turned back to me. He was panting. There was wrath in his eyes but a smile covered his face.

'Let him go,' Egan said to Coonan.

Coonan hesitated, but then released his arm from around my neck and got to his feet. I moved onto my side and went to stand up. I never got the chance. Egan strode up to me, lifted his foot and drove the heel of his boot down onto my face.

Dark Fragments

A second later, I was out cold.

CHAPTER 53

I couldn't remember how I ended up in the hospital. From what I could gather I had only been unconscious for a short while before Cara had brought me around and called the police. They'd arrived in tandem with paramedics and rushed us both off to Birmingham City Hospital.

My mind had blocked from me the period from losing consciousness on the cold, hard ground of that alley and the hours that followed. Instead, the story was relayed to me by a young policeman by the name of Powell as I lay sprawled on a hospital gurney.

I wasn't seriously injured. I'd needed four stitches to a gash on the top of my head, and I had severe bruising on my torso and a concussion. I was achy, I was weak, my head was a mess, but I didn't want to stay there a second longer than was necessary.

'Can I see her?' I said to Powell, who was sitting on a chair next to my bed.

'I'm not sure,' he said. 'It's not down to me. She was worse off than you. I understand they've admitted her to a ward. Internal bleeding I think I heard a nurse say.'

I cringed at his words. At knowing that Cara was suffering. I had to see her.

'Am I free to go then?'

'I don't think that's the best idea, do you?'

Powell had already spent the best part of two hours getting a download from me of the attack. I knew I'd have to make a more formal statement at some point, but I couldn't see any reason I needed to stay in the hospital any longer.

'I'm not staying here if I don't need to,' I said. I propped myself up in the bed and then groggily got to my feet. I'd been given painkillers as well as a mild sedative that hadn't yet worn off and my body felt heavy and somewhat detached.

'Mr Stephens, I don't think this is a good idea,' Powell said, getting to his feet and looking flustered.

I guessed he was probably in his early twenties, and I sensed a naivety and general lack of confidence about the situation he found himself in. He'd clearly been given orders to stay with me and find out what I knew, but it seemed his instructions hadn't stretched much further than that. He was unsure what to do now that I wasn't going along with his simple plan.

'You can't make me stay here,' I said, my tone firm but not confrontational. 'I've given you what you need. If you need another statement, I'll come down to the station, but right now I want to go and see Cara. And then I want to go home.'

'I don't know … but –'

I didn't wait for another response. I headed out, moving toward the A&E reception, dragging my leaden legs as best I could. I barely received a glance from the many busy nurses scuttling about the place. They'd probably only realise I was gone in a few hours when it was time to fill out their next set of checklists.

As I reached the reception I looked around to see whether Powell was following me out and was pleased there was no sign of him. I moved up to the receptionist's desk and was greeted with an awkward smile from the middle-aged woman on the other side.

'Do you know where Cara Andrews has been taken?' I asked. 'She was brought in here a few hours ago but I think she's been taken to a ward.'

The receptionist gave me a hesitant look and then typed away on her computer.

'Are you family?' she asked.

'I'm her husband.'

The receptionist looked up and took a moment too long to scan my battered face before she spoke.

'Ward three, down the corridor,' she said, pointing off to the left, away from the A&E assessment area from where I'd come.

'Thank you,' I said.

I headed toward the ward, again checking around me for Powell. I was so on edge. I wanted to see Cara, but I didn't know what she had told the police of the attack. If she was lucid enough, they were sure to have questioned her, and she had no reason not to tell the police that the attack wasn't random, which is what I had alluded to with Powell, and that I'd known the attackers. I didn't want that. I didn't want the police tracking down Coonan and Egan before I did.

I was a little surprised Dani hadn't been there at the hospital to greet me – or reprimand me more like. Perhaps because it was the middle of the night the word hadn't yet spread that her brother had been attacked by members of O'Brady's gang. That was fine by me. I didn't need Dani's help for what was to come.

I found the ward. The double-doors that led into it were security-locked. I pressed the button for the intercom and waited. When the call was answered I again said I was Cara's husband and a second later the door clicked unlocked. I walked in and saw a gaggle of hospital workers, trainees I assumed, working their way toward me with a casually dressed consultant in front. The timing was perfect and meant I was able to coolly walk past the reception desk at the same time they did without any further questioning from the receptionist.

As I walked further down the corridor it wasn't too hard to figure out which room Cara was in. There was a police officer stationed outside, sitting on a chair with her head resting against the wall.

As I approached she straightened up and got to her feet.

'You?' she said, a look of incredulity on her face.

'Me?' I said, bemused.

I quickly realised she was either one of the officers who had been on the scene or she had seen me in the hospital already.

'You've been discharged?' she asked. 'Where's Powell?'

I ignored both questions. She wouldn't have liked the answers. 'I need to speak to Cara.'

'She's resting.'

I looked through the open doorway and spotted Cara lying on the bed. White sheets were draped over her body and a cannula was attached to her hand. Her eyes were shut and her face was ghostly white, except for her fat, purple bottom lip and her nose, which had turned almost black with bruising.

'I didn't catch your name?' I said, trying to sound relaxed and in control.

'It's PC Trent.'

'Is she okay?'

'I'm not a doctor, but I've been led to believe she should be fine. Eventually.'

'I really need to speak to her.'

'She's sedated. I'm not sure you can.'

I stared at Cara. The noise from my conversation with Trent was making her stir. She shuffled and murmured and then slowly opened her eyes.

'Please?' I said.

'Her husband is here,' Trent said. 'I'm really not sure you should be.'

I looked into the officer's eyes but said nothing. I could see she didn't trust me. I couldn't be sure what she knew of the story of the attack, of my relationship with Cara, but whatever she knew, it was clear I wasn't welcome.

It riled me, though, that she assumed Cara's husband was more welcome than I was. Cara was only still married because he refused to sign his divorce papers.

Just as I was about to turn to leave, Cara came to. She sat up in the bed, rubbing her eyes. She looked over and her gaze caught mine. I looked back at her pleadingly. My heart melted to see her so scared and hurt.

'I think you should go,' Trent said to me, holding out an arm and blocking my way into the room.

'Cara. Please?' I said.

I saw a tear escape from her eye. 'Go away,' she said, beginning to sob. 'Just leave me alone.'

'No. We have to talk. I'm so sorry for what happened, but we have to talk.'

'No!' she shouted. 'No, Ben. Not now. Not ever. I never want to see you again.'

'You heard her,' the officer said.

'You can't mean that?' I said, desperation in my voice.

I pushed Trent's arm out of the way and went to move into the room. Trent grabbed me, twisted my arm into a hammerlock and pushed me up against the wall – a move much like the one Dani had delivered not too long ago. I grimaced in pain.

'She said she doesn't want to speak to you,' Trent blasted. 'And I told you already, you shouldn't be here.'

'Let go of me!'

Trent held me for a few seconds longer. I didn't try to fight back, didn't try to resist at all.

'I'm going to let go,' Trent said, 'and then you're going to walk away from here. Right?'

'Right.'

Trent let go and stepped back. I nursed my arm for a second, looking over at Cara. She'd turned away and was staring out of the window.

'I'm sorry,' I said.

She said nothing in return, didn't even acknowledge my words. There really was little more I could do. Reluctantly, I turned and walked away.

I was hurt. I hadn't expected that reaction from Cara, her stock dismissal of me. And I was angry. With her. With O'Brady. With Egan and Coonan. And, for some unclear reason, with the person I saw entering the ward as I headed down the corridor.

I'd never met him before but somehow I knew who he was. And vice versa, he seemed to clock me.

Our eyes met as he stepped through the ward doors and he stopped in his tracks, his face full of disdain. He opened his mouth to speak to me, but I brushed past him out through the doors.

'Hey, I'm not finished with you!' he shouted, scurrying after me.

He pulled on my shoulder, spinning me around to face him. When he saw my snarling face, it knocked him right back down again.

'Stay away from my wife,' he said, only half as confident as he had been a second before.

'Or what?'

'Or nothing. Just do it.'

'She's the only one who gets to decide,' I said. I went to move away but Dean Andrews grabbed my arm again.

'She doesn't want you,' Andrews said. 'Get that into your thick head.'

Well, I could have argued that point all day long. As it was, the emotion of the situation got the better of me. I lunged for Andrews, grabbed him by the throat and pushed him backward against the wall.

'Touch me again and it'll be the last thing you ever do,' I growled.

Andrews squirmed, trying to break free, my own strength surprising both of us.

'Just leave her alone,' he wheezed.

I held the grip tight on his neck and the look of panic in Andrews' eyes began to grow. But what was I going to do – choke him to death right there in the hospital? What would that achieve?

Reason got the better of me and I let go.

Andrews slumped down. I turned and began to walk away again. I just wanted to leave that place. But Andrews hadn't finished. He still had plenty of salt and he wasn't going to stop until he'd rubbed it all into my open wounds.

'I knew she was having an affair,' Andrews called out to me. His words had the desired effect and I stopped again, though I didn't turn to face him. 'I knew it. She was so happy all of a sudden. Her old self again. In a strange way I was happy for her. I love her. But with someone like you? Look at you. You're a loser.'

I clenched my fists. I wanted to turn back around and finish the weasel off, but I had to stay strong.

I took a step further away, but Andrews just wouldn't let up. He was egging me on. Pushing for a reaction.

'She was pregnant,' he said. His words once again stopped me in my tracks. 'It was mine.'

I turned to face him, my heart in my mouth. I was stunned by the revelation. And confused. And saddened. Still I said nothing.

'Can you believe that?' he said. 'We'd been trying for so long. It tore us apart. We'd split up because of it. She wanted to move on. She was just so desperate to have children.'

I closed my eyes, imagining her pain.

'But I would never give up on her,' Andrews said. 'I would chase her forever. I've always believed in her. In us. All she ever wanted was kids. She was pregnant when she was attacked. She didn't even know. The doctors only found out when they were examining her. She's lost it. She's lost our baby because of *you*.'

I stared at Andrews. I wanted to lash out at him, but it wouldn't have been right. I'd never met the man before, but I'd already hurt him so much. Cara too. And what had happened to her … I would never forgive myself.

I spotted movement over Andrews' shoulder and looked past him to see Powell emerging from around the corner.

'I'm sorry,' I said. 'I'm sorry she was hurt. I really am.'

'Just stay away from her,' Andrews said. 'From her and from me.'

I said nothing more, just turned and left.

Dark Fragments

I hated myself for what had happened to Cara. I'd caused her so much agony. She was a good person. She didn't deserve that.

Her suffering wouldn't go unpunished, though. I was absolutely convinced of that.

CHAPTER 54

'You must have known that Cara would end up getting hurt?' she said.

'Beaten up and raped? I'm not sure how you could expect me to foresee that.'

'I didn't mean that. But you seeing Cara could only ever have ended in pain for her, one way or another, couldn't it? You were in so deep already with O'Brady. And the situation with you and Gemma was far from clear.'

'I know. You're right. But maybe Cara and I really could have been something. Who knows? Perhaps she would have left Andrews for good and we would have been happy together.'

'Do you really believe that? She was pregnant with his child.'

'Yeah, but they had split up. I don't know. It sounds nice, though, doesn't it? That we may have been happy together. Too nice, I guess. Like something that would never happen for me.'

'You could have broken it off, the affair with Cara. When you realised you cared for her, to stop her getting hurt.'

'But I couldn't. I wanted to see her. It was as simple as that. With Gemma gone and no prospect I could see of that ever working out, Cara was exactly what I thought I needed. I wanted to be with her.'

'But you were bringing her into a dangerous world.'

'I know. But that didn't alter the way I felt about Cara. I liked her for who she was, and I thought she felt the same.'

'So you don't think that now?'

'I'm not sure. I was surprised at how easily she was able to remove me from her life.'

'Why did that surprise you? She'd been attacked and raped because of you. She lost a baby too.'

I winced at her words. 'It surprised me because I thought Cara's feelings for me were genuine. Even when someone causes you pain, if you love them enough, you can't turn off the switch just like that.'

'Do you not think perhaps she did have feelings for you, but she had to push you away? That it was a struggle for her to do so, but that was the only course she could see?'

'Maybe. In a way I hope so.'

'You said she was pregnant when she was attacked.'

'That's what I was told. I knew nothing about it. Andrews said that even she hadn't known.'

'What was your reaction on finding that out?'

'I felt two things. On the one hand, I felt an intense sadness for Cara. She desperately wanted children — I can't imagine the pain she must have felt on hearing she'd lost the baby like that. And I felt for the child too, for what might have been. It wasn't my child, but it was still horrifying.'

'And what was the other thing?'

'Hatred. Possibly the purest hatred I had ever felt. I wanted blood. And I knew in that moment, walking away from Andrews in the hospital, that I was going to get it.'

CHAPTER 55

It was the middle of the night when I left the hospital and I was tired and confused. I had two missed calls and a voice message from Dani from earlier in the evening, before the attack. She wanted to speak to me about O'Brady. I could only assume that her lack of contact since then was because she still knew nothing of what had happened. That was good. I had to keep my distance from Dani, from all of them in fact. For now at least.

I'd had no calls or messages from Gemma, though. That hurt. She would surely have heard about the attack? She was my next of kin. Whatever I thought of him, Andrews had been at Cara's bedside almost immediately to be with his estranged wife. Gemma hadn't even called or texted to check on me. She was finally showing her true colours.

As was I.

Initially I headed back to the hotel in Sutton – I needed my car – but the presence of a police panda car stationed in the hotel car park quickly stopped that plan. I couldn't be sure exactly why the police were at the hotel looking for me. Perhaps it was simply a coincidence. I wasn't about to go and find out.

Instead, I headed back to the house. My Yamaha was parked in the garage. I didn't know whether anyone would be home, and even if they were, they'd probably be asleep. Either way, I wasn't planning on saying hello. I wondered whether another police car might be stationed there too. Luckily there wasn't one.

There were no lights on in the house as I approached, no signs of life at all. I opened the garage and quietly rolled my bike out onto the road. After shutting the garage door, I sat on my bike and looked up at the family home. An immense feeling of guilt and regret built up in me as I thought of all the hope there had once been when we'd first moved there as a family.

It had all been a lie, though, nothing more than a far-fetched dream. Sitting on my bike, staring up at the house, I realised with absolute certainty that the dream would never come true now.

There would be no more pretending. No more hiding who I really was. It was time to take back control.

I fired up the engine and pulled on the throttle and the bike edged forward. I meandered along the streets of Sutton, soon moving out of the town and heading east toward the M42 motorway. My mind was bubbling away, though everything around me was serene.

It took me the best part of an hour to reach the twisting country road where Callum O'Brady's luxury home was located, on the outskirts of the leafy, wealthy village of Knowle. I'd only been to his house twice before. Each of those times I had been filled with discontent over my unwelcome but necessary alliance with the man. I'd also been worried for my personal safety, as I was every time I had met with O'Brady or his cronies.

Not so this time.

I parked the bike in a lay-by about a quarter of a mile from O'Brady's house. There was no pavement, no streetlights, and the road was barely wide enough to allow two vehicles to pass. With pain coursing through my body – the painkillers I'd taken some hours ago were steadily wearing off – I kept to the overgrown verge as I walked on in the darkness. My hand nestled inside my jacket the whole way, caressing the cold, hard object that was tucked inside.

Individual properties were dotted along the road, each with extensive plots and nearly all with high hedges, walls and gates screening them from passers-by.

I came to a stop when I reached O'Brady's gates. They were shut. I remembered from my last visit that the ornate eight-foot-high iron gates were electronically secured. Redbrick walls ran along across the front of the grounds, stretching a good thirty yards either side of the gates. A small intercom box was attached to the wall. I knew also that the house had bright security spotlights, though my presence by the outer gates had not yet triggered those.

The security was about as tight as you'd expect for a rich man's home. Not impregnable by any stretch, but certainly visible and deliberate.

I looked through the gates toward the house, which was lit up with sympathetic, soft-glowing lighting that ran up the contoured driveway and around the main building. O'Brady's home was stunning. It was a big, mock-Tudor design with black-painted timber and white render interspersing the red bricks. The lighting brought out all of the property's charm, which was at complete odds with the character of its tasteless owner.

Up the driveway, parked outside the house, I counted a total of four cars. One I recognised as O'Brady's Range Rover – his pride and joy, a highly customised model that looked like an oversized boy racer's plaything rather than an off-road vehicle. The other three cars I didn't recognise, and they made me wonder whether O'Brady had company. I had assumed at least his wife would be home with him, but perhaps some of his gang was too.

As I stood contemplating at the gates my ears caught the sound of a rumbling car engine in the near distance and my heart rate automatically quickened. I moved a couple of steps to my left, toward the wall and out of the faint beams of light that were coming through the gates.

I watched as bobbing headlights came into view. I held my breath, my heart pounding, waiting to see whether the car would slow as it approached the gates, praying that it wasn't more of O'Brady's clan.

As the car approached I was lit up for the world to see in the bright beams of the headlights for all of three seconds. It felt like a lifetime. To my relief, the vehicle thundered past, the slipstream smacking me in the face as it did so. I took a moment to get my heart and breathing back under control.

When I was ready, I moved along the wall to where it abruptly came to an end at the far corner of the plot. Along the adjacent side of the property a dense tree-line marked the boundary with the adjoining farmer's field, but there was no security. The outer wall with the locked gates was as much a visual deterrent as anything else.

I traipsed through sodden undergrowth. My feet squelched and sank into a soft layer of mud with each step. When I was level with the house, I squeezed through the tree-line and then stopped on the edge of a lawn.

Lights were on in two of the downstairs windows at the front of the house. The upstairs was entirely dark. I looked at my watch, squinting in the dim light. It was nearly four a.m.

I had a choice to make. I could sit and wait for O'Brady to make an appearance. It looked like he was home, and certainly someone was up. Being a club owner, it wasn't at all unusual for O'Brady to conduct his business well into the small hours of the night. He kept dogs. Perhaps they were due a late-evening toilet break, or he a cigarette.

On the other hand, did I really want to spend the night in the cold and wet waiting for him to leave the house? I could just walk right up to the door and knock. It was the most direct approach for sure. But doing that I would have no way of knowing what I was walking into.

I kept on moving along the lawn edge until I was at the back end of the property. A minute later a figure stepped out of a door and the piercing rays of the security lights at the back of the house came on. It was O'Brady's wife.

The arc of light swept right around the side of the house. From where I was standing the whole house seemed to be surrounded in a thick white glow. I wasn't in the full beam, but if she looked in my direction, she would surely spot me.

She lit a cigarette and took several long drags. After a couple of minutes she simply stubbed the butt out, then walked back into the house.

The security lights were still on. I took the opportunity to move. I headed right up to the house and pulled to a stop alongside the back end. I crouched down and crept along the back wall.

I heard voices. Male voices. Female too. The back door was still open, I realised. My heart was pumping out of control. Part of me wanted to cut my losses and scarper. I was scared, no doubt about it. But I'd come this far. I had to see it through. I had to make O'Brady pay.

I was just two yards from the open back door. A yellow glow seeped out of the open doorway, cutting a stark contrast to the bright white security lights. I focused in on a man's voice, getting louder. I heard footsteps. I saw the shadow of a figure in the yellow light. I reached inside my jacket and grabbed the handle.

I pulled out the long knife.

I'm not sure whether what happened next was deliberate or an accident. Not that I hadn't wanted it to happen. It was the exact reason I had gone there. But it was pure momentum as much as anything else that caused the actual blow.

As I reached the doorway, Callum O'Brady emerged. We smacked into each other. The knife, held out in front of me, plunged into his stomach, right up to the edge of the handle. About six inches of sharp metal.

O'Brady gasped. He stumbled forward. His arms wrapped around me in an awkward embrace.

'You,' he said.

I pulled the knife out. O'Brady grimaced in pain. The blade was caked in thick, red blood. As was the handle. And the black leather riding glove that covered my hand.

I thrust the knife toward him again. There was a grisly slicing sound as the blade pierced his skin and cut through his flesh. O'Brady's eyes quivered. His face contorted in pain. He stared at me but said nothing.

O'Brady's weight bore down on me as his legs gave way. His arms clung to me. He was hanging on for dear life.

I took the knife out and thrust it into him one more time. Then I drew it out and stepped back and brushed O'Brady's arms off me. He fell to his knees, one hand on his midriff, the other stretched out toward me, begging for my help.

No chance. Never. Not in this lifetime.

My heart was jumping erratically in my chest. My head was spinning. I felt nauseous. It was all too much. I squeezed my eyes shut, trying to regain my focus. It did the trick, if only for a few seconds.

I looked down at O'Brady. Still staring up at me. His eyes were pleading. His mouth was open, but all that came out was a painful gargle.

His gaze never once left mine as he slowly sank to the ground.

A few moments later his body, sprawled before me, went completely still.

CHAPTER 56

I couldn't be sure that O'Brady was dead. I was too scared to check his body. Partly for fear that he might suddenly find the strength, a desperate glimmer of hope for survival, and attack me. I was also fully aware of the ongoing noise from the house. It was only a matter of time before someone realised what had happened.

I ran back to the tree-line, up the side of the house and out into the road. Outside the property I took the plastic bag from my jacket. I stuffed in the bloody knife and the gloves I was wearing, then put the bag back into my jacket. In the cold night air, the implications of what I'd done hit me. I felt the nausea rise again and this time I couldn't fend it off. I hunched over and violently heaved up my stomach contents – the remains of my night out with Cara.

I wasn't thinking straight. I'd never done anything like this before. The attacks on Dove and the man in the club, they were one thing. But this? I'd just stabbed a man. I'd very probably killed him. Not only that, but I'd done it in such a reckless way. I immediately regretted my hastily planned attack.

I was allowed no more time for deliberation, though. As I stood hunched with my head down, waiting to see whether any more bile was about to come up, I heard a woman scream. Seconds later the front door of O'Brady's house opened. More voices. Male voices. Shouting. I looked up through the front gates toward the parked cars. Elvis. Egan. Two others.

I ran.

I ran as fast as I could back to my bike. It was less than a quarter of a mile away. Back in the day, I could have covered that distance in a little over a minute. Even if I could somehow have used adrenaline and pure desperation to accomplish that feat now, I wasn't sure it would give me enough time to get away.

I sprinted down the near-pitch-black road – the only illumination coming from the overcast night sky – doing my best to ignore the agony in my body from the beating I'd taken just hours earlier.

I heard a loud growl as the diesel engine of O'Brady's Range Rover was fired up. The noise gave me the impetus to pump my arms and legs even faster.

Seconds passed and the noise of the engine seemed to disappear. I looked around constantly, expecting to see the twin headlights piercing the darkness right behind me. Nothing.

Perhaps the electronic security gates had given me some extra time. Better still, maybe the car had headed off in the wrong direction. I willed that to be the case.

I soon realised I wasn't going to be that lucky. The roar of the engine suddenly shot through the calm night and almost knocked me off my feet. The monstrous vibrations rocked the road and sent a shudder up through my whole body. I begged myself not to look around again. I didn't want to see how close I was to being mown down.

But I just couldn't resist.

I shot my head around, a split-second move. I was surprised to see no sign of the four-by-four. But I could still hear the rumbling engine, loud to my ears.

I had no time to register any relief. As I turned back around I misplaced my foot. It sank into a ditch at the side of the road. The unexpected jolt caused me to stumble forward. I reached my hands out. I fully expected to tumble into a heap on the road. Somehow momentum or determination or sheer luck kept me on my feet.

My panicked brain was no longer thinking rationally. I looked around again. As I did, the headlights of the Range Rover finally came into view as the car hurtled around a bend in the road.

This was it. They were almost upon me.

But my bike was in sight, a little more than fifty yards ahead. A few seconds. I could make it. I had to. I fished in my pocket for the key. The clumsy movement cost me a sliver of a second.

I jumped onto the bike. Whipped on the helmet. Sank the key into the ignition. The Yamaha roared into life. I wondered whether I might actually make it.

The driver of the four-by-four must have thought the same. The Range Rover's engine whined as the driver dropped a gear and the revs peaked as he tried to eke out every last bit of acceleration. By that point the entire area around me was brilliantly lit up by the lights from the guzzling four-by-four.

I pulled the throttle hard and fast. The bike shot forward. The acceleration was so sudden and severe I almost slid right off the back. I glanced briefly in my side mirror. Objects are closer than they appear. Really? This object appeared to be up my fucking arse already. I was just grateful I had brought the Yamaha – all power and no weight – rather than my car. Immediately I shot away from the fast-moving Range Rover.

As I moved up gears the bike wobbled and I wrestled to regain control. When I finally did, I accelerated again. Only then did I look in my mirrors once more.

I saw I'd already pulled yards away from the heavy four-by-four. I pushed the bike into fourth gear. The speedometer swept past eighty. On the twisting country roads, the Range Rover was no match. I smiled as I realised I was home free.

The driver of the four-by-four had yet to figure that out, though. And that was his fatal mistake.

My bike was made for roads like that. It cornered to perfection, its weight perfectly balanced front to back and left to right. The oversized Range Rover was entirely different. Its giant engine gave it plenty of raw power, but it was heavy and ungainly.

I took a sharp corner at a little over seventy, leaning into it at a dangerously acute angle. The bike stuck to the road like glue.

When I looked in the mirror to see the Range Rover attempting the same corner at speed, it was quite a different story.

It was simple physics. With the driver realising his mistake, I could imagine him frantically pulling the steering wheel this way and that as he tried to right his wrong. Those actions only made the position worse.

The four-by-four swung viciously from left to right and back again, and then seemed to jump into the air as though it had been suddenly thrust from underneath. It rolled over once, then again. With each half-turn the roof of the car and its wheels intermittently crashed and bounced on the ground, throwing it back up into the air once more.

The car finally came to a crunching halt on its side. By that point I'd slammed on the brakes of the bike and come to a dead stop.

For a few seconds I sat motionless, debating what to do. Shouldn't I just get out of there as fast as I could? Part of me was screaming to do so. But I couldn't. I had to know who was in that car.

I had to know whether they were dead or alive.

I cut off the engine and stepped from the bike. As I walked hesitantly toward the stricken vehicle, the first thing that hit me was the noise. The hissing of the battered engine. The creaking of the crumpled metal cabin being slowly squashed under its own weight.

The blood-curdling cries.

As loud as they were, they sounded like just one man's, I realised.

The second thing that hit me was the smell. The unmistakable smell of diesel. But as I crept closer to the mangled heap, another smell hit me. At first I couldn't place it. When I was within a couple of yards of the carnage, I finally realised what it was. Blood. Even in the dull light, the patches of thick wet blood were clear.

I grimaced when I saw the first of the car's occupants. It was the driver. The Range Rover had come to a stop at an almost forty-five-degree angle with its roof and the driver's side of the car crushed into the ground. Amid the wreckage the driver's bloodied head was hanging at an unusual angle, his neck snapped.

I looked over at the front passenger. His eyes were wide open in shock, his deathly stare seemingly fixed on me. But there was no movement. No sign of life at all. A shard of metal from the frame of the windscreen had broken loose and was lodged in his chest. Spatters of blood covered his clothes and everything around him.

He was dead. No doubt about it.

I stepped cautiously around the vehicle. The great hulk of a man sitting behind the driver was unmistakable. He filled the car, making it look like a toy. Elvis. He wasn't moving. He didn't seem to be breathing. But I didn't dare get close enough to check.

Which left just one other. The one who was evidently still alive, judging by the noise coming from his lips, although his screams had by then died down to nothing more than a pained murmur.

It was Mickey Egan.

He was in the rear seat on the passenger side, hanging upside down, his head bobbing out of the smashed side window.

'Help me,' he wheezed.

I walked right up to him and inspected his bloodied and defeated face. He looked back at me, his eyes pleading. I looked in through the broken window. The seat in front of Egan had been pushed back, crushing his legs and his torso. He was wedged in position, the bones in the lower half of his body likely shattered. If he received medical attention quickly, I imagined he would probably survive the crash.

If.

I stood there for a few seconds. Maybe it was minutes, I really don't know. I was in such a daze. Egan was staring at me, trying to speak. Trying to beg for my help. I was frozen. I simply didn't know what to do.

Then something caught my attention and I frowned. The hissing noise from the engine had died down, replaced by a quiet but steady roar. The smell too was changing.

Something was burning.

I looked over at the front of the car. Sure enough, small flames were leaping up from the crumpled bonnet. With the amount of diesel and oil spilled on the road, I knew it would only be seconds before the whole chaotic scene turned into a fireball.

Ignoring Egan's desperate cries, I turned on my heel and ran for my bike, never once looking back.

CHAPTER 57

As I rode away from the scene, all of the mistakes I'd made at O'Brady's house were firing in my mind. My vomit – my DNA – was outside his house. I'd possibly left footprints through his garden. Maybe he wasn't even dead. I could only hope that the fire would burn away any evidence of me being at the crash scene, though either way it was clear I had been in the vicinity.

With a bit of luck at least I had some time on my side. It would surely take the police a while to decipher what had happened. But my life as I knew it was over now. I knew that.

Mickey Egan was surely dead. I hoped Callum O'Brady was too. Including the others in the Range Rover, my actions had killed five men.

I had acted on impulse, spur of the moment. I hadn't sought vengeance against them lightly, though. It might have come about quickly in the end, but it wasn't a moment of madness, or irrational thinking. It was one hundred per cent deliberate – and necessary. The wounds Egan had inflicted had still been fresh. I was angry. I'd wanted to hurt him. O'Brady? Well, he'd been at the forefront of my problems in life for so many years.

I'd accomplished so much in a short space of time. But my business was still unfinished.

I had to dispose of the bloody knife and gloves that were nestled in my jacket, but I wasn't about to just dump them while they were covered in O'Brady's blood and very likely contaminated with my own DNA.

Still thinking through exactly how I would dispose of them, I rode back toward my home, keeping to the quieter A-roads that snaked around Birmingham and alongside the motorways. I made it to the edge of Sutton Coldfield before I dumped the bike outside the gates of a scrap-metal yard and then trudged the couple of miles to my house.

It was only at that point that I felt the buzzing of my phone in my pocket. I took it out to see Dani was calling me. I let the call go unanswered, and then saw I had a half dozen other missed calls from her. Clearly she'd finally heard about the attack on me and Cara.

Or did she somehow already know about O'Brady?

Either way I didn't call her back.

As I neared my home, I took the turning onto the parallel road that ran behind where we lived, and walked down there. It was too big a risk to head straight for the front of the house. I didn't want to run into the police if they were stationed there, waiting for me.

I found the house that ours backed onto. It was a semi-detached with a side gate that led into the back garden. I looked up and down the road – it was entirely deserted – then made my way up the drive of the house. I couldn't see any lights on. I crept up to the side gate.

The gate was locked, but using the adjacent fence I scaled it with ease and was soon creeping through the back garden. I vaulted the back fence into my own garden and stared up at my home. The same feeling of remorse that I'd felt earlier in the evening coursed through me once more as I stared at the bricks and glass and wood in front of me.

This time I managed to quickly put the feelings to one side.

The hope, the dreams, they had never been me. *This* was me. My life had always been intended to run this way. I'd fought it as best I could, but deep down I'd always known that.

The house was entirely dark and I wondered whether it was empty. Certainly when I'd last spoken to Gemma she'd been spending more and more time at her parents' house, getting the help she needed in looking after the children. *My* children.

I wouldn't let Gemma take them away from me.

Suddenly I felt renewed strength and determination. I moved from the fence and over toward the French doors that led into the kitchen. I took the keyring from my pocket and gently slid the key into the lock.

As I turned the key I heard the click as the latch released, and I slowly and silently pulled down the handle of the door, then began to ease it open. I stepped into the kitchen, moving as quietly as I could. The house was dark and still and quiet. I reached behind me and started to push the door.

I was careful. And yet as I steadily pushed on the handle, a gust of wind made the door jerk in my hand and it snapped shut against the frame. I stood, rooted to the spot.

I stared out into the eerie darkness behind the house, but I wasn't really looking. My senses were focused only on any sounds coming from behind me, within the house. At first there was absolute silence. But then I heard creaking and straining as the draught from the outside wind coursed through the old structure. The house was charming and handsome on the outside, but it had always been somewhat creepy and noisy on the inside.

After a few moments I was satisfied that the sounds were nothing more than the wind. And the noise didn't seem to have alerted anyone, if there was anyone to alert at all. I unzipped my jacket and took it off. But as I turned around to face into the kitchen, my heart lurched when I spotted the outline of a person standing just a few yards in front of me.

A light snapped on and I stared, aghast.

'Ben,' Dani said. 'What the hell is going on?'

CHAPTER 58

I placed my jacket down on one of the dining chairs, making sure the plastic bag inside remained out of view. Dani stared at the jacket and for a fleeting second I wondered whether she already knew.

'Where's Gemma?' I asked.

'Asleep,' Dani said. 'At least I think she is, though it's hardly been a relaxing night.'

'What are you doing here?'

'Waiting for you.'

'Why?'

'Because I'm worried about you. We all are.'

'I can take care of myself.'

'Yeah, you always thought that. Even when we were kids you were too stubborn and naive to see that you can't always take on the world on your own.'

'I'm not a child anymore.'

'No, you're not. I'm glad you realise that.'

'Where are Harry and Chloe?' I said.

'At their grandparents' house.'

'Why?' I asked.

'I don't know, they're not my kids.'

I walked toward my sister, toward the doorway that led to the hall. I expected Dani to step aside but she held her ground.

'What are you doing?' I said, taking a step back, giving myself some space.

'I'm not letting you disturb Gemma. She's sleeping. It's been a rough night for her already.'

'This is my house.'

274

'Where have you been tonight?' Dani said.

My mind was on high alert; my eyes were darting here, there and everywhere.

'Where have you been, Ben?' Dani said again.

Her tone made me feel like I was a teenager being berated by a worried parent. Except Dani wasn't really worried about me.

'You care about me all of a sudden?' I said.

'Of course I care about you,' Dani said.

'I was in the hospital. Did you not hear about that?'

'Yes, I heard. I called you as soon as I found out. I called you countless times. I went to the hospital too. My colleagues said you just upped and left. We've been looking for you since.'

'Well, here I am.'

'And where have you been in the meantime?' Dani said, her tone nothing but distrustful. A rich attitude coming from her.

'Here and there,' I said. 'Getting my head straight. It's been a rough night.'

'Are you aware that Callum O'Brady was murdered tonight?'

I stared at Dani, trying not to betray any emotion. I was on edge for sure. Yet hearing my sister confirm that O'Brady was indeed dead made me feel elated.

'No,' I said. 'I didn't know. But I can't say I'm sorry.'

'So you wouldn't know anything about what happened to him?'

'No. Why would I?'

We both stood in silence for a few moments. Dani's glare was unyielding. I questioned whether she would come back at me as good cop or bad cop. But she just stared and didn't say a word.

'What are you doing here?' I said. 'In my house. With my wife.'

'I was looking for you,' Dani said. 'You're getting yourself in deeper and deeper, Ben. I hate to stand by and watch you throw your life away. O'Brady ... I mean ... I really hope you had nothing to do with that. I can't bail you out of something like that.'

'I don't buy it,' I said.

'Don't buy what?' Dani said, looking genuinely confused.

'What are you doing here again? I don't see you for years, then all of a sudden you're best chums with Gemma it seems.'

'I'm not sure what you're trying to say.'

'You know.'

'I really don't. There're police out all over looking for you. After your stunt with O'Brady and the phone, and the attack last night, we knew you were now a target for O'Brady and his crew. We wanted to protect you.'

'I asked for protection before. You told me there was no threat.'

Dani remained defiant. No offer of an apology for what had happened to me. Or Cara.

'I'm here because I needed to find you,' she said. 'Before something really bad happened to you. And if it wasn't me here in your house, it would have just been another officer.'

'But it's not someone else. It's you. Where's Gemma?'

I went to move past Dani but she held firm, blocking the doorway, and pushed me back. I squared up to her and waited for her next move. I wasn't backing down this time.

'Spit it out, Ben,' Dani said, glaring at me. 'What are you trying to say?'

'I know what you did,' I said, my words edged with hatred. 'I know what you did to Alice. You poisoned her against me. I won't let you do it again.'

'You've lost it,' she said. 'I can't believe you would even say that.'

'She told me, Dani. Alice told me everything.'

And then her demeanour changed. Like something had clicked into place.

'Why did you come back here?' Dani said, the suspicion in her voice even greater than before.

She took a step back, beyond the doorway, into the hall. Her gaze never left me. Her confidence was fading for the first time in the conversation. Dani the superstar, the high-flying detective, the perfect daughter. The perfect sister.

Yet she looked ... scared.

And she was right to be. She was my twin after all. She knew everything about me. She really should have figured it out before now. Or maybe she had. Maybe she'd figured it out long ago and was just in shock or some sort of denial.

Dani shook her head. 'Ben, just think about this. Think it through.'

'Oh, I've been thinking this through for years. Waiting for this moment.'

Dani took another step down the hall. I followed her every move. A stunned look now covered her face.

'You and Alice were the two people who were closest to me in the world,' I said. 'You knew how much she meant to me. You turned her against me.'

'I'm so sorry,' Dani said. I knew she wasn't really. 'It wasn't to hurt you.'

'No? I still trusted her after her affair with Fletcher. I trusted that she loved me. She *did* love me. Until you started meddling with her mind.'

'You were sleeping with Gemma, Ben! *You* destroyed what you had, not me.'

'I've always been in awe of you. Everything in life has always been so easy for you, hasn't it? But you've never really cared for anyone but yourself. You don't care what you do to other people.'

'That's just not true.'

'When I found out what you'd done, I wanted to erase it from my memory and move on like it had never happened. I loved you, Dani. But you stabbed me in the heart. I always thought you had my back.'

'I didn't want to hurt you. But I had to do what was right for Alice!'

'Yet look where that got her. If you'd only kept your damn mouth shut.'

'You didn't deserve her!' Dani shouted in anger - or was it jealousy? I'd excelled over my twin sister at *one* thing in life - I'd found a soulmate, someone to start a family with - and Dani simply hadn't been able to take it.

'Do you know what hurt most?' I said. 'The way she rubbed my face in it. Taunting me with what you'd said to her. My own sister saying I wasn't good enough for my wife. My own twin doing everything she could to convince my wife to leave me. Maybe if Alice hadn't been so *nasty* that night, I wouldn't have been so *angry*. I would have been able to control myself ... I would have been able to stop.'

A look of horror swept over Dani's face. She finally got it. She finally understood what had happened. What *had* to happen.

'It was you,' Dani gasped.

CHAPTER 59

I didn't say anything. No confirmation, no denial. I just waited to see what Dani would do or say next.

'It wasn't Egan,' Dani said. 'He killed Hayley Lewis, I'm sure of that. But Alice …'

'Did you really never know?' I said, managing a wry smile. I'd always had my doubts about that. Dani was so close to both us. How could she not have spotted it? 'I loved Alice more than anything. She was the one. *You* took her away from me. You and Gemma both.'

Dani reached into her trouser pocket for her phone. I had no doubt she was calling her colleagues – a request for immediate assistance, or whatever the police's technical term was. Her movements were fast and frantic. She was a bag of nerves. I wasn't going to let her make that call.

'Put it down, Dani,' I said.

'No, Ben. It's over.'

'Put the phone down!' I yelled.

Dani cowered at my words, but a second later a hard-nosed resolve broke across her face.

'No,' she said. 'I'm done looking out for you, Ben. You're not my brother. Not anymore.'

They were her last words.

I lunged for Dani. She only positioned herself for the oncoming attack at the last second. She was too focused on making the call. After everything that had happened, after everything I'd said, she should have anticipated what I was about to do. Perhaps she really didn't think I had it in me. As a child she'd always seen me as weak and in need of her care. As an adult she'd always looked down on me too. Pitied me even. Well, I was about to show her exactly what I was capable of.

Dani brought her free arm up and hunched down, protecting her face and body. She dropped the phone and went for a defensive counter-attack, probably aiming to put me in a hold again. She was nowhere near as strong physically as I was, but I knew she was trained to subdue people twice her size. Not this time, though.

Out on the street, with all the space she needed and in full policewoman mode, I was sure Dani would have quite quickly outmanoeuvred me. But stuck in the doorway she simply didn't have the space. Or the time. And despite everything, she still wasn't expecting me to fight dirty. Her mistake.

With the momentum of my body behind me, I thrust a knee up into Dani's stomach. She exhaled and doubled over in pain. Yet just a split-second later, Dani was already recovering and reaching out to me.

I wouldn't give her even a glimmer of hope.

I threw an open hand toward the side of her head. With Dani caught in the narrow hallway, I had the perfect weapon right there. I slammed her skull into the wall and Dani collapsed to the floor.

The fight had lasted barely five seconds. Just like my dad would have done when he was a kid. Act fast. Deliver the first blow. Don't allow the other guy – or girl as the case may be – to even get started.

I was panting, hunched over, ready to take on any attack that might be coming from Dani. But there was nothing. She was breathing. She was awake. But her fight was already gone.

She let out a long groan. Tried to turn over. Tried to reach her phone. I heard a muffled and crackled voice coming from its speaker. The call had connected. I grabbed the phone and quickly killed the call. Dani's body slumped, her last hope taken away.

Looking down on her, I was reminded of the age-old wisdom that it's better to put a wounded animal out of its misery than to let it suffer. That's what Dani, lying helpless on the floor, looked like to me. A wounded animal.

I picked up a small stone statue from the sideboard next to where Dani lay. Gemma and I had received it as a wedding gift from one of her hideous aunties. The ornament – some sort of modern art depiction of a man with a dog – was equally hideous.

Holding the torso of the stone man in my hand, I looked down at my sister once more. Her eyes made contact with mine. She knew what was coming.

She finally realised what I was capable of.

I swung the ornament down and the thick stone base crashed into the side of Dani's head. It cut into her skin, taking a chunk of flesh with it. Dani's body jolted on impact. Her wide eyes stared up at me. Her face and clothes were spattered with her own blood.

I hit her again.

I imagined her skull caving in from the vicious blow. Dani's body twitched and then, after a few seconds, went still.

CHAPTER 60

I heard a creaking noise. Coming from upstairs. From my bedroom. Gemma.

I placed the ornament back on the sideboard, stepped over the unmoving body of my sister and moved along the hallway. I ascended the stairs quickly, not wanting to lose any of the impetus I now had. Not wanting the flow of adrenaline to stop. And not wanting my conscience – if it still existed at all – to suddenly intervene.

I walked along the landing and pushed open the door to my bedroom. My hands were shaking from anticipation and adrenaline and something else I couldn't quite place.

Gemma was sitting up on the edge of our king-sized bed in a cotton nightie, facing away from me. Her bedside light was on. I got the impression she'd just woken – maybe because of the noise from me fighting Dani downstairs.

I didn't announce my arrival in the room. In fact I'd tried to move as silently as I could up the stairs and along the landing. But Gemma must have sensed my presence. She spun around and jumped up off the bed.

'Ben,' she gasped.

She looked shocked by my being there. My own wife, in my own bedroom.

'What have you done?' she said as she looked down at my clothes, my hands, spattered with blood. A look of panic spread across her face. She took a step backward, toward the door to the en-suite.

'What have *you* done, Gemma?'

She simply shook her head in response.

I began to walk toward her. Gemma took another step back.

'Don't come any closer!' she screamed.

I stopped and feigned confusion. 'What do you think I'm going to do to you?'

'I don't know. I really don't know what you're capable of anymore.'

'What I'm capable of?'

'Where's Dani?'

'Downstairs. Having a … rest.'

I smiled. Gemma cupped her mouth in horror.

'Just one question, Gemma: did you really never suspect me?'

'Suspect what?'

'Suspect what happened to Alice that night.'

It only took a second for my words to click.

'No, no. You couldn't …'

'What happened to her … it was because of *you*.'

I sprang forward two steps. Gemma did nothing but cower away as I reached out with both hands and grabbed her around her throat. She grimaced and snatched my wrists, trying to free herself. I held strong and Gemma soon became frantic, her body twisting and writhing as she tried to fight me off.

Her strength in desperation surprised me. For a moment I thought I might not be able to hold her. I roared as I used all my strength and fury to lift her off her feet and heave her onto the bed.

The terror in her eyes when I landed on top of her said everything. She knew she wasn't getting away.

I squeezed as hard as I could. Gemma was rasping for breath but her attempts quickly became more and more pathetic.

A sudden jolt, a stabbing at the front of my head, took me by surprise. I squeezed my eyes shut and my mind took me somewhere I'd long tried to forget.

To me and Alice. In our home. In our bedroom. Her on the bed. Me on top. My hands around her neck. The look in her eyes a perfect mirror of Gemma's.

Dark Fragments

With Alice, it had been pure impulse. No premeditation. I just hadn't been able to stop myself. Something had taken over my mind and my body in those few fateful moments.

We'd moved on after her brief affair with Craig Fletcher. At least I'd thought we had. I'd forgiven her. I'd wanted things to go back to the way they had been before. But they never had. Gemma had found her way into my life.

Gemma was a mistake. Yet I couldn't get away from her. She would corner me whenever she could, taking any opportunity to rip off my clothes and pleasure me. She was insatiable.

I should have been stronger. I should have said no.

With renewed hatred, I opened my eyes. Together with Dani, Gemma had wrecked my marriage with Alice and ruined my life. If it hadn't been for them …

I squeezed Gemma's neck even harder. Her face was red and contorted and looked like it would explode at any second. My mind once again took me back to how I'd felt as I'd choked the life out of Alice.

I'd never meant to hurt her. If there had been a way to take it back, I would have done. I'd reacted on instinct. Alice had said she was leaving me. She wanted a divorce. She no longer loved me. She said my own sister had finally convinced her!

As I brought my focus back around, I realised Gemma had stopped moving beneath me. I released my grip. The rings of white flesh around her neck were a perfect imprint of my hands. Her ghostly eyes were staring back at me.

With Alice, my first feelings as I'd looked down at her lifeless body were intense regret and grief. Looking at Gemma, I felt relief. I felt freedom.

I turned my back on her and walked over to the sink in the bathroom and looked at my reflection in the mirror. I saw … nothing. No emotion. No humanity. I had given my everything. I was done.

After Alice, I'd broken down in tears, but quickly resolved that I would fight on. I'd been determined to prove that I could still make a life for myself.

I'd picked up my phone and called the one person to whom I could turn in the dire situation. I'd called Callum O'Brady. No-one else would have listened to me in my hour of need. O'Brady helped me because he knew I would forever be in his pocket from that day. I'd put my life in his hands.

O'Brady knew what to do. It wasn't the first time he'd had Mickey Egan clean up after a murder. First Egan had the scene expertly cleaned, removing any trace of fingerprints and handprints from Alice's neck, but also sterilising much of the bedroom, making the scene look like a professional had covered his tracks.

Then he'd arranged Alice's naked body suggestively on the bed, an indication that the killing may have had a sexual motive.

Then came the white feather, such a simple idea. It did its job. It kept the police guessing.

Finally there were the witness sightings of a man behaving suspiciously near our house. Faked, obviously. O'Brady had got one of his men to hang around outside our house that night, acting overtly suspicious in the hope that a busybody neighbour - when it was later realised a murder had taken place - would inform the police. Which is exactly what happened. Using ambiguity over the time of death and when I'd finally called the police to report the murder, we created a convincing set of unexplained events.

Without Callum O'Brady and Mickey Egan, a master of death, I'd never have got away with it.

Hayley Lewis? I still didn't know why Egan had killed her or for what purpose he had staged the scene so similarly to Alice's – perhaps O'Brady was planning to set me up. I would never know the answer to that.

I shook my head and turned on the tap, then splashed my face with cold water, feeling renewed focus and energy. I wiped my hands and face dry, then walked back out into the bedroom.

I stopped.

My heart sank as I looked over at the bed where moments ago I had been choking the life out of my second wife.

Not because of a moment of unexpected grief. That wasn't what I was feeling at all. I had a problem. A big problem. Gemma was no longer there.

CHAPTER 61

I cursed my stupidity. Why hadn't I checked the body? I'd been too caught up in my moment of contemplation.

I saw three options as to where she'd gone. She could have run straight out the front door. She might be hiding somewhere, waiting for help to arrive – which I had to assume was coming following Dani's phone call. Or she was hiding and waiting for her chance to attack. Did Gemma have it in her to do that?

The way the wardrobes were arranged in our room, with numerous shelves and inner drawers, I doubted she'd be hiding in there. And there was nowhere else in the bedroom she could have fitted.

As I crept across the bedroom floor I was filled with anger. At Gemma for thinking she could still win out.

Over my dead body.

I reached the door and cautiously peered out onto the landing. All of the other upstairs doors were open, just as they had been when I'd come up the stairs minutes earlier. There was nothing to indicate that she'd gone into any of those rooms.

I moved up to the banister and peered over the edge, looking down to the hallway below. I could see Dani's feet. She hadn't moved. I was sure she never would again.

That was a relief. It also made me question whether Gemma had yet made it as far as the downstairs. If she had, wouldn't she have screamed or shouted when she'd seen Dani's body?

As quietly as I could, I moved through each of the other three bedrooms. No sign of Gemma anywhere. I crept back toward the head of the stairs where the door to the bathroom was ajar a foot or so. As I neared the entrance, I'd already convinced myself that she must be hiding there.

I decided on a different approach. Rather than creeping into the room, I would explode into it. Take back the element of surprise she'd been hoping for if she was lying in wait for me.

I stood and counted to ten, trying to get my racing heart and my breathing, heavy with anticipation, back under control. Then I thrust open the door and jumped into the room. Ready to attack.

But I needn't have bothered. It took me only a second to realise that the bathroom was empty.

Just where the hell was she? Could she really have made it downstairs and out of the house already?

As I went to turn around, to head back out of the bathroom, she finally gave herself away. I heard a creaking floorboard. It had to be her. I spun around and stepped back out onto the landing and caught sight of the moving figure in the corner of my eye.

I turned and dived toward her. Gemma screamed as I crashed into her. I pushed her back and pinned her against the wall. My hands immediately clasped her throat. I wasn't going to make the same mistake twice. This time I was going to finish Gemma off for good.

But I was too focused on punishing her. I should have expected what was coming. I spotted her hand arcing toward me, the shining metallic object in her grasp, too late.

My hands, gripped tightly around her neck, put up no defence as she plunged the nib of the fountain pen into the side of my neck. The fountain pen Alice had bought me as a present on our first anniversary.

Gemma jerked the pen out and I screamed in pain, immediately releasing her. I whipped a hand up to the wound, from which blood was already pouring.

She thrust the pen toward me again. At least my hand was there to protect my neck the second time around. The pen sank into the flesh on the back of my hand, becoming wedged between the bones there.

I yelled and launched my head toward Gemma. I caught her square on, forehead to forehead. There was a loud thwack and everything in front of me bounced and became blurred.

I'd never head-butted anyone before. I thought in that moment I must have misjudged it. It did at least take away some of Gemma's fight. I heaved my wobbly body up and off Gemma and yanked the pen out of my hand, shouting out in pain again.

Gemma crawled up the wall, trying to get away from me. I was snarling. Demented with anger. Gemma, on the other hand, looked petrified. But sometimes looks can be deceiving.

And looks had always been one of Gemma's biggest weapons.

She sprang into action, launching herself at me. We grappled for just a few seconds. I quickly realised just how weakened I'd become from the wound to my neck, which was gushing thick blood all down me. I should have been able to overpower her, but I struggled for control.

Then all of a sudden I felt something tug at me from behind. A short, sharp yank on the neck of my jumper. With my body moving backward from the unexpected pull, I went to place my foot behind me, but it connected with thin air.

I began to tumble ...

As I crashed and banged downwards, I saw two figures at the top of the staircase. Gemma. And Dani.

I landed in a heap at the bottom of the stairs. Everything was spinning. I tried to get up but couldn't. The world around me felt so distant.

I opened and closed my eyes a few times as I looked up at my wife and my sister. Neither said a word. Gemma just sat down on the top step, pulled her knees into her chest and stared, while my sister stood alongside her, glaring down at me.

A flicker of light caught my attention. I looked up at the ceiling. A blue light. Flashing intermittently. Its beam was coming in through the small frosted window on the front door. My eyelids were heavy.

Dark Fragments

I gazed back at Dani. Then at Gemma. The look on her face had changed.

As I closed my eyes one last time, I saw her smile.

CHAPTER 62

'Are you sorry for what you've done?'

'What do you mean by sorry?'

'Well, I asked you before about regrets. But what I'm trying to get at is whether you feel any remorse for your actions?'

'Remorse?' I said. 'I feel a lot of remorse. I'm remorseful that I won't get to see my children growing up, for example. I love them more than anything. But it's more complicated than just saying I'm remorseful for a specific action.'

I looked around the room. At the prison officer standing at the thick metal door. Over to the small window that had a sturdy metal grate in front of the glass. I looked down at my hands, cuffed together. I looked at my prescribed clothing, the only attire I would likely ever know.

'Am I sorry?' I said. 'Look at where I am. Of course I'm sorry.'

'So you're sorry that you were caught. Is that it?'

'No, that's not it at all. When I look back, I see my whole life has been filled with regret and remorse. I've made so many mistakes, and each only plunged me further into the mire. Kind of like a snowball running down a mountain – it starts off small, and with each roll it picks up speed and grows and grows, and eventually you have a boulder the size of a house. It causes an avalanche of snow that thunders down and destroys everything in its path. That's my life. That's the only way I can explain how it got so out of control. I was always so busy trying to rectify the past mistakes that I just kept on making more and more.'

'But it sounds like you only regret that you didn't end up with the happy life you'd craved for so long. What about all the people that you hurt? The people you killed? What do you feel for them? For those who loved them?'

'I was sorry for Alice. Killing her was a mistake, a huge mistake. I regretted it immediately, and I've regretted it every day of my life since. I knew I would never get over it. It destroyed my life.'

'And Egan and O'Brady? The others who died in that car?'

'They deserved it. They would have killed me. O'Brady was a despicable human being.'

'Yet he helped you in your hour of need. He helped you to cover up the fact that you'd murdered your wife.'

'It was the only thing I ever asked of O'Brady. He got back more than his fair share from our knowing each other. He milked me for years.'

'And what about Gemma and Dani?'

'They both lived to fight another day, didn't they?'

'But you tried to kill them both.'

'I tried. I failed.'

'You don't feel bad for trying to kill your sister and your wife?'

'No. They were responsible for what happened to me. For what I did to Alice. It was my hands that took her life, but it was their actions that caused it.'

'You still believe that?'

'I'll always believe that. You asked if I have regrets. Yes, I have regrets. I regret that I wasn't able to kill them too. In fact, I wish I'd done it years ago. Rather than going crying to O'Brady for help and spending the next seven years of my life in misery, I should have ended it there and then, wiped out the lot of them.'

'Some would say that your lack of remorse is quite startling.'

'It's not really. Everyone dreams of punishing the people who've wronged them. Anyone who says otherwise is a liar.'

'People may say such things in passing or think about hurting others, but very few people would justify hurting and killing others in real life the way you have.'

'The only difference is that I decided to take control. Where other people wallow in their own self-pity, at least I tried to make things right. You know, I never wanted any of this. I didn't want my wife to cheat on me, or my sister to turn her against me. I didn't want to strangle Alice in a moment of madness. I certainly never wanted to meet a man like Callum O'Brady. And I never wanted to end up in a place like this.'

'You don't think you deserve to be in prison?'

'I think it's inevitable, given the path I chose. Do I think it's fair? I'm not sure on that one. I know I committed crimes, and I understand there are consequences. Whether or not I agree with those consequences is another question, and I'm not sure I know the answer. I don't want to be here. The prospect of spending the next fifty years locked up isn't exactly appealing. But I've got plenty of time on my hands to figure that one out.'

We both went silent for a few moments while she caught up with her notes. I stared over at the prison guard, who was glaring blankly into space in front of him. He never once twitched, never once looked over. I wondered whether he, whether any of them, ever bothered to listen in to these conversations. I wondered what went through their minds.

'It's been suggested that you acted with diminished responsibility,' she said.

'Suggested? It was the crux of my lawyer's defence.'

'But the jury didn't believe it.'

'Apparently not.'

'What do you think? Do you believe you were acting with diminished responsibility?'

'Do I think I'm insane, you mean?'

'That's not the correct terminology, but yes, essentially that's what I'm trying to find out. That's been the purpose of these sessions.'

'You're asking me whether I think I'm insane? How could I ever answer that? And how would you know what to make of the answer? It's like asking someone whether they're a liar.'

She thought about that for a moment. I knew the comparison wasn't exactly the same, but it wasn't far off.

'If I admit I'm insane,' I said, *'doesn't that take some forethought and knowledge of what insanity is? Which would then suggest that I'm cognisant of my behaviour, which means I'm not insane. If I say no, then what the hell am I? A psychopath? Aren't psychopaths insane?'*

'Well, this is where the terminology isn't helping the question.'

'It was your question.'

'And whatever answer you give is valid. It's not a trick.'

'But I don't know how to answer it.'

She jotted down another note and then sat back in her chair.

'Just one more question,' she said. 'What I want to know is why you committed these crimes? And I don't mean the answer about getting revenge against people who wronged you. That's a motivation. I want to know how you can reconcile actually taking the actions. What is it inside you that made you kill those people?'

'My father told me a fable when I was younger,' I said. 'I think it comes from the Native Americans or some other similar culture. The story goes that there's a battle inside us all between two wolves. One is evil. It represents anger, resentment, greed, lies and jealousy. All of the bad things in humanity. The other is good. It represents happiness and joy, peace, hope and kindness. Empathy.'

'You think there's good and bad inside us all? That's what you're saying?'

'Yes. Anyone is capable of doing the things I've done.'

'But not everyone does.'

'No, not everyone does.'

'So why you?'

'Because one wolf always wins out in the end.'

'And what makes one wolf succeed over the other?'

'It's simple. In the battle of good over evil, the wolf that wins is the one that you feed the most. And really, there's nothing more to life than that.'

THE END

<u>Acknowledgments</u>

I'd like to keep this short and sweet and thank all of those people who have helped and supported my writing career so far. Hopefully you know who you are, but a special mention has to go to my parents, whose (almost) unwavering support has driven me for many years, my wife, for tolerating me and letting me get away with murder (not literally), my editor, Charlie Wilson (aka The Book Specialist), who never fails to tell me when my writing is a load of crap, the team at Bloodhound Books, who I am sure will help make this book the biggest success it can be, and finally all of the readers and reviewers and bloggers who have taken the time to read my work (particularly those who keep coming back for more).